REMEDY:
D.E.T.O.X.X.
AMERICA

All the Best to Judith
Harold Kuester
11/29/08

HAROLD KUESTER

PublishAmerica
Baltimore

First printing

PublishAmerica has allowed this work to remain exactly as the author intended, verbatim, without editorial input.

All characters in this book are fictitious, and any resemblance to real persons, living or dead, is coincidental.

ISBN: 1-60672-216-6
PUBLISHED BY PUBLISHAMERICA, LLLP
www.publishamerica.com
Baltimore

Printed in the United States of America

DEDICATION

To democracy: "the worst form of government except all the others that have been tried." *Sir Winston Churchill*

"All the others" includes government dominated by market fundamentalists, who assert that the market is perfectly self-correcting, omniscient, and God-like, capable of producing the best of all possible worlds. They ignore Lord Acton's famous dictum: "Power tends to corrupt; absolute power corrupts absolutely."

ACKNOWLEDGEMENTS

Many thanks to my wife Mimi, my daughter Sonia, her mother-in-law, Sara Pfaffenroth, and to Shirley Kozlowski for their invaluable assistance in preparation of this novel.

Thanks also to the host of philosophers who remind us that present views of economics and society are merely a few of many possible alternatives, some of which may prove superior to our own.

PROLOGUE

Among the white birch and hemlock trees of the Minnesota north woods, the radio telescope staff of Global Communications and Internet Services monitored and recorded radio and television programs beaming in from the planet Pisces II. After translation, the programs were rebroadcast on GCIS commercial internet stations. The shows were adored by Earth audiences and were generating huge profits, a gold mine for the company.

"Hey, Bill," called out Dan Dietrich, "I'm picking up a signal on a new frequency. Do you want to record it?"

"Hell, yes," replied Bill Schmidt, Director of Operations. He came over and took a look at the screen. "Obviously not a commercial broadcast."

"Right. Lots of diagrams. Any idea what they're about?"

"Not off the top of my head. Those Pisces aliens sure got us beat when it comes to science and technology. Maybe this is one of their tech channels. If so, our company could make big bucks selling the stuff to interested corporations. When you've finished recording, get it to Sam Cohn or one of the other translators immediately. Make sure they send it to the big boys as soon as possible."

As Bill turned to leave, Dan said, "Hold on, there's something else."
"What?"
"I think the video's sending a warning about a spaceship."
"And?"
"Dunno for sure, but it seems to be headed for Earth."
"Let the big shots worry about it. I've got enough on my plate."

Day One

Chapter 1

Peter Abelard sat up, stretched, and looked down at Julia, sleeping, her silky brown hair inviting his touch. Caressing the long luxurious strands, he could not resist gently kissing her slightly parted raspberry-red lips. Her eyes fluttered open slowly as her arms sleepily encircled his neck, drawing him closer. Suddenly, with a quick grin, she flipped him over, and her warm, soft body forced him down into the sheets. Ripping open his pajama top, she half-kissed, half-bit his hairy chest.

The alarm's shrill buzz rudely interrupted his dream. Twisting sideways on one elbow, a silencing hand slammed down on the demonic device. He arose slowly, unenthusiastically.

Shaving and showering, he thought back on his first encounter with Julia. They met at a space station organizational session at GCIS headquarters. The attraction had been instant and mutual. Despite his initial reticence, the relationship had become serious. He quickly learned, to his dismay, that Julia was an old-fashioned girl who believed that sexual intimacy should be reserved for marriage. Surprisingly, he soon realized he cared for her so deeply that waiting was not a problem—except in his dreams. Besides, a recent automobile accident had crushed several vertebrae and forced her into a body brace. The injury would mend, but she—and he—would have to be respectful of her injury for several months.

"God, I love you," he murmured, glancing at her photo as he slid open his cubicle door.

Inspired by visions of Julia, he strode down Outer Main, the corridor running along the outer circumference of the donut-shaped space station. The fast, hard pace of his work at Global Communications and

Internet Services had begun losing its appeal—until Julia. Their shared interests and passions had rejuvenated him. Living in close proximity to her on the space station seemed like living in paradise.

Intent upon seeing her before his shift began, he sped down the corridor. Only the rotating space station's artificial gravity prevented him from taking flight. The crew members he passed greeted him with the friendly, informal camaraderie that develops spontaneously within small groups working together on a common project.

Arriving at the communication center, he quietly tiptoed up behind where Julia sat, speaking intently into the phone. Who is she talking to, he wondered, security? As the conversation ended, he brushed aside her silky brown hair with a flick of his hand and lightly kissed the nape of her neck.

Tensing in surprise, almost knocking a cluster of papers off her desk, she spun around, annoyed. "Peter, can't you see I'm working?"

"Sorry," he apologized with mock sincerity. "I'm on my way to the radio telescope. How about lunch?"

Even as she glared at him, her expression softened, "I guess so. But…"

"I'll get you back on time, promise." Holding up his right hand, "Scout's honor."

"No excuses?"

"Promise."

Turning to leave, he blew her a kiss, remembering with fondness that mad, happy social whirl they had enjoyed shortly before rocketing up to the space station for their current tour of duty. Still, Julia seemed now different somehow. Their relationship was not exactly a secret, but they hadn't made any special effort to bring it to everyone's attention. Was she upset by his public demonstrations of familiarity? Or was it the strain of her duties on the station? Should he even mention it? He started to say something, but fearful of offending, didn't, even though he was acutely aware of the pitfalls awaiting couples who fail to communicate openly and honestly, who keep secrets.

He was reminded of his seemingly affectionate parents, who had divorced when he was a vulnerable nine-year-old, wondering if he was the cause. His father, an astronomer, had sought to interest him in the riddles of the universe, including the possibility of extraterrestrial life. However, young Peter had been more drawn to electronics. His mother had encouraged the latter, hoping, he later learned, to deflect him from his father's obsession with astronomy and academics, which she regarded as contributing to the breakup of their marriage. As a young adult, he came to realize that he was drifting through mere semblances of relationships, his parents' example having disabused him of romantic fancies—until now.

Refocusing on the task at hand, Peter clambered up a stairway on his way to the solarium in the "hole" of the space station doughnut. The artificial gravity lessened noticeably as he approached Inner Main, the corridor running around the perimeter of the "donut hole." Exiting the stairway, he "moon-shuffled" toward the nearest solarium hatch.

Thinking of the radio telescope reminded him of his friend Sam Cohn. A grade school buddy, Sam had helped Peter cope with his parents' divorce. They had kept in fairly close touch over the years and, more recently, Sam had convinced him to accept a position at GCIS. Part of Sam's job included teaching the Piscean language to company personnel, including Peter, who knew that he had been chosen to work on the space station because of his electronic and Piscean language expertise.

Leaping upward easily, Peter grasped a handhold beside the solarium hatch door, refusing to use the ladder-like steps built into the wall in favor of this more gymnastic entry. Opening the hatch, he felt his usual thrill at the sight of the solarium. The giant ball of water suspended in zero gravity at its center always awed him. Sunlight flooded in through the solarium's transparent "top" and "bottom," producing a dazzling display of color as it interacted with the liquid crystal. Pausing for a moment before the sparkling watery jewel, his eyes focused on the plants and fish within, essential to the space station's air and food supply. He noted the reassuring hum of the evenly-spaced speakers dotting the walls of the spherical solarium, constantly bombarding the ball of water with sound waves which maintained its shape and position in the wondrous zero-gravity world. He felt the air swirling around the stationary ball as it made tiny ripples and indentations in the water's surface. The motion of the air was generated by the spin of the spherical solarium, attached as it was to the rotating space station proper.

Kicking off from the hatch door, which had automatically closed behind him, he deftly propelled himself out into the space between the huge ball of water and the solarium wall. Surfing the air currents was tricky. The moving air could cause unintended collisions with the wall or splashdowns in the ball of water. Soaring near the water's surface, he became one with the plants and fishes flowing by beneath, thankful for this enchanting shortcut to work.

Too soon the spell was broken. Emerging from the solarium through another hatch, he again felt the tug of weak artificial gravity. As he shuffled along the far side of Inner Main, he spied security officer Arthur Huston, peering out a space station porthole. Peter could not help feeling intimidated by the taller, more muscular Huston, rumored to be a former Special Forces officer. As Peter approached, the austerely neat red-crew-cut head snapped in his direction, the fierce, freckled face breaking into a grin.

"Damn, wish I was back on my bike in the mountains!" he exclaimed. "Love Colorado!"

"Same here," sympathized Peter, imagining Julia's hand in his as they strolled down a mountain slope strewn with brightly-colored flowers.

For several minutes, the two men gazed silently at the distant bit of Earth visible above the solarium from their geosynchronous orbit, some twenty thousand miles over the mid-Pacific equator. Earth, suspended in the stark blackness of space, sparkled like a blue gem and looked delicate and fragile.

* * * * *

In the radio telescope control center off Inner Main, Peter ran the diagnostic program which checked for malfunctions. The system was configured to enhance transmissions from Pisces II and beam encrypted versions to GCIS in Minnesota. The control center's airlock permitted easy access to the telescope dish suspended on girders in the vacuum of space above the solarium. Security hatches prevented unauthorized entry both from the space station proper and from the airlock. Once everything checked out, Peter activated the system, which included a special gyroscopic unit to keep the dish locked on target.

Signals from Pisces II had first been detected twelve years earlier at a mountaintop radio telescope research facility in Hawaii. Although the government attempted to suppress it, word of the discovery soon leaked out. Corporate media giants battled the government and one another to obtain legal rights to the signals. GCIS was the first to successfully translate the alien language. The company's position as dominant player in the commercial Internet broadcast of translated alien programs was currently uncontested, with Kenneth Lacey's United News Services a distant second.

Two types of alien signals, known simply as the "strong" and the "weak," had been detected at the Hawaii research facility. Astronomers speculated that one pole of Pisces II always pointed toward Earth and thus that the other pole always pointed away. They hypothesized that the strong signals came from the side of the planet facing Earth and the weak signals from the side facing away from it. Currently, only the strong signals were intelligible when received by radio telescopes on Earth, and thus, so far only the strong signals could be translated and rebroadcast on Earth commercial Internet radio and television.

Hence the GCIS space station. Its radio telescope was intended to capture intelligible weak signals for the first time. In order to maximize reception, the telescope dish was shielded from both earth- and sun-based radiation. Experts expected the best reception when the mass of the earth lay between the space station and the sun, blocking still more solar radiation.

"Fantastic!" exclaimed Peter. Monitoring the strength of the now coherent weak signals being sent to Earth for the first time, he pondered their trek through the vacuum of space. The journey took two years—two light-years, that is—traveling at 186,000 miles per second, twelve trillion miles, an unimaginable distance.

Yet he knew the alien star, named after its discoverer, the American astronomer Alfredo Pesce, and until recently hidden by galactic clouds, was closer to Earth than any other. When the seven planets of the star were discovered, they were named Pisces I through VII, as "Pesce" was Italian for fish. The names seemed even more appropriate after it became known that inhabitants of the star's second planet, believed to be responsible for the strong signals, were air-breathers who possessed fish-like gills running down both sides of their upper bodies, remnants of an evolutionary past. The occasional joking references to the gills on Piscean radio and television had first called them to the attention of Earth audiences. They were usually analogous to terrestrial jokes dwelling on the resemblance of hairy men to apes. Surprisingly, these gills were the only known major anatomical difference between Pisceans and humans.

Earth biologists were unable to account for the pronounced resemblance of the two species. How could evolution be regarded as a largely random process, they wondered, given such pronounced resemblance? Of course, religious fundamentalists and UFO true believers knew, each in their own way, how to account for the resemblance.

Because he was busy adjusting the radio telescope, Peter made no attempt to actually listen to a weak signal. He simply encrypted the now intelligible signals, and transmitted them to Earth. GCIS required encryption in order to prevent the pirating of this potentially lucrative new commodity.

Peter suspected that audiences loved the current strong-signal Piscean shows because it was comforting to watch otherworldly beings who shared not only human looks but also good old Yankee free-enterprise values. One of the most popular alien shows, "Lifestyles of the Rich and Richer," entranced audiences with the dream that one day they too would strike it rich and lead luxuriously indulgent lives.

Before coming onto the space station, Peter and Sam had begun the difficult task of mastering Piscean strong-signal speech, with its strange clicks and chirps, in addition to translating it. On sudden impulse, Peter chose a weak signal at random, turned on a speaker, and listened for the first time. It was sufficiently distinct that he could discern individual words. Imitating the utterances as they were spoken, "Aieee click pop drrr," he heard both familiar sounds and familiar words.

"Yes!" he yelled, exuberantly. "It's Piscean! Those weak signals must be coming from the other side of Pisces II!"

Chapter 2

"This living wage thing might be your last chance to make it to a major market," Liz Brock, Watertown, Iowa's popular TV anchor, reminded herself as she hurried on stage, well aware that age still mattered in the broadcast news business, at least for women. She had applied generous makeup to a lovely but no longer youthful face.

"Three...Two...One," called out the director as a camera zoomed in on Liz, who had seated herself at an onstage desk before the studio audience of her live weekly talk show.

"Good morning. I'm Liz Brock, your Talk-of-the-Town host. Our principal guest today is Robyn Sherwood, leader of the Living Wage Movement." The camera panned to an attractive strawberry blond with deep blue eyes seated beside the desk.

Liz continued, "I also welcome Charles Phelps, our network news anchor. Mr. Phelps is in Watertown covering the Living Wage Movement and has graciously consented to be with us today." The camera panned to a distinguished-looking gray-haired man seated to Robyn's right.

"Also on our stage today is Watertown's Mayor Jim Meyer." Mustached, graying, and slightly paunchy in a dark three-piece suit, he smiled and waved at the audience.

Liz rose and strode toward the studio audience. "And, last but not least, I would like to welcome our town's civic leaders who are here in the studio with us today." The camera panned to a group seated front and center as the audience clapped.

Liz returned to her desk, faced her three guests, and began: "The Living Wage Movement as we know it started right here in Watertown, as a reaction to working conditions at our local MegaSmartMart. Tell us a bit about that, Robyn."

"Well Liz, I started working at MegaSmartMart when I was in college. Like me, most employees were part-time. We earned little more than minimum wage and had practically no affordable benefits. Store management dictated work hours and work conditions. We had minimal input.

"Some of us college students started speaking up. We were naïve. We believed that management would listen, would be reasonable, would play fair. They weren't, and they didn't. They began firing us for the flimsiest of reasons. When you work for MegaSmartMart, freedom of speech doesn't exist. You're expected to shut up and follow orders."

"Must have been rough," sympathized Liz.

"Right. I was a twenty-one-year-old single mom, going to school and supporting myself and my child. It's rough even when you're living at home with your folks.

Always having an eye for a sympathetic cutaway, Liz motioned to a cameraman, who panned to Robyn's six-year-old son sitting in the first row, vigorously kicking his feet up and down and banging his heels into the seat.

"Your son is adorable. What's his name?"

"Nicholas. He was born at Christmas."

"Hi, Nicholas," called Liz. The boy smiled shyly and kicked even harder. Turning back to Robyn, "You shared with me prior to the show that the stress of losing your job contributed to your breakup with your boyfriend. Nicholas's father?"

"No."

"You were a senior in high school when Nicholas was born?"

"Yes," Robyn paused, irritated at Liz's attempt to steer the discussion toward her personal life and answered philosophically, "Life changes. People change. Couples grow apart. My friend and I were both working hard at getting through school and that was all we could handle. I guess we just couldn't work hard enough at us."

Pausing and smiling winningly, she returned to her main topic. "I started college intending to become a social worker. But education affects a person in unexpected ways. I came to realize that many of society's ills are systemic and that social workers often can't address the real causes, the root causes. I switched from social work to economics. In grad school, I switched again. I decided to get a law degree and do my bit to humanize the system.

"So you didn't leave MegaSmartMart quietly," commented Liz.

"No, I didn't. None of us did. We were outraged! We consulted with local political activists. They helped us organize a petition drive to place a law raising the local minimum wage on the next county election ballot. Business leaders campaigned hard against it. They claimed that higher prices and higher unemployment would result. But the law passed by a landslide."

"So what happened next?" Liz prompted.

"MegaSmartMart and the other chains threatened to pull out of Watertown," Robyn replied. "So we encouraged groups in surrounding counties to promote living wage laws there, too. The business community spent huge sums to counter our efforts, but they failed miserably. Laws similar to ours passed with large majorities in the surrounding counties. Thank goodness, at least around here, a real living wage isn't considered to be a radical idea."

"And as of now, how far has the movement spread?" Liz asked.

"There are active chapters all across the country, although the majority are still in neighboring states such as Minnesota and Wisconsin. Many groups have successfully worked for laws similar to ours."

"Mr. Phelps?"

"Ms. Sherwood: how did all this translate into a campaign to raise the national minimum wage? Certainly you must have been aware of the job losses and other negatives which would result."

"I must admit we started to get scared," Robyn said soberly. "Could our movement have created an economic monster? We began researching past national minimum wage increases. None of them resulted in the unemployment and other dire consequences that opponents had predicted. Instead, our minimum wage laws were creating economic booms. More people had more money to spend, and they were spending it. We were ecstatic! So, getting back to your question, that's when we began entertaining the possibility of persuading Congress to raise the national minimum wage."

"Mr. Mayor?" Liz queried.

"I don't believe things are as neat and simple as you claim, Ms. Sherwood," said the mayor. "The jury's still out on the long-term effects of the new minimum wage laws here. We do know that the number of jobs in our community has fallen considerably. Isn't that too high a price to pay?"

"Yes, Mr. Mayor, the total number of jobs has decreased," replied Robyn. "But most of those job losses were to part-time teenage workers, and to adults who no longer need to work at two or three jobs just to get by. Most importantly, the total income of our community has increased, and that money will create more jobs."

"Aren't you just sending jobs overseas to Third World countries?" the mayor replied.

Robyn said, "It's true that wage increases here make some of our workers and companies less competitive in the global market. But isn't our primary, our first responsibility to our workers, to our standard of living?"

"Perhaps," Phelps interjected, "but isn't protectionism ultimately irrational? It limits trade. It hampers global markets by restricting their efficiency. Sounds like you're in favor of government regulation, not a free market."

"We aren't talking either-or here," Robyn retorted. "It's clear that we need a market economy. But history shows us that an under-regulated market fosters monopoly, corruption, and inequality. These are evils which should not be tolerated in a democracy.

"As my educational emphasis switched from social work to economics to law, I've come to see the United States as the land of a small, controlling, wealthy and powerful elite. Our so-called 'free economy' puts obscene wealth in the hands of a few. The fact that a former CEO of MegaSmartMart is president of the United States means that most citizens still don't understand. Hubert Hedges was no friend of workers as CEO of MegaSmartMart, and he certainly is no friend of the average citizen as president of the United States."

Robyn laughed bitterly. Liz, looking strained and uncomfortable due to Robyn's disparagement of the establishment, smiled silently at her guest.

"That reminds me," Robyn continued. "Some of us thought of a new name for our movement to highlight that we are about much more than merely a living wage."

"What was that new name?" Liz queried.

"It's an acronym—'DETOXX'. It stands for 'Defeat Economic Tyranny and Outlaw eXecutive eXcess'. We wanted to make it clear that the goal of our movement is economic and social justice and the protection of constitutional rights. But the name DETOXX didn't communicate clearly enough for many of our members. So we abandoned it, and stayed with Living Wage Movement."

"We'll be right back," Liz interjected, as the show's director cut to a commercial.

During the interim, Phelps said to Liz and Robyn, "After the break, I would like to continue the line of questioning I began, if I may." They agreed. Everyone grabbed a bottle of water from the stagehand who was circling the table with a tray. The stress of doing a live show had made the guests thirsty, although Liz and Phelps, the experienced TV hosts, kept busy writing notes on their pads as they waited for the signal that the commercial had ended. The bottles were collected again just as the countdown began.

As soon as the show went live again, Liz called on Mr. Phelps.

"Back to the income disparities you were talking about," Phelps continued. "Aren't you advocating class warfare, Robyn? Isn't that un-American?"

"No, Mr. Phelps, I'm advocating economic justice," Robyn responded with obvious irritation. "Calling it class warfare is parroting the establishment party line. It's economic injustice that pits class against class, and there's nothing un-American about pointing that out. The wealthiest 5% have too much of everything. They earn as much as the bottom 95%. If average consumers—that bottom 95%—had more money, they would spend much of it. Such spending would create more income and more jobs, exactly what's been happening everywhere our living wage law has passed. Those economies are booming because the average citizen has more money to spend."

"Let me ask you something, Mr. Phelps," said Robyn. "How patriotic are our American-owned international companies when they send investment money and jobs wherever in the world the most profit is to be made? How patriotic is it to ignore the need and the duty to supply our own citizens with jobs? How patriotic is it for companies to set up offshore postal drops posing as 'corporate headquarters' in order to avoid paying U. S. taxes?"

"A company can't stay in business if it doesn't make money," Phelps responded forcefully.

"Paraphrasing the words of Jesus regarding the Jewish Sabbath," said Robyn, "Are the people meant to serve the economy or is the economy meant to serve the people?"

Without waiting for Robyn to elaborate, Liz jumped in, "Our local Living Wage Movement is spearheading a Labor Day rally in Washington, D.C. to demand a substantial increase in the national minimum wage. Their bus caravan leaves here the day after tomorrow. Movement members are encouraging sympathizers from across the country to join them in Washington. I've even heard, Robyn, that your Washington rally might attract crowds comparable to the civil rights marches of the 1960s."

"We hope so," Robyn replied. "Ours is also a civil rights movement, economic civil rights. If you work hard, you deserve to earn, you have a right to earn, a living wage."

"And now for a word from our sponsors," said Liz.

The debate between Robyn and Charles Phelps continued during the commercial break.

Back on camera, Liz turned to the studio audience, "Time for questions."

As the discussion or debate progressed, neither side conceded any ground to the other. With difficulty, Liz prevented the arguments from getting out of hand, successfully maintaining a veneer of civility and politeness.

* * * * *

After the show, Robyn walked across the station parking lot to her car. Hearing the strains of a Brandenburg Concerto, she retrieved the phone in her purse. Hardly able to hear due to the noise of a nearby car engine, she put a finger to her ear and shouted, "Hello. Robyn Sherwood speaking."

"Tom Cartwright, Robyn."

"Yes, yes!" she blurted out excitedly. Continuing in a calmer, more subdued voice after a moment, "I heard you speak at a meeting of the American Progressive Party in Des Moines a year ago. We chatted briefly in the reception line."

"Sorry, I don't remember," he said apologetically.

In an even, measured tone, she said, "Lots of people. I'm not surprised."

"The station you just appeared on is one of ours. I learned of the interview and decided to listen in—with considerable interest, I might add. I'm calling to inform you that your cause has my total support and, if I'm any judge, that of the American Progressive Party."

"I'm very, very happy to hear that, Mr. Cartwright. The Living Wage Movement appreciates your support and that of the Party. We need all the help we can get."

"Congratulations on the gem of a job you did in articulating and defending the position of the Movement."

She blushed. "I'm flattered. Thanks. Every bit of positive recognition encourages us in our struggle."

"Then extend that congratulation to your members. However, may I offer a piece of advice?"

"Yes, please do."

"Consider keeping your comments as close to the middle of the road as conscience permits. You'll alienate the least number of potential voters. Of course, if you're speaking to the faithful, that's another matter."

"Thanks. I know I go overboard at times. Ever since I was a teenager, I guess. Got me into more trouble than I care to remember."

"I know it's not easy, but the most reasonable propositions start sounding radical if there's too much righteous indignation behind them. But I also called to tell you I'm thinking of attending your Watertown sendoff rally and your Labor Day rally in Washington, and to ask for details."

Robyn outlined planned events. She concluded, "I'm certain our supporters would be overjoyed if you were one of our speakers, Mr. Cartwright.... Perhaps our principal speaker?"

"Call me Tom."

She blushed, even though no one was near.

"I'd be happy to consider your kind offer. Looking forward to meeting you...again, and let's talk before the Labor Day rally. Is this the best way to reach you?"

"Yes."

"All right, then, I'll be in touch."

"Thanks for your support."

Chapter 3

Accessing the New York Stock Exchange's main server, Sarah Stevenson conducted a routine check of the system. Everything appeared normal. She thought of the good old days and daydreamed about what the frenetic activity on the market floor must have been like before the computer takeover.

Her aptitude for computer systems and high finance had been nurtured as an undergrad at Smith and hailed as a grad student at Harvard. Exploiting her technical expertise, her redheaded good looks, her prim and proper New-York-socialite charm, and the heritage of a family used to moving comfortably in the highest social echelons, she had successfully fought her way up the corporate ladder of major New York investment firms at a young age. Recently, she had embarked upon still more challenging work at the New York Stock Exchange. She was now the confident, upbeat *wunderkind* responsible for the smooth operation of the automated Exchange. Though appreciative of its benefits, she was also somewhat disappointed; "push-button warfare" lacked the glamour and excitement of hand-to-hand combat.

A computer's warning wail interrupted her reverie. She called to her assistant, "Find out what's up."

He responded with that slightly flirty look, as he often did. Although she felt a certain attraction, she knew better than to reciprocate. Having dated an analyst briefly while working at another investment firm, the explosive ending of the relationship had underscored the generally-accepted wisdom of looking outside the workplace for one's social life. Still single, she was aware of a sometimes-undesired power to intimidate men, which tended to stifle any potential romantic inclinations.

Increasingly desiring more from life than her job could provide, she would freely admit, except to her mother, that the long hours and constant jockeying for power were taking their toll.

"Someone on the floor needs help," her assistant advised.

Bringing the trader's screen up on her own, she spoke into the intercom, "What's the matter?"

"Don't know exactly," came the agitated reply.

"Give me some idea," she encouraged.

"Something could have gone wrong with the last transaction."

After reviewing the data, she said, "Everything looks fine. What made you think so?"

"I couldn't track the price. The screen went blank."

Sarah knew very well that the system was complex and bound to have a glitch every now and then. She also knew it was so highly redundant that its sophisticated diagnostic programs could detect and correct almost any error—short of a general system failure.

"Switch to a spare terminal, have yours checked, and relax," she reassured him, masking the annoying anxiety which plagued her even at the mere prospect of a potential mysterious error and a loss of complete control.

Chapter 4

Peter heard background static as he fine-tuned another weak signal. Glancing anxiously at the equipment, he was relieved that it did not appear to affect signal strength. Looking at the video screen, he was surprised to see several aliens wearing hoods that completely hid their faces, except for one unhooded individual who seemed to be the leader. His large intelligent eyes and strikingly handsome human appearance drew Peter's attention.

Despite his alien language training, Peter had difficulty following the rapid and apparently highly idiomatic exchanges. "Income should be [or would be]…with disastrous consequences. Government could be counted on…" Accompanied by violent shouts and gestures, the topic was obviously controversial.

Without warning, on a signal from one of the hooded aliens, they all jumped up and ran from the room. The camera followed, but without audio signal. A wild chase down several corridors ended with a leap through a window into and down a fabric tube. The camera followed, and emerged in what appeared to be a narrow alley between tall buildings. Hoods lay on the ground near the fabric tube as several figures disappeared around the corner of a building at the far end of the alley. When the camera reached the corner, no pedestrians were in sight, only vehicles speeding along a busy thoroughfare.

Shortly, the original room was back on screen. The unhooded alien, still in his chair, was surrounded by highly agitated uniformed personnel holding what seemed to be weapons. Appearing unperturbed, he held up a disk. Despite the commotion, there was still no audio signal. After a brief heated exchange between the seated alien and a uniformed alien who appeared to be in charge, the seated alien pointed in the direction taken by those who had fled.

The scene faded. When the picture returned, now accompanied by sound, the same alien wearing a new set of clothes was seated in what appeared to be a different, studio setting. He spoke rapidly and was difficult to understand but seemed to be talking about some sort of economic crisis.

Suddenly, Peter's chair moved, interrupting his viewing and sending him sprawling.

"Ow!" he exclaimed, as his knee painfully struck the metal floor.

The floor heaved. An explosion? He had heard nothing. Soon, the heaving began to subside. The room continued to move erratically, but he managed to get to his feet. He noticed that the radio telescope equipment had ceased to function.

Peter knew that the space station's propulsion system allowed it to maintain orbit, but that it could not rapidly alter the motion of the massive station. Something else must have happened. But what? The artificial gravity seemed weaker. Could the rotation of the space station have slowed? The air pressure had not dropped. But that did not mean much. The control center's hatches provided airtight seals. He decided to put on his spacesuit as a precaution.

"Damn," he muttered, as the continuing erratic motion of the room made putting on and fastening the suit difficult. Finally, suit on, he shouted into the helmet radio, "Peter Abelard here. Come in!…Anybody!"

Silence.

* * * * *

Senses on full alert, Peter crept slowly and cautiously down the passageway connecting the radio telescope control center to Inner Main, thankful that the emergency lighting was still working. Thudding sounds caused him to stop and listen. Hearing nothing more, he cracked open the hatch to Inner Main, ducking instinctively at the sight of water. When it failed to cascade down upon him, he straightened up, observing that the corridor was partially flooded. A side passageway off Inner Main was also flooded.

"The solarium!" he gasped, imagining a rush of water sweeping down Outer Main toward Julia and the others. "Oh my God!" He screamed into the helmet of his spacesuit. "Anybody? Please, anybody at all. Come in!"

Moving as quickly as possible through the knee-deep water covering the floor of Inner Main, his shock and fear grew at the sight of other flooded side passageways leading to Outer Main. Half-jumping, half-running, he made his way to the nearest solarium hatch. Now he was certain that the artificial gravity had grown weaker, well aware that a shift of mass to the outer portions of the space station "doughnut" would slow its rotation.

Approaching the nearest solarium hatch, he was horrified to see it wide open. Peering in, he was sickened by the sight of the solarium's empty immensity, its walls littered with limp water plants and flopping fish. Reason told him that Julia and many of the crew were dead. Feeling faint, he put a steadying hand against the hatch, and became aware of the silence. The speakers lining the solarium sphere were no longer emitting their steady hum.

Terrified by what he might find if he dove down to the now-submerged communication center in Outer Main, Peter sought an alternative, desperately, subconsciously wishing to avoid the inevitable. His gaze shifted from the speakers to the transparent portion of the solarium known as the dome. An intense desire to know what had happened in the solarium seized him. Kicking against the wall, he soared toward the surveillance cameras. He removed the videodiscs from the cameras and stuffed them into his spacesuit utility pack.

Hearing a crackling in his headset, he moved toward the center of the dome and turned up the volume.

Hearing nothing, he spoke loudly into the helmet microphone, "Peter Abelard here! Come in!"

The faint, but familiar, voice of ground control answered, "What's happening up there? Everything went dead."

With an emotional torrent of words, he explained.

"Christ!" came the reply.

* * * * *

A hard kick against the dome sent Peter flying toward the solarium control center. A cursory examination detected nothing amiss. The computers were functioning. "Must be on emergency power," he muttered, staring at the blinking lights. "Move it!" he suddenly cried to himself. Love and conscience dictated that he dive to the apparently submerged communications center. With determination, he turned to kick off. As he did so, he became aware of movement on the far side of the solarium. A spacesuit emerged from a pressure hatch and waved as it soared in zero gravity across the solarium toward him.

"Thank God," he thought, "someone else is alive."

Fumbling in its spacesuit utility pack, the figure landed awkwardly on the solarium wall some distance away. Its right arm suddenly pointed at Peter, whose helmet jerked violently to the side, slamming him into the control center computers. A sharp report and gouge along one side of his helmet told Peter that he had been struck by a bullet. Jolted by the force of the discharge, the figure, in the adrenalin intensity of the moment, appeared to tumble backward in slow motion, one hand reaching for the pistol, which also tumbled backward.

Opting to take no chances, Peter propelled himself rapidly to the nearest solarium hatch. After landing with a splash in Inner Main, he retreated to the radio telescope control center, running and jumping through the water. At the hatch, he changed the entry codes just to be safe.

Inside, his thoughts raced. Thankful that the emergency electrical system and ceiling ventilation fan still worked, he picked up a phone and, heart pounding, dialed the escape capsule bay nearest Julia's workstation. To his deep distress, but not to his surprise, no one answered. Next, he tried the workstation itself. Nothing. Finally, he dialed the other escape capsule bays. No answer.

He slumped into a chair. The emergency earth-link phone rang. "Peter, Peter are you there?" He recognized the voice of Bill Swanson, vice president in charge of the weak-signal project.

"Yes, yes. We need help," Peter said, his voice choked with emotion.

"Switch to encryption," Swanson instructed.

Instantly furious at Swanson's greater apparent concern for security than for the welfare of the crew, Peter silently complied with clenched jaw before shouting, "Damn it, Bill, we have a catastrophe here!"

Swanson calmly insisted that he describe what had happened. Peter did so, all the while experiencing increasing anger and frustration at the barrage of unanswerable or irrelevant questions.

Finally, after the description of the shooting in the solarium, Swanson asked, "And that's when you decided to head for the radio telescope control center?"

"Yes!" Peter almost shouted, irate at Swanson's seemingly matter-of-fact attitude. Finally, he opted to ask a question of his own, "Any transmissions from the space station besides mine?"

"Not to my knowledge," Swanson answered slowly. "Why do you ask?"

Peter balled his fists in frustration. "At least one other person's alive," he uttered through a tightly clenched jaw, "the guy who shot at me. Seemed like a reasonable question."

"Sorry. Back to your situation." Swanson agreed that, for his safety, Peter should remain where he was. They also agreed that he should evaluate the condition of the space station by accessing as many systems as possible from the radio telescope control center. Swanson concluded, "Keep us informed. And Peter, we are doing everything we can. We want you to know that. We are deeply concerned about you and the crew."

Peter struggled to remain civil, "Thanks."

After signing off, he sat breathing hard. With considerable effort, he focused on what needed to be done next. Removing his spacesuit, he disconnected the equipment from the dead wall outlets and reconnected everything to the emergency system. Testing as many of the space station's systems as he could from the control center, he discovered that the battery-powered emergency system, fed by the station's solar panels, was one of the few still functioning. Assuming very few survivors, he calculated how long the existing air supply would last. Peter felt a lump form in his throat as he wondered about Julia and the others. Not knowing was pure torture.

Seeking diversion, he contacted Swanson and reported his findings. "No telling how long the emergency power system will last," Peter concluded, staring at the spinning ceiling ventilation fan.

"Good job," said Swanson. "We'll get back to you."

Deciding it was best to keep busy, Peter began recording alien weak signals. Once more, he noted a faint static while adjusting the equipment. It ended abruptly, only to begin again. As before, it did not significantly interfere with the signals. Unfortunately, the recording equipment required little attention once properly adjusted. Soon, he was alone again with his thoughts.

Seeking another diversion, he thought of his private collection of weak-signal recordings. He'd made them while initially adjusting the radio telescope equipment but had been too busy and under too many time constraints to view or listen to any. He pulled them out and stuffed the discs into his favorite old backpack.

Reminded of the solarium disks, he removed them from his spacesuit utility pouch. Inserting one into a player, he waited impatiently for it to load. The screen revealed a normal-looking solarium. Collapsing into a chair, he watched, longing for Julia and feeling terribly alone.

Needing to occupy himself with something else, anything else, he calculated how long it would be before a relief ship arrived. That, of course, depended on how much the corporation was willing to spend. The government could send a ship in two days. The corporation's own ship would take twice as long, at least. He reasoned bitterly that Swanson would likely choose the latter alternative, both because it was cheaper and because GCIS would retain total control of the situation on the space station.

While watching the image of a normal solarium, he thought of the fish and plants matting its wall, remembering that the transparent portions were free of debris. Why? It occurred to him that, if the speakers holding the ball of water in place failed, the rotation of air caused by the spinning solarium walls would gradually induce the ball itself to rotate. The centrifugal force of the spinning ball plus the cohesion of its water molecules would cause it to flatten into a giant pancake.

After a moment, he muttered, "No, not good enough," reasoning that it would take a long time for the movement of air in the solarium to generate enough rotational motion in the massive ball of water. However, if only the speakers on the wall failed, and not those on the transparent portions, the ball of water would rapidly be squashed flat, moving outward toward the solarium hatches in a matter of minutes. Once there, the water could somehow have shorted out the electrical system, opening the hatch doors. Propelled outward by the centrifugal force of the spinning space station, the mass of water would rapidly flood the corridors.

Movement in the solarium video attracted his attention. A tiny figure floated across the solarium toward its control center. Something about the figure seemed familiar. It left the control center and disappeared off screen. Momentarily, the giant ball of water flattened into a pancake, moving outward toward the solarium wall. Once the hatch doors were inundated, they opened and water gushed through.

"Yes!" he exclaimed, believing that something finally made sense. The speakers on the walls had apparently failed, while the speakers on the two transparent domes had continued to function, squashing the ball of water into a pancake. Then why didn't I hear them afterward? he thought. The only explanation which came to mind was that they failed subsequently, before he got there.

Quickly backing up the video, he watched for a second time the tiny figure enter and leave the solarium control center. It again seemed familiar. Zooming in, he was shocked to recognize the clothes.

They were his.

But I was never in the solarium control center alone, he thought, recalling that two days before, the solarium crew chief, wearing a blue diving suit, had offered to show him around.

All was the same, except the crew chief and his blue diving suit had vanished. "Damn," Peter shouted angrily, wondering who the hell was trying to frame him.

Chapter 5

Maggie Blevins loved the rough-and-tumble of investigative journalism, and she was anxious to get started on her current project. She recalled with fondness her first job, as reporter and later editor of Chicago's Hyde Park High School newspaper. It was a valuable experience because Hyde Park remained socially, economically, and racially diverse, due in large measure to the proximity of the University of Chicago. She knew that her parents, owners of a thriving Hyde Park deli, had intentionally sent her to public rather than private schools, hoping that the exposure would broaden her outlook and acquaint her with people from diverse backgrounds. In the process, she developed a sympathy for the underdog and a taste for taunting the elite. After obtaining college degrees in economics and journalism, she became a reporter for a New York Internet daily—Gaia—a job which seemed more like indulging in her favorite sport than like work.

Today, she was on her way to her newspaper's library. She had begged for and won her editor's grudging consent to continue investigating the possibly illegal activities of certain politically-oriented issue ad organizations. Such organizations were required by law to operate independently of any political party or candidate and to disclose funding sources. As long as specific issues were addressed without reference to political parties or candidates, the organizations could spend virtually unlimited amounts of money on advertising or otherwise advocating their causes.

Big joke, these organizations, she thought as she walked into Gaia's library. Anybody with half a brain knew which political party and which candidates an issue ad favored. Her suspicion was that several wealthy political activists, who wanted their contributions to be kept secret for fear of compromising the ads, had somehow circumvented the law and "laundered" their contributions to the organizations. Scott Smith, her editor, had given her so little time to work on the project that she had decided the library's huge databases and super high-speed internet links would be the quickest, most efficient way to obtain information.

She quickly checked the membership lists of various political issue ad organizations but was disappointed when she failed to detect any pattern suggestive of illegal activity. She was also disappointed when she could not identify the employers of all the members and again when she was unable to find any pattern suggestive of criminality.

Changing tactics, she investigated the officers and boards of directors of the employers that she had just identified. This search proved easier because such information was a matter of public record.

"Bingo!" she exclaimed, startling nearby library patrons.

* * * * *

Maggie greeted her editor as she entered his office, "Hi, Scott. Busy?"

Grinning broadly, he looked up at her from his desk, "Just added a new market, Indonesia. *Gaia* is now the largest circulating electronic newspaper in the world."

Maggie saw Scott Smith as the epitome of East Coast old money, down to his black garter socks. Thirtyish, darkly handsome, a Harvard grad, he was still single but clearly would not stay that way. She'd been attracted, and so, she knew, had he. What man wouldn't be, she thought. She was a well-rounded, vivaciously-muscular, curly-haired-brunette who ran four miles every morning.

One evening in a bar, over a couple too many drinks, she had realized that she was sitting across the table from a shallow, pompous elitist. They'd dated since, but the relationship was definitely on hold, at least as far she was concerned. Am I too idealistic, too picky? she wondered. Would Mr. Right even want somebody like me?

Scott's voice intruded, "What's on your beautiful mind?"

Pompous ass, she thought. "Those issue ad organizations."

"What about dinner tonight?" he asked, changing the subject. "I've found a new Italian restaurant. You'll love it."

Vacillating, Maggie hesitated.

"Think about it. What have you got?"

She removed several computer printouts from her briefcase. "I've got more. The important stuff is underlined."

He shuffled through the printouts. "What does it all mean?"

"It means that those five men," she said pointing to various sheets, "are the ultimate employers of every member of every independent issue ad organization I've been able to trace. They serve on the boards of every company that employs those members."

"You've traced…," he paused. "What? Eight…ten percent of the members?"

"Fifteen percent," corrected Maggie. "Fifteen percent of thousands of names."

"And on that basis you're drawing what sort of conclusion?"

Maggie ignored the expected put-down. "Wouldn't it be interesting to know how many of the members of these issue ad organizations received pay raises, bonuses, or promotions after becoming contributing members?"

Scott, she noted, seemed to develop instant indigestion. "Don't you have another assignment on deadline?" he queried.

"Cartwright and the American Progressive Party." Keep your big mouth shut, she told herself. But the temptation was too great, "Heard of Kenneth Lacey?" She already knew the answer. Kenneth Lacey, Scott Smith's uncle, was also CEO and chairman of the board of United News Services, *Gaia's* parent corporation—the same Kenneth Lacey whose name appeared prominently in her printouts.

Chapter 6

Tom Cartwright rose and sat on a table facing GCIS's senior engineering staff. "So? Is the construction of the instantaneous communication device described in the transmission feasible?" Nods, all around. "Then, let's get to it. We've got to beat our competitors to the punch if we're going to claim ownership."

"Right," replied the chief engineer. "Let me bring you up to speed. The Piscean transmission asserts that an ICD is possible because the ultimate attainable speed in the universe far exceeds that of light. It claims that superluminal conduits can be created, so signals can be sent almost instantaneously between any two points in the universe as long as a continuous force field link has been previously established. The continuously repeated transmission describing the device is supposedly such a link. A Piscean ICD operating on Earth will presumably transform the link into an actual superluminal conduit."

"What's the construction timeframe?"

"About twenty-four hours. The mechanism itself is actually surprisingly simple. We have access to similar basic hardware. The connections and configurations, plus the software, are new and different but easily replicated."

"So, you have everything sorted out and are ready to proceed?"

"Yes. But you need to know that we don't fully understand the device. It's possible that it could pose some sort of danger. We don't see anything troubling in the specs, but we should be cautious."

"What do you suggest?

"The device needs the support of certain of our computers. However, we need to separate it from the rest by a special firewall."

"Fine. Let's get going. The sooner the better."

An engineer at the back of the room stood and said, slowly and deliberately, "Tom, some of us are concerned that what we're doing might be illegal, that it might violate some national security statute."

"I understand your concern. We've already sent copies of the communication to both the administration and the military. Both advise us to take it slowly, but no one is telling us to stop, which means they haven't been able to come up with any legal reason to force us to do so. However, they also haven't come up with any good or legal reason why we shouldn't proceed. Unless they do, we intend to go full speed ahead.

"Other comments? Questions?"

A second engineer stood and glanced at the others around him. "The Piscean communication also warned about a spaceship heading toward Earth. It said the ship was armed and dangerous."

"Yes, that's correct." Tom said briskly. "We forwarded that communication to the military, and they're looking into it. As of yet, I haven't heard anything."

"Isn't it possible that our space station was attacked by that spaceship?" replied the same engineer.

"Anything is possible." Cartwright started to get annoyed with his people's reluctance. "But right now we don't have any evidence of an external breach of the integrity of the space station. We think that whatever went wrong happened as the result of something onboard."

"We all know that the solarium water flooded the rest of the station," offered a third engineer. "It was only held in place by sound waves. A spaceship could've jammed and disabled unshielded electronic equipment from a considerable distance, without firing a shot."

"True," said Cartwright. "We know that the solarium computers automatically switched to emergency power when things went wrong. They have been tested from Earth and are fully functional. But we don't know exactly what happened, and we won't know more until a team is sent up to the space station. I'll relay your concern to the military. But I'm not willing to wait on the ICD while we sort out everything else."

"Other comments or questions?"

There were none.

"Then let's get started. As soon as you finish, we'll get together, turn on the juice, and see what happens."

Chapter 7

"Wow," mouthed James Archer, newly-appointed chair of the Securities and Exchange Commission, to himself as he surveyed Michael Murphy's luxurious New York Stock Exchange office. The SEC's authority now extended to the internet, at least within the confines of the United States. Because most communications, including business and banking transactions, now took place over the Web, the Commission's regulatory powers had expanded considerably. Internet speed, security, censorship, and viruses continued to be major concerns.

"Now, what can we do for you?" boomed Murphy, the forceful, graying chairman of the Exchange, after concluding a phone conversation. Walking around his large mahogany desk, he vigorously shook Archer's hand, causing him to wince. Ushering him to a chair, Murphy sat facing him.

"I'm here in my official capacity, and at the president's request," said Archer.

Murphy leaned back in his chair, "And?"

"We want your help in placing undercover agents." Murphy, a former CIA chief, was well respected within governmental circles.

"Why?"

"Several prominent investors recently met privately with the president. Their portfolio managers were complaining of irregularities in the market."

"People who lose money often think that there's some giant conspiracy working against them. They don't consider the possibility that the conspiracy might just be their greedy fingers at war with their tiny intellects. Is that all you have?"

"Yes," confessed Archer.

"Pretty flimsy evidence for initiating a major investigation, wouldn't you say?"

"Yes and no," replied the SEC chair, struggling to match Murphy's self-assured tone. "We can't simply discount the collective judgment of highly competent and prominent financial advisors."

After a lengthy silence, Murphy said, "I have never refused a president when the country's welfare might be at stake."

"The president and I appreciate your support."

"However, one Watergate and one Enron are one too many."

"The Attorney General and the Congress are being advised of our every move."

"Glad to hear that," said Murphy. "Before we get down to business, there's someone I want you to meet. Sarah Stevenson. She may be able to help you in your investigation."

* * * * *

Sarah entered Murphy's office. The Exchange chairman was in the midst of yet another phone conversation and motioned for her to be seated. She found herself beside an attractive, trim and fit dark-haired man. However, when he introduced himself, she was put off by his obvious sense of self-importance. She also had the feeling that she had met him somewhere.

As Murphy's phone conversation continued, they quietly introduced themselves, and found they had much in common. Both had attended prestigious east-coast colleges, and both held graduate degrees from Harvard.

Did I meet him at Harvard? she wondered. He may be a bit pompous and conceited, but he's a charmer and definitely a hunk. She saw no signs of a ring.

When Murphy's phone conversation ended, he asked, "Have you two introduced yourselves?" They nodded. "Fine. Sarah, please show Jim around and familiarize him with our operation."

She waited for some further explanation of Archer's presence, but none was forthcoming.

"By the way," Archer said to Murphy as he and Sarah rose to leave, "Ken Lacey sends his regards."

"Tell him the same for me," said Murphy. "Lacey introduced you to the president, right?"

"Yes. He's been a mentor and a good friend."

At the door, Murphy casually remarked, "Sarah, that call was from Alan Thompson. A broker is complaining about a transaction. Check with him when you get a chance."

"Certainly."

Sarah led Archer through a maze of mainframe computers. A large round computer to one side of the room attracted his attention. Sarah explained that it was a new mainframe linking together various components of the Exchange system. Entering a room filled with rows of computer cubicles, which seemed to extend to the horizon, Sarah continued describing the Exchange system.

"Very impressive," Archer acknowledged.

"Much of our software is written in-house."

"I'm rather interested in your software," he said as they strolled along.

Sarah blushed at the apparent double meaning, but hoped it wasn't obvious.

Archer stopped, turned toward her, and said apologetically, "I'm sorry. I said that poorly."

Sarah, still more embarrassed, responded in her most professional voice, "No offense taken." She turned, partly to hide the liquid warmth of another blush and the attraction from which it flowed. "Let me demonstrate a few of our software capabilities in my office."

With Archer seated beside her, she demonstrated several programs. When she finished, he asked, "What about that Thompson thing Murphy mentioned? Might be instructive if I saw you in action."

Sarah was not eager to investigate a complaint in front of an audience. Some unforeseen glitch might pop up. It was impossible to totally eliminate them from complex systems. She liked being in control, and the prospect of sorting out problems in front of an audience made her feel anxious. However, since no reasonable excuse for refusal came to mind, she felt compelled to say, "Sure," with a forced smile.

She called Thompson, who told her, "The broker complained of price irregularities at the time of the transaction."

"Anything else?"

"No."

He gave her the account identification code. She entered it and the transaction appeared on her computer. "Looks good," she remarked to Archer. "Here are the figures," she pointed to the screen, "and here are the price averages at the time of the transaction. The sale price was on the low side but within parameters at the time of the sale."

"What was the exact time of the transaction?" asked Archer, staring at the screen.

"We never know," Sarah had to admit. "The computer hardware is highly parallel. As you're no doubt aware, such operations are processed asynchronously as the appropriate data become available via other computer components, rather than according to the precise beats of an internal clock like the old computers. In other words, we know only the approximate time of a transaction."

"So you are unable to exhaustively follow a transaction?" queried Archer thoughtfully.

"Correct. But the software is extremely sophisticated, and the system is highly redundant, so it's easy to detect errors or discrepancies."

Staring at the screen, Sarah sensed the onset of her anxiety, never too far below the surface. As a consequence, she failed to tell Archer of her amazement that the transaction details had been saved instead of just the usual concluding summary. Among the details was a sudden, very brief, sharp drop in the market price of the stock in question. Never before had she seen such a microburst drop. She had no idea who or what could have triggered the special high-speed memory required to save these details. Perhaps some error or anomaly had activated the system's defenses?

After returning her guest to Murphy's office, she stood in the foyer wondering about Archer, with the realization that neither Murphy nor Archer had given her any hint of what brought the SEC chair to their door. Was the SEC conducting an investigation? Was Murphy under suspicion? Was he secretly cooperating? She felt her anxiety slowly build until the induced tension caused her to jog down the corridor, heading for the cafeteria and a soothing dose of chocolate.

* * * * *

When the conference between SEC chairman Archer and her boss ended, Sarah felt compelled to tell Murphy about her findings regarding the Thompson complaint. She emphasized the improbability of the microburst drop in the price of the stock and the mysterious triggering of high-speed memory. Murphy praised her perceptivity but dismissed the microburst as a "blip" in the market and the triggering of high-speed memory as an accidental random occurrence. He advised her to run a thorough check of the new software she had programmed into the Exchange system, suggesting that she might not have taken every contingency into account, thus allowing unforeseen erratic and disruptive operations. He warned her that the Exchange could be held legally responsible for system malfunctions if investors lost money to which they were legitimately entitled. Otherwise, he said he considered the matter closed but encouraged her to report any other unusual occurrences, especially any recurrent ones.

Sarah turned to leave, but hesitated for a moment. Anxious and uncertain of what, if anything, Archer and/or Murphy were up to, Sarah intuitively realized that she needed to be certain about one thing. "I remember reading somewhere that Jim Archer's wife also works for some governmental agency, but I can't remember which. Do you happen to know, Mr. Murphy?"

"It's about time you started calling me George. You're making me feel like an old fogey. I believe he and his wife divorced recently. It made the news briefly. They had a row at a formal diplomatic reception. Apparently, she accused him of subordinating their marriage to his political ambition. Unfortunately, that's a facet of life with which I'm only too familiar. She was the one who filed for divorce. That's all I know. I really can't say what sort of chap he is."

"Thanks," said Sarah, slightly embarrassed, yet pleased.

* * * * *

Sarah returned to her office anxiety-ridden, unconvinced that Murphy was right but sure he wasn't telling her all he knew. Aware of possessing a certain stubbornness and love of puzzles—a trait she knew she shared with other systems analysts—she calculated the probability of a microburst drop in a stock price, and found it to be astronomically small, something like the probability of all the air molecules under a table moving in the same direction at the same time, sending it smashing to the ceiling. After tinkering with the Exchange system for the better part of an hour, she succeeded in enabling it to track such microbursts, having diverted an entire mainframe and super fast memory to the task. She soon discovered other microbursts. To her surprise, many stocks had actually been sold at the greatly reduced microburst prices. Could the Exchange be held legally accountable for the losses to the sellers?

What about earlier this morning? she wondered, disappointed that the super-fast memory had not been triggered for other transactions that morning. Even if it had, the system could only save complete information on a limited number of transactions. Since super-fast memory systems were fiendishly expensive, only a limited version had been installed. It had been difficult to convince the Exchange board to pay for even such a version. The permanent record of most Exchange transactions consisted only of final results. Those rare instances in which complete records were kept usually involved criminal investigations.

Returning to her task, Sarah continued to search for additional microburst stock price changes and, more importantly, for patterns. She discovered that purchasers at the lower microburst stock prices were mainly large pension and mutual funds, not surprising given the amounts of money they invested.

However, one account showing numerous microburst transactions caught her attention. Owing to media coverage, she was familiar with the name of the group—the Living Wage Movement—but little else about it. Bringing up its trading record, she saw that the size of its purchases and sales were miniscule in comparison with market averages.

But, calculating the organization's day-end profits, she blurted out in a half whisper, "My God! 430%!"

Checking the organization's trading record for the past few days, she was astounded to find that its profits for each day were never less than 400%. Such luck—if it was luck—was a statistical near-impossibility. Murphy had recently mentioned rumors of weird goings on. Was that the reason for Archer's visit to the Exchange? Could the LWM be the key to understanding what was going on? Was she caught up in a giant fraud scheme? Was she being set up?

Staring blankly at her computer screen, she wondered what to do. Finally, she saved the results of her search to several disks. After slipping them into a briefcase, her fingers flew over the keys, restoring the initial system configuration and erasing as much of her trail as the software would allow. Then she left the building.

Chapter 8

Peter stared at the ceiling ventilation fan in the radio telescope control center, pondering various possible sabotage scenarios. Absent-mindedly his eyes wandered down the streamer dangling limply from it. Suddenly, he sat bolt upright.

"Holy hell!" he shouted, jumping up out of his chair. Reaching for the Earth-link phone, he contacted Swanson, "Bill, I can't stay in the radio telescope control center. The emergency ventilation quit."

"What are you going to do?"

Peter was once again infuriated by his calm tone. "Don't know. I like breathing, but I don't particularly want to get shot." As they discussed options, Peter became increasingly irate; Swanson seemed to downplay the danger in his situation. Suddenly eager to rid himself of Swanson, Peter said, "Let me mull things over," and abruptly signed off.

He gathered some of the most recent weak-signal recordings and stuffed them into his backpack with the others. He put on his spacesuit but not the helmet, opting to conserve the suit's air supply. With difficulty, he slung the backpack full of discs around his shoulders and over the suit's air tanks. Propping open the security door in case he needed quick re-entry, he crept cautiously to the Inner Main hatch, swung it open a couple of inches, and peered out into the corridor. Hearing and seeing nothing, he opened it farther, glancing about warily and listening. He then opted to leave the relative safety of the control center and venture into the corridor.

Tiny ripples undulated through the water covering the corridor floor. Peter froze. A second set of ripples. Vibration? A third set. He was certain that he had not sensed vibration. Could his adversary have shut off the ventilation and be in the corridor, waiting? The sick feeling in his knotted gut made him feel like a fugitive in a movie.

Silently, he closed the hatch and made his way back to the radio telescope control center, latching the security door. After considerable deliberation, he decided to contact Swanson, telling him that he intended to exit the radio telescope control center through its small airlock, walk across the outer hull of the space station, and re-enter through the airlock near the auxiliary communication and control center on the far side of Inner Main.

"Watch yourself," cautioned Swanson. "Good luck." He signed off.

"Good luck?" thought Peter angrily, glad that he hadn't revealed his real plans and that he hadn't told Swanson about the water ripples. "This isn't a game! It's my life!"

Making his way back to Inner Main, he quietly opened the hatch and again peered intently at the water covering its floor. Soon he saw the ripples become waves. Hanging from the hatch by one hand, he extended his body out into the corridor and glimpsed a figure in a spacesuit shuffling away.

When the spacesuit was out of sight, Peter hooked his feet around the hatch, relaxed, and allowed the weak artificial gravity to extend his body toward the floor of the corridor. As he did, he could see farther and farther along its curve. Fully extended, he again saw the spacesuit, standing in front of a port window. Sometimes the helmet remained motionless and sometimes it bobbed up and down. He guessed the person was alternately listening and speaking. When the apparent conversation ended, the spacesuit shuffled away down the corridor.

Gently lowering himself into the water covering the floor of the corridor, Peter moved slowly in order to minimize wave creation. Entering the nearest solarium hatch, he noticed motion and ducked back into the corridor.

"Must not like getting his feet wet," he mused.

Peeking through the hatch, he watched the spacesuit glide across the solarium. When the figure exited, Peter moved cautiously from hatch to hatch, eyes never leaving the one through which the spacesuit had disappeared. At that hatch, he stared at the gently rippling water in Inner

Main, easily detecting the direction his adversary had taken. Hearing nothing, he moved silently into the hatch. He surveyed the corridor. The spacesuit was not in sight. Gradually extending his body out into the corridor as before, Peter saw nothing.

Reentering the solarium, he pushed off and soared to the next hatch. Staring once again at the water in Inner Main, he listened and looked for ripples. None were apparent. He moved into the hatch, halting when he saw the watery reflection of a spacesuit. His adversary was standing beside the auxiliary communication and control center airlock, gun in hand. "He must know what I told Swanson," Peter whispered.

His thoughts were distracted by a body in the water. The corpse faced upward, a bloodstain in the middle of its chest. He recognized a solarium crewmember. Had the man been impaled on something by the rushing water, or had he been shot?

Sensing movement, Peter glanced up. The reflected image of the spacesuit was splashing through the water, its dark helmet looking straight at him.

With a gasping rush of adrenaline, he scrambled back through the hatch to the solarium. Kicking furiously at the wall, he propelled himself to the nearest hatch, putting on his spacesuit helmet as he flew. Entering the hatch, he heard a ping and saw sparks.

"Damn fool!" his mind screamed, imagining the bullet punching a hole in the solarium wall.

With all his might, he propelled himself through the hatch, landing with a splash on the floor of Inner Main. Churning through the knee-deep water, he dove into the first submerged side passageway leading to Outer Main.

The weight of the spacesuit aided his descent. Glancing up, he saw a dark helmet peering down at him. Lines of air bubbles streaked downward. He felt three bullets hit his suit, but the water was too deep for them to do any harm.

As he watched, the other spacesuit performed a low-gravity, slow-motion dive. He propelled himself downward faster, but his foe rapidly closed the distance. Swimming furiously, Peter felt a hand grasp his ankle. He desperately kicked at it, but with a yank, it pulled him closer.

Feeling his adversary tear fiercely at his backpack, Peter realized that he was after the air hoses. Luckily, they did not come loose. The backpack and the disks seemed to be protecting him.

With a sudden, violent twisting motion, Peter sensed the odds turn as he tore loose his pursuer's air hoses. But to his surprise his adversary did not immediately abandon the attack and swim for the water's surface. Only after a few long moments did he stop and start swimming upward. Peter considered grabbing a leg and holding him down, but hesitated too long and missed his chance.

"Maybe the biggest mistake you ever made," he thought to himself, cursing silently.

Without further delay, Peter continued the descent. Although full of plants and swimming fish, the water was relatively clear, in spite of its recent violent agitation. Reaching Outer Main, he noted that the safety hatch was open. Titanic II, he mused bitterly, knowing that the hatches were designed to close automatically if the pressure dropped, but, not, apparently, if the pressure rose, which must have been the case as the water rushed in.

Suddenly, his heart twisting, he made his way as quickly as possible toward Julia's workstation. He thought about the nearby escape capsule bay, wondering how difficult it would have been for her to swim, encumbered by her body brace from the accident.

Passing a dead body floating in the gloom, surrounded by a school of small fish, Peter was thankful that it was a relative stranger; he was aware that actually witnessing violent death is far more psychologically devastating than seeing it on a video screen. Encountering several more bodies, he kept a tight rein on his emotions, trying to harden himself against the prospect of what he might find at Julia's workstation.

Farther down the corridor yet another body caught and held his gaze in its grisly embrace. Open eyes stared from a face frozen in death. Sadly, he recognized his boss, Gene, who was—had been—in charge of the space station. As he came closer, he noticed part of one leg was missing. Strange, he thought, his face shows fear but no pain.

As he stared at the corpse, the torn serrated stump of a leg suddenly screamed, "Predator!" His mind flashed to the sharks used to control the population of smaller fish in the water ball, and to visions of Julia fighting for her life. Scanning his surroundings, Peter searched anxiously for signs of sharks. None were apparent.

I need protection, he thought. An air vent grill dangling from the ceiling caught his attention. He detached it and made several quick motions to get the feel of it in the water, then connected leads from the spacesuit's auxiliary power pack to opposite ends of the grill. The fabric of his spacesuit would insulate him from any surges of electricity he would use against a predator.

"Damn well better work," he muttered.

With the grill firmly in hand, he continued his slow-motion shuffle down the corridor. Julia's workstation was still some distance away. Each step through the watery gloom seemed interminable.

As he neared his destination, a shark suddenly appeared and came straight at him. Reflexively, he brought up the grill. The shark swerved to his left, and he switched on the auxiliary power pack's strobe setting, sending intermittent surges of electricity through the grill. His meager knowledge of shark behavior dictated that he hold the grill at arms length in front of him.

As if in response, the shark circled closer and closer, its unblinking eyes appearing serenely confident. He thrust the grill at its snout. It jerked away, but the lash of its tail knocked his legs out from under him. The grill's electric leads came loose as he fell. Scrambling to his feet, he moved to the wall to protect his back while fumbling with the leads. With a slight flick of its tail, the shark came for him. He raised the grill. The shark bashed into it, pinning him against the wall. Then it swam away. Managing to reattach the leads, he brought up the grill as the shark came straight at him. Spinning to the side at the last instant, it collided violently with the wall.

"Yes!" Peter shouted triumphantly.

Bouncing off the wall, the shark swam in the direction of a safety hatch. Peter followed, swinging the grill from side to side, intent upon herding it through and closing the hatch. As he neared, it shot to the ceiling and darted behind him. Sensing a tearing in the left leg of his space suit, he yanked it away, turning and bringing the grill down on the shark's snout. It seemed to "trip" over itself getting away. Glancing down, he was relieved to see only a slight tear in the suit, but relief turned to horror when a tiny crimson cloud emanated from it.

"Damn!" he hissed, envisioning sharks in a feeding frenzy.

As he watched, the crimson cloud elongated into a ribbon. He felt a gentle tugging at his spacesuit. It became stronger. He had difficulty maintaining his footing. Then the surging water swept him down the corridor, ridding him of all thoughts of sharks.

Chapter 9

Peter shouted obscenities as the force of the water bashed him into the edge of a metal girder. Desperately, he grabbed at a hatch as the current swept him along, clinging to it with difficulty as plants, fish, and human bodies struck glancing blows. Forcing himself to think, he could not recall any change in the motion of the space station, only in the motion of the water. Therefore, the water must still be in the outer circumference of the spinning space station. The current could only be the result of water venting out into space through a cargo hatch.

Instantly, he became focused on the fact that his torn spacesuit would not protect him in the vacuum of space. His blood and other body fluids would boil. He would, quite literally, explode. An involuntary shudder almost broke loose his grip.

As he expected, Outer Main soon began emptying of water. When there was only a flow around his waist, he was able to stand, still clinging to the hatch. Struggling with the hatch door in the current, he managed to close and secure it. Moving quickly to the hatch at the other end of the compartment, he managed to close and secure it as well. Alive for now, he thought.

Peering through the tiny hatch window, he saw the water level rise as it flowed against the door. However, the level was of less concern than the prospect that it might begin to boil, indicating that the air pressure in the space station was dropping toward the vacuum of space. As he continued to watch, the unexpected happened. The water level covering the floor of Outer Main stabilized at about two feet. More important, it showed no sign of boiling. He ran back to the first hatch. The water level there had stabilized as well, and without boiling.

Glancing at a gauge on the sleeve of his spacesuit, Peter surmised that the air pressure drop was consistent with a venting of water out into space, speculating that his adversary had initiated the venting from the station's auxiliary control center in Inner Main. It made perfect sense. At the least, he would not be able to hide as easily. At the most, he would be flushed out into space and certain death.

"Now what do I do?" Peter murmured.

Resolving to continue his search for Julia, he hurried back to the far hatch, opened it, and sloshed his way with determined steps down the corridor to Julia's workstation. He knew it was unlikely that he would find her body due to the venting of the water. But he still felt considerable relief upon not finding her. Rummaging around the workstation searching for clues, he was soon forced to admit he wasn't accomplishing anything.

Hoping that Julia had somehow reached the nearby escape capsule bay, he ran and jumped through the water to it. The bay airlock did not respond to its electrical controls. Fortunately, there was manual backup. Inside, the bay appeared dry, except for the airlock water which had entered with him. The water quantity seemed to indicate that he was the first person to have entered the bay since the disaster. However, a glance at the row of escape capsules revealed that one was missing. His heart raced. Speculating that much of the water which had entered with her would have flowed into the outer airlock when she launched the capsule, he assumed the rest had evaporated.

Grabbing a large wrench, he destroyed the bay surveillance camera and exited. Back in Outer Main, he pushed a small piece of metal obtained from the bay workshop into an unobtrusive spot in the airlock's manual gearbox, hoping his adversary would waste time trying to get into the bay, expecting him to be inside.

On the lookout for sharks even in the shallow water, Peter warily sloshed down Outer Main, putting distance between himself and the escape capsule bay before heading up one of the side passageways leading to Inner Main. At Inner Main, he stopped. Seeing and hearing nothing, he made his way to a solarium hatch. After assuring himself that no one was in the solarium, he kicked off and sailed across, trusting that the destruction of the surveillance camera had confused his enemy.

Exiting the solarium, he headed for another escape capsule bay. Once again he had to manually open the airlock doors. Before entering, he removed the gearbox crank handle and took it with him. Inside, he quickly disabled the surveillance camera and hoped it would be some time before his adversary would try to enter.

This bay also appeared dry. The rows of escape capsules were in place, ready to be hoisted onto the launch track that led to the outer airlock and the vacuum of space. He punched the capsule hoist buttons. No response. At least they did something right, he thought, thankful that the bay was designed to operate both electrically and manually.

Pushing the hoist to the capsule nearest the outer airlock, he attached it and released the locking devices holding the capsule in place. The hoist chain moved easily in his hands, and soon the capsule wheels were resting on the launch track. Opening the outer airlock, he pushed the capsule to its launch site. Returning to the bay, he removed his backpack and damaged spacesuit. When he saw the first aid kit there, he opened it to smear some antibiotic cream on the tear in his leg. He then donned a new, undamaged spacesuit from the bay's store.

Backpack in hand, he reentered the airlock. Closing the airlock hatch, he threw his backpack into the capsule. Every crewmember had been drilled in the operation of the capsules and had taken flying lessons, but that preparation now hardly seemed adequate. Glancing at his watch, he noted the time and manually armed the catapult. He had ten minutes before the outer airlock hatch opened and the capsule launched. Seated in the capsule cockpit, he ran the program which checked all systems. The indicator lights turned green. Everything was go. Closing and latching the capsule hatch, he strapped himself in, took a deep breath, and waited.

* * * * *

The catapult launch was successful. But it felt like a disappointingly slow, poor imitation of the carrier launches seen in videos. As the capsule glided away from the space station, Peter retracted its wheels. Gazing at the debris surrounding the space station, he tried not to dwell on the sight of corpses that had exploded as the body fluids boiled. He could not help looking about for Julia. But he was greatly relieved when, upon leaving the debris field, he had not seen her corpse, which would have been identifiable in part because of her body brace.

Activating the capsule's guidance program, he determined the craft's exact location and calculated various glide paths to pre-selected landing sites on Earth. Where should I land? he wondered, aware that by now he was quite likely a suspect in the space station disaster. Fatalistically, he set the glide path for the company's Minnesota site. After the retro rockets kicked in, he reluctantly contacted GCIS headquarters.

Bill Swanson's calm voice answered, "We've been expecting to hear from you, Peter. Our instruments indicated a launch. Are you onboard a capsule?"

"Yes. I've programmed it for Minnesota." His pulse quickening, he asked, "Were any other capsules launched?"

"We're not certain. There may have been a launch shortly after the disaster."

"Any transmissions?" Uncertain about whether to trust Swanson, he did not mention the capsule missing from the bay near Julia's workstation.

"No, none. Keep this frequency open. We'll get back to you."

Looking through the cockpit window, Peter gazed at the space station and its surrounding spiral rings of debris. From this distance, the horror of what had transpired was not apparent. Rather, he was reminded of Saturn. As he continued to watch, a dark speck appeared against the brighter halo-like background of debris. "Guess who?" Peter thought, not in the least surprised. Switching the capsule radio to auto scan, he heard only static.

Abruptly, the static ceased. "Bird dogging," said a monotone voice.

Peter did not recognize the voice. "Knowing my landing site won't do him any good," he told himself, aware that the docking of space vehicles, such as escape capsules, was almost impossible without computer assistance and that the capsule computer systems were designed for landings, not orbital interceptions. When the dark spot was no longer visible, he settled back in his cockpit seat, trying to relax before the ordeal of reentry.

Sitting with eyes half-closed, the heat shield alarm alerted him to initial contact with Earth's atmosphere. Located on the underside of the capsule, the heat shield was designed to withstand the high reentry temperatures resulting from atmospheric friction. A second alarm alerted him to the need for course correction. Because the capsule was now in the atmosphere, course correction could be accomplished using mostly conventional airplane controls, at least in the initial stages of reentry. Peter instructed the computer to make the necessary adjustments to the capsule's stubby little wings and tail. The response was immediate.

"Almost like surfing," he thought, remembering his days at the beach in California.

He was enjoying the gentle massage of capsule reentry vibrations when he felt a sudden jolt and was jammed back into the cockpit seat cushions. Without his seat harness, his shoulder would have slammed into the side of the capsule. He grabbed the control stick and struggled to right the tipping vehicle, mindful that the upper body of the capsule would rapidly overheat if exposed to atmospheric friction.

"What the…," he shouted, looking backward through the cockpit window. Another capsule had rammed into his. That feat of interception should have been practically impossible with the simple capsule computer control systems. Switching on the thruster rockets, he attempted to distance himself from it. The response was sluggish.

"Damn it!" he shouted. The capsules seemed locked together. Shifting weight, he attempted to rock his vehicle. Again, the two capsules responded as one. He wondered if his enemy had intended to damage the tail. That would make reentry dangerous, if not impossible.

Puzzling over how the interception had been possible, he soon felt foolish. "Of course," he chided himself. Once the capsules entered Earth's atmosphere, guiding the capsule became more like flying one airplane toward another than docking orbiting vehicles in the vacuum of space.

Nursing a bruised ego, he felt his capsule shift. Fearing that the locked-together capsules might burn up, he decided to help his foe. When the capsule rocked one way, he threw his weight the other. When he felt the thrusters of his foe's capsule push in one direction, he directed his thrusters in the opposite direction.

"Looks like we cooperate or cook," Peter's radio squawked.

Was the voice familiar? He could not be certain. In any case, it was an offer he could not refuse, "Agreed."

Working together, they lined up the capsules for re-entry, deciding upon a shallow angle of descent in order to minimize atmospheric stress. Bits of the heat shields on the undersides of the capsules began to burn loose, creating a glowing trail. The capsules vibrated erratically, requiring constant attention because they could not be perfectly aligned.

Peter was arm-weary when the vibrations finally lessened. Minutes passed before the electromagnetic interference decreased sufficiently so he could obtain a satellite location fix. As expected, the capsules were hundreds of miles off his intended original course due to the glide path change.

Because he was now traveling at airplane speed, Peter chose to deploy his capsule's parachute in an effort to separate the two craft. He pulled the chute release but felt nothing. Release mechanism's damaged or jammed, he concluded.

His body started straining against the seat harness, first one way, and then another. Wondering whether the other capsule had deployed its parachute, he turned to look but could see nothing because it had grown too dark. He seemed to be tumbling, but that made no sense. A deployed parachute exerted a sudden slowing force, followed by a floating sensation. Instead, his capsule seemed to be gyrating wildly. One moment he felt as if he were falling, the next rising. The instruments indicated that his senses were not deceiving him.

"What's happening?" his mind screamed.

A violent flash lit up the sky, answering his question. A second flash revealed the presence of the other capsule beside his.

The intensity of the buffeting increased. Suddenly, the stubby wing of the other capsule crashed through his cockpit window, pinning his helmeted head against the seat and causing him to fear decapitation. As suddenly as it had appeared, the wing vanished. Due to the altitude, he knew he would have blacked out were it not for his spacesuit.

Grabbing the stick, he dove into the thunderstorm updraft, attempting to distance himself from the other capsule. The up-and-down motion continued, but the instruments indicated that he was slowly descending. At eleven thousand feet, he broke free of the updraft. Gradually, the rain ceased, and lights on the ground became visible through scattered clouds.

Sighting the glow of numerous lights, he headed for it, seeking illumination for a safe landing. The capsule's tail responded sluggishly. Damaged, he thought, also noting that the capsule did not glide well. It was descending more rapidly than he would have liked, despite his best efforts. No doubt the shattered cockpit window was largely responsible. Only increased speed would slow the rate of descent. He decided to hold off increasing his speed by diving until the final descent.

The glow became a small city. He saw the distinctive lights of an airport but judged it too far away to be of any use. Surveying the farmland below, he could make out large fields of what he took to be corn, soybeans, and wheat and decided to land in a wheat field, guessing that it would provide a more consistent and more slippery landing surface than either corn or soybeans.

Waiting until the last moment, he lowered the retracted landing wheels and dove at the wheat field. The acceleration gave him better control and, when the dive ended, a slower rate of descent. He tried for a perfect three-point landing. Touching down, his knees bashed painfully into the control panel, but otherwise the field felt relatively smooth. When the capsule came to rest, he was thankful just to be alive. Leaning back in the cockpit seat and trying to consciously relax, he gazed upward at illuminated clouds slowly drifting along.

Without warning, the capsule radio came to life, abruptly ending his attempt at meditative tranquility. His body jerked involuntarily, sending throbbing knees bashing painfully into the control panel yet again. "The suspect is believed to be in the vicinity," blared the radio speaker.

"Respond immediately to any sighting of a strange-looking small aircraft. Take all necessary precautions. However, be advised that, at this time, there are no formal charges. Repeat. No formal charges."

Chapter 10

Computer on her lap, Maggie Blevins watched Tom Cartwright acknowledge the standing ovation greeting his appearance at the podium of the Minnesota convention of the American Progressive Party. She wasn't enthusiastic about covering Cartwright, and Scott knew it. She felt a twinge of regret at so blatantly calling attention to Ken Lacey's involvement in her issue ad story. She did not know whether Scott talked to his uncle about politics, but he had certainly wasted little time taking her off the story and sending her packing to Minneapolis.

Bastard! Maggie thought. It's never censorship. It's lack of reader interest or some other lame excuse. I'm going to keep digging anyway. Cartwright is just a temporary detour. Mr. Scott Smith is ancient history if he doesn't get down on his knees and apologize—and probably not even then.

Reluctantly, her focus returned to Cartwright. She knew little about him, except that he was an enormously wealthy businessman who had directed the explosive growth of GCIS. He'd become involved with the fledgling company about the time the internet in all its manifestations—cable, fiber optics, satellite, and more—achieved truly high-speed capability, resulting in its expansion to include virtually unlimited full-motion video and high-quality surround sound sent in real time to millions of customers. GCIS quickly became the leader in the field. Some likened it to Microsoft at the turn of the century.

To Maggie, it seemed as if Cartwright was a bundle of contradictions. Why would he help found the American Progressive Party? A big business, Reaganomics party, yes, but the APP? It claimed to be a party of the people, a guardian of middle- and lower-class interests, hardly usual fare for a billionaire.

Maggie knew that Cartwright's generous financial support was a major factor in the party's considerable success. In Minnesota alone, one United States senator, several House members, and a goodly number of state legislators and local officials were party members. Nationally, the party constituted 9% of the Congress, enough to be decisive on close votes and certainly enough to make the other two parties take notice.

After a round of acknowledgments, he began his speech, "Although the election is more than a year off, I want you to be the first to know that I'm here and now declaring my candidacy for the presidency of the United States on the American Progressive Party ticket."

The convention exploded in cheers, clapping, stomping, and waving of banners and placards.

When the pandemonium died down, Cartwright continued, "The U.S. economy has become toxic for most of our citizens. Yes, I said toxic. I see seven alarming trends poisoning our economy, our country, us. What are they? Trend one: the exportation of huge numbers of American jobs to low-wage countries. Trend two: the increasing percentage of low-wage jobs throughout our country. Trend three: the stagnation of the real wages of the average worker. Trend four: the buying power of the minimum wage at its lowest level in recent memory.

"Are you alarmed yet, folks? There's more. Trend five: the concentration of wealth and power in fewer and fewer hands. Trend six: the enormous and growing disparity between the income of the wealthy and the income of the average citizen. And finally, trend seven: the stagnation of the labor union movement. Traditionally, unions have been a powerful voice for change leading to greater social and economic justice. Today, only 6% of the work force is unionized.

"These trends are all alarming, and they are all interrelated. Changing one requires changing them all. The design of the car needs to be changed, not just the oil. The lobbyists and the special interests are dragging us down. As president, I'll do my best to change the country, to change the system responsible for the problems just outlined. I won't just change the oil."

Scrutinizing his ruggedly handsome features, Maggie experienced a sudden rush, sensing the dynamism of his message and his magnetism for the first time. News videos didn't do him justice, she thought.

Prolonged cheers and applause echoed throughout the hall.

When the audience quieted, he went on, "President Hedges would solve our economic woes by decreasing taxes for the rich and reducing the size of government. Just the sort of party line you'd expect from a former CEO of MegaSmartMart. He contends that decreasing taxes for the rich will stimulate economic growth. It's the old trickle-down economics. Been there, done that, several times, as a matter of fact. It didn't work then, and it won't work now. President Hedges' most ardent supporters, a small group of extremely wealthy individuals, are working behind the scenes to see to it not only that these horrendous trends continue, but that they grow and grow and grow. Before jumping on the Reagan bandwagon, the elder George Bush, called this 'voodoo economics.' I agree, George. You had it right. Our current president lied about how well the economy is doing, and he has lied about the size of the government. It has grown more than under any president since Ronald and George W.

"If we don't act, the middle class will continue to shrink, and eventually it will disappear. Bill Gates' father had it right a while back when he declared on a Bill Moyers PBS television interview show that you can have either an extremely wealthy elite or a democracy, but you cannot have both. He was on that show opposing the revocation of the so-called "death tax," which in reality was an inheritance tax affecting only the richest 2%. The elder Gates believed that really large estates should be taxed at a rate of at least 50%. Our founding fathers, who opposed the establishment of a European-style aristocracy on our shores, would agree. I'll have more to say about the evils of extreme wealth as the campaign proceeds.

"Let me emphasize once more: the system needs to be changed. The American Progressive Party advocates fundamental reform. We promote growth that benefits all our citizens, not merely a wealthy few. Deming, that well-known twentieth-century business analyst and reformer, advised against just looking at the facts. He urged business leaders to look at the system, to look at the theory responsible for the facts. Deming was right then, and he's right now. The system, the theory, needs to be examined and drastically changed.

He spread his arms and shouted, "What needs to be changed?"

Back came the thunderous reply, "THE SYSTEM NEEDS TO BE CHANGED."

"Yes, THE SYSTEM NEEDS TO BE CHANGED. The current administration and its supporters claim that the so-called free market will solve all the ills of society. It won't. Only intelligent direction of the market—and I stress the word 'intelligent'—will solve the problems caused by the ruinous trends which are destroying our country. Make no mistake: we need the market. There is no substitute for the market. But the market can be either the servant of society or the master. For the American Progressive Party, the choice is clear, and the answer is obvious. The market must serve the people, must serve society. We need to detoxify our economic system! We need to win the next election and return our country to the people."

The stomping and cheering delegates rose to their feet as one.

Day Two

Chapter 11

Sam Cohn had been at GCIS for a frenetic thirty hours, and he was exhausted. First, he had helped deal with the space station disaster, only to learn that Peter was a suspect. Next he had been involved with building the Piscean instantaneous communication device. Finally, CEO Cartwright's televised acknowledgment of the space station disaster had resulted in a deluge of inquiries.

At the moment, Sam's attention was focused on the Instantaneous Communication Device, or ICD, as the engineers were calling it. The GCIS Board had charged him with editing its follow-up letter to U. S. President Hedges about the device. He had a finished draft in hand.

Sam pondered the implications of the Piscean communication. The aliens had not provided a complete explanation of how the device operated. Thus company engineers could not eliminate the possibility that it might pose some sort of danger. In order to protect itself, the Board had volunteered to share all information with the military but had agreed with management's decision to retain control over the soon-to-be-completed actual construction. The Board's concern, voiced only in-house, was that government involvement might tie up construction for months. Also, GCIS was determined to establish sole proprietary ownership by constructing the device before its competitors.

Sam leaned back in his desk chair and closed his eyes.

* * * * *

In a restaurant across the street from Watertown's small, drab bus station, Peter nervously dialed Sam's number on a borrowed cell phone.

69

Mindful of the escape capsule radio transmission he'd heard after landing, he knew it was risky to call Sam. But who else could he trust?

The phone seemed to ring forever before the answering machine clicked on. He hung up.

Five excruciating minutes passed. He dialed again. After two rings, he was overjoyed to hear Sam pick up.

"It's me," Peter whispered in Piscean. "Can't talk long."

"Where the hell are you?" Sam hissed, in Piscean. "You're wanted for questioning."

And for murder, Peter thought grimly. He rapidly explained his situation, his concern for Julia, and his belief that the space station had been sabotaged.

"You've got to give yourself up," Sam said emphatically. "If you don't, you'll look guilty."

"Maybe I should," Peter conceded. "But I don't know who to trust." Not even you, he thought with a silent groan. "Have any other escape capsules turned up?"

"Not that I know. I haven't heard much lately though, not even rumors. But I do have one piece of real news." Sam briefly described the Piscean ICD.

Peter feigned interest, but quickly returned to his concern for Julia and his own situation. "Please find out what you can."

"I'll do my best," Sam promised.

Using a code known to both, Peter gave Sam the number of a public phone in another nearby restaurant, and a time when he would be waiting for a call. After Sam hung up, Peter sat very still, his hand over the mouthpiece, listening. Hearing nothing, he returned the phone and immediately walked out, fearful of a possible trace of his call.

Chapter 12

"We've received the grudging approval of the government," Cartwright said as he stood facing the senior engineering staff. Looks of relief appeared on the faces of several. "Now, let's turn the thing on."

The ICD was hooked into portions of the GCIS computer system in order to provide sufficient computing power, but separated from other programs and hardware by several firewalls. Company engineers agreed that the device possessed very high-speed capabilities. Some even expressed concern that it might overload the firm's supercomputers.

After a thumbs-up from the chief engineer, Cartwright announced, "Here goes," and initiated the start-up sequence.

The ICD's control lights flashed and a distinct hum could be heard. The video screen sputtered and hissed. A young adult male head appeared, looked surprised, and called to someone off camera.

Shortly, an older male appeared and, speaking in English, said, "Greetings to the people of Earth."

"Greetings to your people," replied Cartwright. "We are pleased to communicate with your planet."

After initial niceties, preliminary arrangements were made for video conferences. Next, Cartwright inquired about the dangerous spaceship mentioned in the ICD communication. He was told in no uncertain terms that the spaceship was a governmental matter which would be discussed only with representatives of the United States government. He agreed to try to set up a meeting. Finally, the Piscean informed him that he had the authority to make the databases of his world available to Earth.

"Thank you," said Cartwright. "We appreciate your kind offer." It was common knowledge that access to Piscean information systems could greatly benefit terrestrial science and technology. "Please understand," he continued, "that it will take time to make similar Earth resources available."

The Piscean smiled and nodded. He urged that the ICD not be shut down, advising that this would permit Piscean engineers to monitor the device and inform GCIS engineers if problems arose. He also offered to begin downloading reference information about their databases, explaining that this would permit terrestrial librarians and scholars to begin familiarizing themselves with Piscean information systems.

After consulting with his staff, Cartwright agreed.

Chapter 13

Robyn Sherwood drove up to the Watertown station just as a bus was arriving from Des Moines. Recognizing several young Living Wage Movement members waving and calling to her, she waved back with enthusiasm and a broad smile.

"Ready to stick it to the Washington wascals?" she shouted.

"Yeah!" came the resounding reply.

As the passengers disembarked, Robyn greeted several with hugs. Conversation was animated. Everyone wanted to learn the latest about the bus caravan and the Labor Day rally.

Peter stood on the fringe of the group, feeling old and conspicuous with his new clean shave and closely-shorn hair. However, his scuffed black leather vest, faded jeans, and T-shirt did not seem to attract attention. After purchasing the outfit in a Goodwill store, he had spent the night in a newspaper recycling dumpster. He had slept, then shaved his beard and trimmed his long hair in order to alter his appearance.

Peter recognized Robyn at once because of all her newspaper and TV exposure. Initially, the Living Wage Movement had struck him as kooky. But over time, media jokes about Robyn and her Merry Movement increasingly seemed like obnoxious caricatures. He decided to pose as one of the new arrivals, motivated both by the police officers scrutinizing people in the bus station and by the realization that traveling with the LWM to Washington might be a good way to put some distance between himself and the downed escape capsule.

"You from Des Moines?" asked a young man standing beside him.

"Nah, up near ISU," Peter lied.

"Student?"

"Graduated. Looking for a job."

"What kind?"

"Computers."

"Much luck?"

"Not much."

"Pretty tough, huh."

Before long, the two were jabbering away like old friends.

After the luggage was unloaded, half the group piled into Robyn's van. The other half waited to be picked up on her return. Peter made certain he was among the former group.

He found himself seated beside an attractive young woman. He said politely, "Hi, I'm...Pete," offering his hand.

Failing to reciprocate, she merely looked at him. At length, she said, "Hi, I'm Sarah. Traveling light, I see."

"Yeah. Last-minute decision."

Me too, she thought, reminded of calling in sick to the Exchange. "Remembered to bring your toothbrush, I hope," she said, eyeing his scruffy leather vest.

"Sure did." Peter patted his tiny duffle bag.

When the van arrived at the Movement's storefront headquarters, it was crowded with other recent arrivals. Robyn introduced the small staff before heading back to the bus station.

Alice, a staff member, addressed the new arrivals. "We've made sleeping arrangements with local organizations. Make sure your name is on a sign-up sheet and don't forget the name of the organization and its address." After all had done so, other staff members passed out additional signup sheets for tasks that needed to be done in preparation for the Washington Labor Day rally.

"Oh, you're also interested in computers," said Sarah.

Peter noted her surprise. Probably assumed that, since I look like a biker, I couldn't be interested, he concluded. "Runs in the family," he replied, pleased that a woman who looked like a fashion model had more than two brain cells to rub together.

Each group was further subdivided. "Anybody good with a spreadsheet?" Alice asked the computer group. Several raised their hands. "How about internet stuff?" Sarah and Peter raised their hands. "Only two?" Alice asked disappointedly.

As other tasks were assigned, Peter and Sarah paid little attention. Each was preoccupied with a personal agenda.

Chapter 14

GCIS Vice President Swanson greeted SEC Chair Archer as he was ushered into a room adjacent to the ICD.

"Are you the Swanson in charge of the GCIS space station project?" Archer asked.

"I am."

"How bad is it?"

"Most of the crew is presumed dead."

"I'm sorry."

"The water in the solarium flooded the rest of the station. We don't know why."

"This isn't the best timing, I know, but I need to be briefed on the ICD. I need to determine what impact, if any, the ICD might have on our nation's communication systems. I am to report my findings directly to the president."

Swanson provided a general description of the device's functions and played a video of the conversation between Cartwright and the Piscean.

Then Archer said, "I'd like to see the device and have an engineer provide me with technical details."

"This way, please," said Swanson.

When Archer saw the device, he stared at it silently. Without explanation, he turned to Swanson and demanded a room and privacy.

"Certainly," said Swanson, leading Archer to a small empty office.

Once alone, Archer contacted the Justice Department on his cell phone. "This is James Archer, SEC chair. It's an emergency. Let me speak with whoever is in charge."

Momentarily, "Jim, John Walker."

"Oh, John. Good to hear your voice. Let's encrypt.... I need the green light for an investigation—no, make that two investigations—one at the New York Stock Exchange and one at Global Communications and Internet Services in Minneapolis." He described the round ICD at GCIS and the almost identical round computer at the New York Stock Exchange. "Maybe it's just a coincidence. But we can't be too careful. After all, GCIS administers many Internet services for our financial institutions. Its system might even be involved in the weird goings on at the Exchange, if, indeed, there are any. You've heard the rumors, haven't you?"

"I have. Your request sounds reasonable. I'll contact the attorney general and get back to you ASAP."

A few minutes later, he called back with the Attorney General's word that authorization would be forthcoming and that an investigation could proceed as long as legally borderline surveillance procedures were submitted for judicial review prior to execution.

Archer then called Harold Evans, his second-in-command at the SEC. Deciding to conduct the investigation at GCIS himself, he directed Evans to take charge at the New York Stock Exchange. "Low-profile this," he told Evans. "Fill in Murphy, the head of the Exchange. Oh, and Murphy's assistant, Sarah Stevenson, was investigating some glitch when I visited the Exchange. There didn't seem to be a problem, but check with her anyway. Find out if anything has turned up since."

Next, he called Alexander Turner, the president's chief of staff.

"Jim," said Turner, "what can I do for you?"

"I know you guys don't like surprises," Archer began.

After receiving his briefing, Turner said, "Thanks, Jim. The president will want to be kept fully informed."

His business completed, Archer exited the small office and walked over to where Swanson was waiting. "Arrange a meeting with Mr. Cartwright, immediately!"

* * * * *

Once he and Archer were alone, Cartwright asked, "What's up?"

The SEC head described the remarkably similar appearance of the round computer at the New York Stock Exchange and the round ICD. He shared his suspicions about the weird goings on at the Exchange. If both devices were involved and if the ICD succeeded in hacking into Global Communications systems, the result might well be catastrophic.

"Sounds pretty wild," said a skeptical Cartwright.

"Yes, it does. I'll be the first to apologize if I turn out to be a damn fool, but it's my official duty to pursue this matter. We need to determine the signal's authenticity. Could just be dealing with criminals."

"Well, at least that's something we can look into. My people and I'll get right on it."

"Mind if mine sit in?"

"Not at all," replied a tight-lipped Cartwright.

"I assume that a firewall separates the ICD from your other programs."

"Of course," replied Cartwright testily.

Archer persisted, "How reliable is the firewall?"

"Set up by the best in the business."

"Nevertheless, under the circumstances, let's double-check," Archer replied resolutely.

"Seems like a waste of time and money," said Cartwright curtly. "But of course you'll have our full cooperation."

Chapter 15

Robyn spoke into the computer microphone, "The buses are leaving tomorrow morning around 11:00. Will you be ready?"

"Sure will," said the voice at the Washington end of the Internet connection.

"Great. See you at the rally."

Robyn heard the crash of breaking glass. Whirling, she saw a whiskey bottle with burning wick and shards of the front window hurtling through the air. The bottle didn't break as it hit the floor, but a pool of flame spread rapidly. Robyn grabbed the bottle and tossed it back through the jagged hole in the storefront window. The bottle shattered as it struck the pavement in an explosion of flame and screech of tires. With the help of Movement members, she used a rug to smother the flames on the floor, but not before the front window curtain caught fire. They tore it down and dragged it outside.

By the time the police arrived, a crowd had gathered. Robyn recognized the two responding officers from her MegaSmartMart picket-line days.

One officer walked over to her while the other addressed the crowd, "Anybody see who threw the Molotov?"

"Two guys," came the reply.

"They ran down the alley," a bystander shouted, pointing across the street.

Others agreed.

"What did they look like?" asked the officer.

"Dressed in black," yelled another bystander. "Only saw them from the back. They were running, and then, poof, they just disappeared."

"What do you mean?"

"Just what I said, officer. Poof! They seemed to vanish into thin air."

"Was the alley dark?"

"Not that dark. I couldn't believe my eyes."

The officer asked for and received more detailed descriptions. Walking over to the police car, he radioed in what he had learned, leaving out the strange-sounding disappearance of the suspects.

"I'd like to shake your hand, ma'm," said the other officer. Robyn took his outstretched palm. "Crime sure went way down after your living wage law passed." Releasing her hand, "Received any threats lately?"

"Who's counting?"

He nodded sympathetically, "Doesn't take much to stir up the kooks. Think of anything different that made a threat stand out?"

"No, not a thing," Robyn replied soberly.

"We'll keep an eye on your place tonight. Let us know right away if anything needs to be checked out."

"Most people I talk to are sympathetic."

"Yes, I know, but you can't be too careful. We'll keep a sharp lookout. You do the same."

"Will do. Thanks again, officer," she said, shaking his hand a second time.

* * * * *

After the trauma of the firebombing had abated and the front window was boarded up, Jeff, a staff member, gave Sarah and Peter a tour of the jumble of electronic equipment at the rear of the storefront. "Here's the info about our web sites and contacts," he said, holding up a battered red notebook. "If you have any questions, just ask. Familiarize yourself with what we've got and organize things as best you can. Decide which hardware and software we should take to Washington. But please…no drastic changes, at least not without checking with me first, OK?" They nodded. "I'm still officially in charge, but you'll be doing all the work. Got my hands full with other rally stuff."

During the tour, Sarah had noticed a round metal computer box. It looked like the round computer at the New York Stock Exchange, though much smaller. Taking the monitor off the computer and placing it on a nearby table, she examined the exterior but found no manufacturer's name or other identification.

"What's wrong?" Peter asked, as she began removing the computer from its box.

"Peculiar-shaped box," Sarah replied, warily. "Just taking a gander at the guts."

"Peculiar design too," Peter said after Sarah had removed the computer. "Can't tell what's what."

"Yes," replied Sarah, grateful for confirmation of her own judgment. Damn! she thought after a more thorough examination. "No identification inside or out. Probably homemade, or some small manufacturer."

"Probably," agreed Peter.

"I'm going to check on it." She walked over to Robyn. "Pete and I are wondering about that round computer over there," she pointed. "Neither of us knows the model or design. Anybody that can tell us about it?"

"It was a gift," answered Robyn. "Anonymous friend. We talked on the phone, but he didn't want to give his name. The computer's pretty user-friendly. Even I don't have trouble. He's been helping us invest Movement funds. Pretty successfully, too. We use the computer to act on his investment advice."

"How long?" asked Sarah.

"Don't remember exactly. Not very."

"So nobody really knows much about it?"

"Guess not," said Robyn. "Nobody's complained. Like I said, it's user-friendly."

Deciding not to inquire further for fear of arousing suspicion, Sarah thanked Robyn and returned to the rear of the storefront, wondering where the Exchange had gotten its round computer. It had already been installed by the time she assumed her responsibilities.

Selecting a computer on the rear wall obscured by a clutter of equipment, she sat down on a rickety desk chair in front of the monitor.

"Got to get on the 'net and let my friends know where I am," she lied over her shoulder to Peter.

Accessing the New York Stock Exchange's inventory listing, she obtained the round computer model number and the company from which it had been purchased. Next she located the Minuteman Corporation online and searched through its catalog.

"What the...?" she mouthed in silent astonishment. The machine listed in the catalog bore no resemblance to the one at the Exchange.

* * * * *

While Sarah was occupied, Peter searched in his backpack for the solarium discs. Putting one into a video player, he watched as a view of the solarium lit up the screen. He studied it for a moment, then fast-forwarded until his image appeared. Watching himself approach the solarium control panel, he looked for any telltale sign that the image of the solarium crew chief had been edited out. To his disappointment, he could detect no trace of an edit. Dejectedly, he watched the video end and the screen go blank.

Reliving the events on the space station, he searched for something that might prove his innocence. Suddenly inspired, he turned to another computer and entered the address of Global Communication's software library. The library was used regularly by GCIS's worldwide staff. However, he needed a personal identification code other than his own. Fortunately, he knew the code of a fellow employee and entered it.

Downloading an audio editor, he searched in his backpack for a particular disc of Piscean recordings. Donning earphones, he listened for a faint static. Isolating the static, he saved it as a separate audio track. From another disk, he loaded the company encryption program used on the space station.

After playing the isolated static track using the encryption program, he whispered, "Damn!"

Then he noticed subtle gaps in the wave patterns of the static track and decided to fill them in as best he could using the audio editor. After several passes, he had eliminated the gaps to his satisfaction. Opening the encryption program a second time, he played the restored static track.

"Damn!" he whispered again.

In desperation, he simply played the restored static track without using the encryption program. To his surprise and elation, he heard, "It must be silenced…. Use your own judgment…. Whatever support is required. Do your job!"

The voice was unfamiliar. What was it talking about? The space station? His mind raced.

Chapter 16

President Hedges' campaign chairman, Jerry Roamer, ushered two members of the Faith Fellowship for Freedom into his office. As they seated themselves, he said, "Glad to see you again, Jeremiah, Micah. What can I do for you?"

"We're here to let you know that we intend to picket the LWM rally on Labor Day," said Jeremiah. "People need to be reminded that they ought to earn their keep instead of getting a minimum-wage handout from the government."

"Yes," said Micah, "Jeremiah and I grew our businesses from scratch by hard work. We earned every penny."

"Our workers," added Jeremiah, "were paid what they were worth on the open market, and my company was paid what our products were worth to our customers. In a free society, people should be paid what they're worth. 'Do unto others as you would have them do unto you,' that's what our Lord said."

"Yes, yes," said Jerry Roamer. "Love God, love your neighbor, be honest and moral, and remember that God helps those who help themselves. But, tell me, why exactly is it that you're here?"

"We wanted to warn you that things might get a little out of hand at the Labor Day rally," said Jeremiah.

"When the Lord's cause is your cause," said Micah, "righteous indignation, the sword of the Lord, must at times be wielded."

"Yes," said Roamer. "But violence is neither the professed policy of your organization nor of the Constitution of the United States."

"Of course," said Micah, "we don't advocate violence. But violence is always possible at such events."

Romer stared at them for a long moment, then said, "Either side could spark it." They nodded in silence. "Anything else?" They shook their heads no.

Standing and shaking hands, Roamer opened the door to his office and led them out. "Thanks for your support. We're counting on you and your people at the next election."

"You bet," said Jeremiah.

* * * * *

Jerry Roamer walked into Vice President Carlton Sweeney's office. "Hello, Carlton."

"What's up?"

"Some of our staunch supporters were just in to see me. They're going to picket the LWM Labor Day rally."

"And?"

"They're concerned that violence might break out."

"Fill me in."

"They're concerned that some of the more…faithful might get carried away with the…righteousness of their cause."

"I hope you told them to preach restraint."

"I did."

"They can't be held legally responsible for the violent acts of a small minority acting on its own. Can't avoid crazies in politics. But maybe a greater police presence is in order."

"That would seem prudent."

"Something else?"

"Perhaps we can take advantage of the situation?"

"A few clean dirty tricks?"

"Any objections?"

"All's fair in love and politics. Just exercise discretion and good judgment."

"Always."

"Looking forward to watching the rally on television."

"'Bye. Thanks for the input."

After returning to his office, Roamer picked up a cell phone and dialed. "I would like to speak to Mr. Lacey…. Ken, Jerry. I have something that might interest you." After they had activated their encryption devices, Roamer described his conversation with the vice president and concluded, "So anything to discredit the LWM is fair game."

"Anything? I get nervous when people use language like that."

"Within reason. You know what I mean. Anyway, we'll need good media coverage."

"I'll see to it that you have plenty of coverage. Just don't let things get out of hand."

"Thanks, Ken. Worry not."

Chapter 17

That afternoon, Cartwright reassembled the two teams responsible for checking out the ICD. GCIS vice president Swanson headed the team responsible for determining whether Pisces II was the source of the signal. Archer headed the second team, responsible for determining whether the device was capable of hacking into Global's systems.

"Mr. Archer, any comments before we begin?" Cartwright asked. When he shook his head, Cartwright turned to Swanson, "Proceed, Bob."

Swanson began, "In order to authenticate the signal, we established a checklist. First we investigated the direction of the signal. It proved to be consistent with a transmission from Pisces II. We checked and double-checked the other items on the list with similar positive results.

"After that, we brainstormed. Ted," he pointed to an engineer sitting in the third row, "noticed that the frequency of the signal seemed to change slightly.

"We conducted a careful examination, and he was right. We consulted with the Global Communications staff responsible for handling routine Piscean strong signal transmissions. They suggested that the frequency changes were very likely Doppler effects due to the motion of Pisces II relative to Earth.

"As you are no doubt aware, the frequency of a signal changes when the source of the signal moves toward or away from the observer. It's similar to the variability of the pitch of a whistle on a moving train. The pitch is higher if the train is moving toward the listener and lower if it's moving away. The pitch also varies depending upon the speed of the train.

"So in order to determine whether the changes were the correct Doppler effects, we ordered a detailed comparison of the transmission's changing frequency pattern with the Doppler patterns of other Piscean signals. They checked out for the most part. However, there was one difference. We detected small frequency jumps rather than the smooth, continuous Doppler frequency changes characteristic of other Piscean signals and of Doppler effects in general.

"This discrepancy made us suspicious. We conclude that the broadcasting device responsible for the ICD transmission is most likely not located on Pisces II. We think it is in near-Earth space. We suspect that the circuits of the device are subject to tiny random electrical fluctuations, which would explain the small frequency jumps.

"We can easily test this hypothesis. The device would have to move in space in order to maintain the direction of Pisces II relative to us as Earth rotates on its axis and orbits the sun. If that is the case, the device could only compensate for the motion of one location on Earth at a time, in this instance the location of Global Communication's dish antenna. So detection of the signal from other locations on Earth should prove conclusively whether or not it is a fraud because the direction of the signal would vary."

"What's the quickest way to check that out?" Cartwright asked.

"We thought about contacting some of our competitors who may also be receiving the ICD signal," replied Swanson. But we decided against it because they'd probably figure that something was up and simply refuse or give misleading information."

"We don't even know," interjected Cartwright, "whether our competitors are receiving the transmission."

"Instead," continued Swanson, "we decided the best course of action would be to contact astronomers in the northern hemisphere and have them monitor the direction of the signal with their radio telescopes."

"Good work," congratulated Cartwright. The other team applauded. Turning to Archer, he said, "Now, it's your turn."

Archer began, "I wish that our findings were as definitive. We first attempted to determine how many Global Communications systems the ICD could have accessed. Initially, we detected no breach of security.

However, as the investigation proceeded, we identified a possible chink in the company's armor."

Archer noted Cartwright's shocked reaction.

"Global Communications' software library is constantly accessed by company employees throughout the world. The library is protected, but any determined hacker could break in because the library is not within the corporation's main defensive firewall. We thought it prudent to assume that the device had hacked into the library because access to Internet connection was permitted in order to facilitate the downloading and sharing of files describing supposed Piscean information systems.

"The Global Communications library files themselves contain little confidential information. However, during the time an employee's computer is connected to the library, a hacker could conceivably access files on that employee's computer. Because those files change, there's no knowing what, if any, files were hacked into. In other words, the device could have already gained access to our country's Internet financial services. Since there's no way to prove or disprove this, we recommend that the device be completely isolated from all systems immediately, most particularly Internet systems."

Chapter 18

"Hello, my name is Maggie Blevins," she told Cartwright's secretary, slightly breathless after her trek through the GCIS labyrinth to his inner sanctum. "I'm a reporter with the Gaia news organization here to interview Mr. Cartwright. I have an appointment."

The secretary examined her computer screen, "Yes, there you are. Let me check with Mr. Cartwright. Please have a seat." She picked up her phone, "It's Jennifer. Reporter Maggie Blevins has an appointment with Mr. Cartwright." After a moment, "Mr. Cartwright regrets that he must keep you waiting for a few minutes. Would you care for some coffee or tea?"

"Thanks, coffee would be great." Sipping the hot brew, she reviewed her hastily assembled notes. The news files on Cartwright left many unanswered questions.

Maggie was about to ask Jennifer a question when Cartwright appeared—tall, leathery tan, jeans—reminding her of an old Marlboro commercial.

"Hi, Maggie," he said with an air of easy familiarity, as if they were old friends, without a hint that minutes before he had been dealing with the potentially fraudulent and dangerous ICD. "Come on into my office. Can Jennifer bring you anything?"

"I'm fine, thanks," Maggie said, holding up her cup.

He ushered her toward a couple of stuffed chairs. She was surprised by the simplicity of the décor. "Shoot," he said after they were seated.

Maggie glanced at her list of questions. Looking up, she confessed, "I'm new on this beat. Looks like I'll be covering your presidential campaign for my news organization, Gaia. I'd like for our readers to get to know you better. I'd like to get to know you better. What experiences shaped Tom Cartwright? What about your passions? That sort of thing."

He fingered his chin, "Well, I was born here in Minnesota, a small town called Pinedale. Lots of places around here named after the Dale family," he said with a broad grin. "Family of three boys. My father was a hard worker, a building contractor and a fair man, though sometimes too quick with his fists. He worked long hours, so my mother was pretty much the one who raised us. Both my parents were political liberals. Some of that seems to have rubbed off on me, at least lately.

"Learning came easily. I got a scholarship to Carleton College, a small liberal arts school in Northfield, Minnesota. Not many liberal arts colleges left. Too bad. My spies tell me that Frisbee is still more popular on campus than football. I had a double major, economics and philosophy. I guess I was both a utilitarian and an idealist.

"My college sweetheart and I married right after graduation." He hesitated. "When Rhonda died, it was rough. My kids and I owe a lot to friends and relatives who helped us through those terrible times." He paused, shifting his weight. Maggie knew his wife had died relatively recently and empathized.

Resolutely, he continued, "After I finished graduate degrees in law and business at the University of Minnesota, Rhonda and I left Minneapolis for big, bad New York City. I wanted experience in the communications business. Luckily, I found work with a small company on the move, becoming the business manager back when all I knew about most electronic gizmos was that they plugged into wall sockets. At the time, the company was applying for patents on a device that would allow video viewers to see a 3D image without wearing special glasses. We were incredibly successful, and our little company grew into an international corporation. At the same time, the Internet became truly high-speed. The number of possible simultaneous real-time video and audio transmissions became virtually unlimited. In a few short years, our 3-D device revolutionized the Internet video business. In the process, I matured and learned enough to be named CEO.

"Due to patent protection, only our Internet sites offered true, high-quality 3D transmissions. Any stations that signed on with us were guaranteed a national audience, a national market. Subsequently, we also patented an advanced form of surround sound 3D audio. We were able to produce true surround sound anywhere in a room, not merely in the so-called "sweet" spot. Since our Internet sites offered a far more appealing brand of television and radio than our competitors, our Internet television and radio business exploded.

"Our patented decoders were yet another source of income. Viewers needed our decoders in order to properly receive 3-D video and audio signals. Because of these and other patents, we became one of the largest and wealthiest international companies. Along the way, I discovered that I really missed Minneapolis and moved company headquarters back home."

Cartwright paused and leaned back in his chair. Maggie, taking it to be a signal for her to jump in, said, "I have a few more questions." He nodded. "About the time your company became really successful, you got involved in right-wing political causes, which is generally par for the course with successful businessmen. Then, at some point, you switched sides, and now you support liberal political causes, such as the American Progressive Party. Why? What caused the change?"

"I'm embarrassed to admit it now, but a few hundred million inflates the ego so much that when you're invited to join the Club it seems only natural."

"What club?"

"The Club. For all practical purposes, it's an organization made up of the people who run things, the good ole boys. Its members pretty well control world trade organizations and corporations. They don't care whether you're a Democrat or a Republican as long as you support the 'right' causes. Some who know about the Club believe its members have a secret plan to rule the world. That just ain't so. They're only shortsighted business types interested in making a buck, who justify, or perhaps a better word is rationalize, their extreme wealth by claiming that the so-called free market is God's gift to humanity. Only their version of the free market, they claim, can maximize production and lift the world out of poverty, despite the fact that, to date, this just hasn't happened.

"You heard my speech last night?" Maggie nodded, pleasantly surprised by his candor. "Things may be getting even worse. The Club sees nothing wrong with paying workers here and abroad as little as possible. Of course, workers in developing countries are paid far less than workers in industrialized countries. Club members claim that low pay is better than no pay, ignoring the fact that such practices do little to raise wages or standard of living. Eventually, they even drive down wages in industrialized countries.

"With the help of family and friends, I came to realize that such practices are simply wrong, that a free market doesn't automatically solve the ills of society. I also came to realize that economic policies which affect everyone are everyone's business and should be openly discussed and voted upon.

"The Club doesn't believe in public discussion and formulation of economic policies. Several years ago, it created the Bilateral Freedom Institute, bilateral referring to the producers and the consumers of goods and services. The organization is essentially a propaganda front, promoting the view that regulation of trade is unnecessary, even detrimental. Business, they claim, is most efficient when markets are essentially free from government regulation, thus allowing producers and consumers to do as they please." He paused.

"Chances are you haven't heard of the Club or the Institute."

"No, I haven't," confessed Maggie.

"They go almost unnoticed by the mass media. Why? Because some media are controlled by Club members, and other media are afraid of losing advertising dollars.

"When you come from a middle-class background, as I did, wealth and power can easily go to your head. As I said, if it weren't for family and friends, I might still be a Club member." He paused. "I'm not going to pretend it wasn't pretty intoxicating for a while, running the world, but Rhonda sat me down one day and said she didn't know me any more. She said she was seriously considering leaving me. Said I was no longer the man with whom she had fallen in love. That was like pouring a bucket of ice water over my head. She helped me see that I'd become the very sort of person I'd despised as a student.

"I withdrew my support from the Club and the Institute, though I made an effort to remain on speaking terms with at least some members." He chuckled. "Not surprisingly, that proved to be increasingly difficult after I helped found the American Progressive Party. Although Club members supported politicians in both of the major political parties, they couldn't find much to support in the Progressive Party. George Murphy, chair of the New York Stock Exchange, is the only one whom I still regard as a friend, but then he never was a true-blue Club member."

Cartwright glanced at his watch, "I apologize, Maggie, but I'm going to have to cut this short. Today's a busy day."

"Thanks for the interview. Hope we'll get to know one another better during the campaign."

"Absolutely," smiled Cartwright. "Feel free to come see me anytime."

"Thanks for the information about the Club."

As they shook hands, he put one arm around her shoulder, partially embracing her. Maggie felt the same attraction she had experienced at the Minnesota party convention. Careful, gal, she cautioned. He wouldn't have gotten this far if he wasn't a world-class charmer.

Chapter 19

Under SEC chairman Archer's direction, GCIS staff undertook the task of contacting radio telescope facilities in the northern hemisphere. Each was to be given the coordinates of Pisces II and the broadcast frequency of the presumed fraudulent communication in order to determine whether the signal was coming from the same point in the sky as that occupied by the planet and its star. Archer insisted on personally contacting several facilities.

He made his first call. "Hello. This is James Archer, chair of the Securities and Exchange Commission. To whom am I speaking?"

"Dr. Ted Wilson, director of the Mesa Verde radio telescope facility."

"Dr. Wilson, I am calling regarding a possible national emergency. We would like you to immediately direct your radio telescope to coordinates we will provide, and listen on a certain frequency. We are interested in the precise point in the sky from which the signal is originating and in any changes of location. The signal may not be originating from the precise coordinates we provide."

"Your request will seriously disrupt our telescope schedule, Mr. Archer. What sort of national emergency are we talking about?"

Archer drew a slow, irritated breath. "I can't reveal the details for security reasons. But if you doubt my identity or my authority, please call the Washington office of the Securities and Exchange Commission."

"Well, I guess if it's a national emergency," Wilson capitulated. "Give me the coordinates and frequency, and I'll contact you as soon as I have something to report."

During the next hour, Archer contacted three other academic radio telescope facilities, making the same request. Not all were as cooperative as Mesa Verde. One simply refused, complaining that its research would be adversely affected. Another complied but complained of possible loss of grant money. The last demanded confirmation and asked to speak to the president.

Exhausted, he was sitting with eyes closed, when the phone rang, "James Archer."

"Dr. Ted Wilson, Mesa Verde radio telescope. We conducted a thorough scan of the sky in the vicinity of your coordinates and have been unable to detect a signal at the frequency you indicated."

"Really?" Archer's obvious puzzlement attracted the attention of those nearby.

"Yes, we scanned a wide section of the sky without success."

"I apologize for interrupting your normal schedule, but please conduct another scan over an even larger area. Our national security is at stake."

After a silence, Wilson replied, "All right. I'll do as you ask, but I'll be sending a request of my own, for compensation, to your office."

"Fair enough," Archer replied.

Chapter 20

By the afternoon of the day she had begun her spy career, Sarah was amazed to find herself the temporary acting treasurer of the LWM. Robyn, among her other duties, was treasurer, but lately she had not found time to oversee the accounts, so pressing was the business of preparing for the huge Washington Labor Day rally. She and Sarah had been chatting about the rally and related internet activities when the conversation shifted to more personal topics and Robyn learned of Sarah's work experience. Wasting no time, Robyn had approached the governing board members, insisting that Sarah was the perfect person to temporarily assume the treasurer's job, thus allowing her to concentrate on the rally. Board members had insisted upon examining Sarah's credentials, of course, but a cursory check plus phone calls soliciting recommendations were sufficient to convince them that Sarah should be appointed temporary acting treasurer. She felt guilty about not mentioning her most recent work experience and including George Murphy in the list of references, but she wanted to avoid questions concerning her absence from the Exchange. Her official installation had occurred during lunch with the Board. Afterward, she and Robyn visited the Movement's bank in order to have her certified. Robyn remained the official treasurer with ultimate authority and responsibility.

Sarah was flabbergasted at the speed with which she, a complete stranger, had been entrusted with legal access to the Movement's accounts. Employees at the Exchange went through a long security check before they were allowed significant access, much less being entrusted with important security codes. Of course, the LWM was a smaller, more informal organization, operating largely on the basis of personal trust rather than the strictures of legal fine print. However, although she was happy to have the authority to conduct ordinary business and thus have access to the accounts, she was relieved that Robyn's counter-signature was required on all but minimal transactions.

Everyone was pleased. Robyn was pleased to find a competent volunteer who could make decisions without constant consultation. The Board was pleased with Sarah's credentials, and Sarah was pleased to have the opportunity to investigate the Movement's finances.

After returning with Robyn to Movement headquarters, Sarah began systematically checking LWM accounts. She knew that Robyn and the Board relied heavily upon their stock market guru for trading advice. On the basis of her previous day's experience, she expected to find more unusually high profits. A steady flow of buy and sell instructions had been executed that day via the round computer by members of the staff entrusted with the task. As expected, today's trading was amazingly successful. She wondered why the guru didn't lose money part of the time just to make it look good?

The similar appearance of the Exchange round computer and the LWM computer continued to disturb her, especially after her discovery of the discrepancy between the computer model listed in the Minuteman Company catalogue and the Exchange machine. If only I had examined the guts of the machine at the Exchange, she chided herself, I would have some idea if the designs are similar.

"My God!" she mouthed as she examined other Movement accounts. Using the computer mouse, she paged through account after account. "Over nineteen million!" she exclaimed in a harsh, horrified whisper. It had all been deposited within the past few hours and did not come from stock trading. What's going on? she thought with alarm. What have I gotten myself into?

Using Exchange system codes, she gained access to bank databases and tried to trace the transfers to LWM accounts. Even with the codes, it was difficult. What was not traceable was the identity of those responsible for the transfers, nor could her efforts determine whether the transfers were legal. Fearing that someone was manipulating both the banking systems and the stock markets, Sarah, for the first time, questioned the wisdom of her reluctance to contact Murphy about her suspicions.

Chapter 21

"We've shut it down, Mr. President," SEC chair Archer announced into his encrypted phone. "We now consider the so-called instantaneous communication device to be a fraud, although we lack definitive proof."

"What do you mean, 'lack definitive proof'?"

"Radio telescopes in the Northern Hemisphere have been unable to detect the signal. In other words, we've been unable to verify our hypothesis that the signal is originating from a transmitter in near-Earth space.

"However, as a result of this negative outcome, we did a more careful check of the ICD signal. We found that the signal was undetectable even a short distance from Global's dish antenna, meaning that the beam was very narrowly focused. Such focusing would require a larger, more sophisticated device out in space than we had previously suspected."

"What are you suggesting?"

"The ICD message indicated that a dangerous spaceship was approaching Earth."

"Why would the spaceship be the source of the signal if a warning about it was mentioned in the message? Doesn't make any sense. Does it?"

"It would make sense if the criminals were attempting to deceive us. The instant communication device message would initially appear to be friendly. Our building of the device would allow the criminals to more easily hack into our systems, perhaps even into our military systems. By then, it wouldn't matter if we discovered and destroyed the spaceship or whatever the hell is out there."

"So where are we?" the president asked with obvious irritation.

"Unclear. My second-in-command has been investigating a computer at the New York Stock Exchange which is very similar in appearance to the so-called instantaneous communication device at Global Communications. He just informed me that some stock prices may have been manipulated electronically by an outside party. So we've also shut down the round computer at the Exchange. However, since our systems have very likely been infected, the illegal activity may well continue."

"If we're not on top of this soon, Jim, I'll have to declare a national emergency and suspend market operations. I really don't want to do that. People might get the impression that we're in the middle of another financial debacle, such as the one created by Congress when the laws regulating business and banking were so weakened that the result was Enron, WorldCom, and a general increase in corporate corruption. It's the sort of bad publicity that a business-friendly president like me needs to avoid."

"Sir, it's not just our stock markets. Our banking systems may have been compromised as well."

"Oh, no," the president groaned.

"There have been mysterious unauthorized transfers of funds. So far, we haven't been able to identify those responsible or detect a pattern."

Archer quickly summarized the transfers that his staff had been able to trace mainly from the accounts of wealthy individuals and organizations to other accounts, such as pension and mutual funds. He admitted he had no evidence so far that a criminal individual or group had profited from the transfers.

"Whatever needs to be done, do it now!"

"Yes, Sir. However, our investigations require the full cooperation of other agencies, such as the military, the FBI, and maybe even Homeland Security. I also need your authorization to have military satellites search for the device—or spaceship—responsible for what we believe to be the fraudulent alien signal. Our best guess is that it's constantly maneuvering in order to maintain its position relative to the GCIS dish antenna and Pisces II and that it's some distance from Earth. Also, since the source of the signal has not yet been detected, we should probably assume that it has some sort of sophisticated means of making itself difficult to detect."

"Real high-tech criminals from the sounds of it. I'll instruct governmental agencies to cooperate with your investigation. Contact the Pentagon and FBI and tell them what you need."

"Thank you, Mr. President."

As Archer was considering his next move, a shout from across the room attracted his attention. "Someone's tracking fund transfers," called a Global Communications staffer assisting Archer's people. "Whoever it is knows high-level codes."

"Codes? What codes?" asked Archer.

"The person is accessing bank databases through the New York Stock Exchange."

Instantly, he contacted Harold Evans at the Exchange. "Evans, someone is using the Exchange system to track fund transfers. Get on it. Find out who."

As he waited for Evans' response, Archer reviewed the growing list of suspected illegal transfers of funds and stocks, convinced that there would be numerous transfers until the criminals finally effected a theft of money out of legitimate institutions and into their own pockets. He expected that the trail would be difficult to follow. One set of transfers particularly attracted his attention. Noting the recent increases in LWM account balances, his face became animated, and he shouted to staff members around him, "I may have found what we've been looking for, a place where the criminals are actually preparing to steal money. I wouldn't be surprised if a radical fringe group like the LWM was capable of almost anything."

His phone rang, "What?...The LWM. Doesn't surprise me." Listening again, he slowly repeated Evans's last words, "The only person besides Murphy who possesses that much knowledge of codes is Sarah Stevenson. Damn, I should have paid more attention, asked more questions. She was a real charmer, a real distraction. You have no idea.... Now she's nowhere to be found.... Yes, tell Murphy. At least we know where to start looking."

Chapter 22

Sam Cohn walked unannounced into Bob Swanson's office. Surprised, the GCIS vice president motioned for Sam to be seated as he continued watching a political issues ad. It looked to Sam as if it had been pirated from an episode of that ancient science fiction classic, *Battlestar Galactica*.

"*Why did the space station disaster occur just as it was about to relay intelligible versions of weak signals to earth?*" An exploding space station filled the screen and the speakers boomed with the sound. "*Perhaps the signals would have confirmed that liberal fear-mongering is nonsense and that the strong, vibrant free-market economy of Pisces II proves it. Who would benefit by withholding this information from the American people? The Committee for the Protection of American Rights and Freedoms wants to know. Don't you?*"

"Got to keep abreast of the latest lies," said Swanson, turning off the TV. "What can I do for you, Sam?"

"Is Peter going to be charged?"

"We still don't know exactly what happened. Why do you ask?"

"I hear there may be other survivors."

"We're still investigating. As far as we know, Peter is the only survivor. Other escape capsules may have been launched, but, as far as we know, only one landed safely. We believe it was Peter's.

"Look, Sam, I know you and Peter are close, but take some friendly advice. If he contacts you, encourage him to turn himself in. Don't become an accessory."

"Accessory to what?"

"The space station may have been sabotaged. He could have launched other escape capsules to divert attention from himself. Maybe not. He should turn himself in. Tell his side of the story."

Sam sat mute and motionless. At length, he said, "I'd like to examine the weak-signal recordings that Peter transmitted just prior to the disaster."

"Unfortunately, most of the transmissions were garbled. But we do have one clear recording. Mr. Cartwright has a copy, and he may have some language questions for you. I'll get a copy to you."

Swanson stood and walked to the office door, indicating that the conversation was at an end. Sam left. He felt uneasy.

* * * * *

At LWM headquarters, Robyn sat before a semi-circle of staff members, doing final planning for the bus caravan sendoff. "Do we have adequate sound equipment?" she asked.

"Yes," volunteered a bearded young man to her right.

"You have a call, Robyn," Sarah shouted from the rear of the storefront.

Robyn excused herself and walked over to Sarah, who handed her the phone. "Robyn Sherwood speaking."

"Hello, Robyn, Tom Cartwright."

"Hello…Tom."

"Could you use an outside agitator at tomorrow's bus caravan sendoff?"

"Absolutely!" As Sarah watched, Robyn's face grew radiant and animated. "American Progressive Party candidates are always welcome, especially the presidential candidate. Your appearance will help boost our visibility and our credibility."

"What time tomorrow?"

"About ten…. I realize this is short notice, but would you consider saying a few words?"

"No problem. It would be an honor and a privilege. Can't run for the presidency unless you're prepared to give unprepared speeches whenever the opportunity arises."

"I…we really, really appreciate your support."

"Fit me in wherever you think best, and, Robyn,…the other reason I called is because I need to speak with you privately tomorrow. I know you're on a busy schedule, but could you make a little time available for me?"

"Of course!" Robyn's puzzled expression aroused Sarah's curiosity. "I'll look forward to it."

"Fine. Until then. All my best."

Chapter 23

Peter jumped to his feet at the first ring of the nearby antique pay phone, "Hello."

"Whooo issh thisssh?"

"Who do you want?"

"Aaa Aaanniee," the music and crowd background noise made it difficult for Peter to hear.

"Anybody here named Annie?" he called to the few late-night patrons at the fast-food restaurant. There was no response. "You must have the wrong number."

"Sah sah sorry."

Peter hung up and returned to his booth. It felt good just to sit and enjoy a burger, fries, and coffee.

The phone rang. Again, Peter jumped up, "Hello."

"Whooo issh thisssh?"

"If you want Annie, you've got the wrong number."

"How di did you ou know?"

"You just called. You have the wrong number."

He sat down and ate the last of his fries. Sam is late getting back to me, he worried, fearful that his friend might have been compromised somehow. How long was it safe to wait? Peter really wanted to talk to him. A wave of his coffee cup brought the server over. As she poured, he noticed a car drive into the parking lot. A man got out and walked toward the restaurant.

"Oh, hell!" Peter mouthed silently.

Shrinking back in the booth, he watched out of the corners of his eyes as Huston, the space station security officer, came in and sat down at the counter. Stunned, his heart pounding, he realized that it must have been Huston who tried to kill him and who had been in the other capsule.

When Huston did not immediately react to his presence, Peter's muscles relaxed a little. But his mind raced. What was Huston doing here? Was Sam's phone tapped? Had Sam betrayed him? Taking a deep swig of the weak black coffee, he told himself to keep calm. Huston did not appear to be paying attention to anyone in particular.

Slapping several coins on the counter, Huston ordered coffee to go and inquired about a bearded person. The description fit Peter's appearance on the space station. When the server and those at the counter indicated that they had not seen any such person, Huston stood to leave. When he was at the door, the phone rang. Pausing, Huston picked it up. Peter tensed. "Yes?" he said quietly. Looking past Peter toward the customers at the counter, he asked, "Anybody here named Annie?" Receiving no acknowledgment, he spoke curtly to the person on the phone and hung up. Without looking back, he walked out to the car.

As Huston drove off, Peter noticed another person in the car, but could not make out much else because it was too dark.

He considered leaving, but thought better of it, thankful that he hadn't when the phone rang again. Springing to his feet, he grabbed for the receiver, almost dropping it, "Hello."

Sam's voice and a torrent of alien speech brought renewed hope and joy.

"Anything new?" Peter asked impatiently in a harsh whisper.

"Swanson seems convinced you're the only survivor," replied Sam.

"I just saw Huston!"

"What???"

Peter explained.

"Swanson also thinks that you may be responsible for the disaster. If Huston is alive, that changes everything."

"Yes, but where does he fit in? He must be the one who shot at me. And what about those edited solarium videos? Must also be part of the conspiracy trying to frame me."

"Maybe, maybe not," cautioned Sam. "You can't identify the person who shot at you. Correct?"

"Yeah, but right now Huston's the only suspect."

"Who should we tell about Huston?"

"Don't know…. Maybe we should just sit on it for the time being. Whatever you do, don't tell Swanson. I don't trust him."

"Okay."

Peter paused. "Listen, Sam, I just had an idea. What about bugging Swanson's office? It would be great to find out what he knows and why he thinks I sabotaged the space station."

Silence.

"Sam," Peter said soberly, "I realize this could make you an accessory."

Silence.

"I'm being unfair. I have no right to ask you to sacrifice this much for me."

"You're right," said Sam, "this could get me in big trouble."

"Sorry," said Peter, "forget it. My head isn't screwed on right anymore."

"Maybe not," said Sam, "but I know you are innocent, and I know you're my best friend. What the hell! I couldn't live with myself if I didn't do everything I could to prove your innocence. I'll do it. I'll bug his office."

"Thanks, buddy," Peter's voice cracked with emotion.

"Better cut this short. I'll check on Huston and see what I can find out. Remember last New Year?"

"Yeah."

"Call tomorrow and give her your number. She'll call me, and I'll get back to you on a secure phone."

"Good luck with Huston!"

After tipping the server, Peter left the restaurant. Halfway across the parking lot, a car raced up and screeched to a halt. Alarmed, Peter almost ran. Two men wearing black suits sat in the front seats.

The driver asked, "Hey buddy, did you see a big guy with a military hair cut?"

Peter stared at the man, wondering why anyone would be looking for Huston if no one knew he was alive?

"Twenty bucks for your trouble," said the driver.

Aware that his hesitant behavior had given him away, but having no reason to cooperate, Peter pointed, without describing, or even mentioning, the car, and said, "He went that way."

The man jabbed a twenty into his hand. "Thanks, pal."

As the car pulled away, his heart continued to race and his attention was drawn to the passenger in the front seat. A feeling of déjà vu came over him. "What the hell is going on?" he said softly, mystified. "Are they with Huston, or hunting him?"

* * * * *

Through the undamaged portion of the boarded-up window, Peter could see Sarah and Robyn in the back of the storefront.

"Hi," said Sarah as he entered. "How's my bit and byte buddy?"

"Tired. Can I still get a ride to where I'm supposed to sleep?"

"The last ride left about fifteen minutes ago," said Robyn. "I'm afraid you're stuck with us for the night."

"Sleeping bags and two beautiful women. What else could a man want?" He laughed halfheartedly, deeply, desperately desiring Julia.

"That's the spirit," said Robyn. "We'll be safe. The police are patrolling. We've got to get up early, so who wants the bathroom first? I need to take a shower, but I don't mind sharing. Peter? Sarah?"

Peter, surprised, said quietly, "You go ahead. I need to just sit and unwind."

Neither objected.

To Peter's continuing discomfort, they did not close the door. Memories of Julia swept over him. He moved to a chair away from the bathroom. In the presence of these two vibrant, attractive women, he felt as if he was in hell, the hell of life without her.

He reminisced about their final week on Earth and the play they had attended at a small avant-garde Minneapolis theater. On the recommendation of a friend, Julia had purchased the tickets. He remembered in particular the play's strident presidential press conference, which made him realize that he still had much to learn about her.

"Amy Jones, Los Angeles Sentinel. Mr. President is it true that you support legislation abolishing the national minimum wage?"

"Yes. Such legislation would benefit American workers."

"How so?"

"It would help them compete with workers in countries where people live in mud huts and come to work barefoot."

Although the audience, including Julia, laughed and hooted, he had not been amused. Why had she insisted on this particular play?

When the president recognized another individual, reporter Jones persisted, "Mr. President, many experts believe that abolishing the minimum wage would be bad for American workers."

"Better to have a job than to be able to feed your family."

More hoots and "Bronx cheers" from the audience.

The president's press secretary walked over and whispered in his ear.

"Sorry," the president said to the reporters, "I must leave. I have an important engagement."

"What's more important than a press conference?" another reporter called out.

"The CEOs of fifteen of the largest U. S. corporations are in my office," the president replied as he turned to leave.

"Why the meeting?" shouted reporter Jones.

"The CEOs are unhappy. Executive pay is only a thousand times that of the average worker, plus stock options are being taxed. They're threatening to quit in protest."

Peter remembered how Julia and the audience had roared with laughter, clapping and cheering as the cast stood in a line, joined hands, bowed, and filed off stage for intermission. He seemed to be the only one who was not amused.

Overjoyed when the play finally ended, he was convinced that Julia's friend—the one who had recommended the play—must be one of those far-out nutty liberals.

Afterward, they had walked hand in hand to Jerry's Pub, choosing a two-person table in a dimly lit corner. When Julia was seated, he remembered bending over and gently caressing her cheek. She looked up, pulled him close, and planted soft, warm, lingering kisses, her hands cupped over his ears.

Reliving the heady emotions of that moment, he vividly remembered asking her, "What about seeing each other every possible minute until we leave for the space station?"

She looked at him pensively, flashed a broad grin, and in a soft, sexy voice murmured, "Absolutely, my love, every possible minute." For long intimate moments, their eyes, then lips met.

So engrossing was his reverie that he convulsed in startled surprise when Robyn suddenly materialized beside him wrapped in a towel. She coaxed, "Go take a shower."

"Uh—Still relaxing," he stuttered. "I'll give Sarah a chance to finish."

Shortly, Sarah poked her turbaned head out of the bathroom, "Your turn."

As he entered, they briefly brushed against one another. Her warmth sent something like an electric shock coursing through his body. Turning slightly, she smiled, adding to his discomfort.

After doing his teeth, he removed his shirt and splashed water on his face and upper body. He hadn't intended to shower, but his itching body inspired a change of mind. Slipping unseen into the shower, the soothing warm water prompted him to hum with eyes closed.

"What's that tune?" Sarah called through the shower curtain. A spasm shook his body at the nearness of her voice, causing him to drop the soap. "Oops, didn't mean to startle you," she apologized.

"Old Devil Moon," he said in as nonchalant a voice as he could muster while staring through the shower curtain in his self-conscious nakedness at Sarah's shadowy, indistinct figure at the washbasin. "Big day tomorrow," he said, in an effort to relieve some of the tension in his taut muscles.

"I'm looking forward to it," Sarah replied, her speech garbled by a mouth full of toothpaste. She rinsed, then said, "I'm beat. See you in the morning."

"Goodnight," he called. "Sleep well."

When he was certain that Robyn would not also reappear, he quickly stepped out of the shower, fearful both for himself and for Julia as he toweled. His attraction to these two women in Julia's absence aroused feelings of guilt. What had she been wearing yesterday morning, beside the body brace? He could not be certain. How ephemeral love and life suddenly seemed.

Chapter 24

"This is James Archer, chair of the SEC. General McNulty is expecting my call."

"One moment, Mr. Archer."

"General McNulty."

"Anything to report, General?"

"That depends on your point of view. We trained several of our spy satellites on the location indicated by your people, but we came up with zip, nada, nothing."

"Describe the search, please."

"Sure. We checked for the signal frequency you indicated and for other types of radiation. We surveyed the area with our highest-resolution telephoto equipment, and with high-frequency Doppler radar. There was no evidence of any device."

"How large an area did you search?"

"Large. If anything is out there, it would have to be practically invisible."

"I trust you will continue the investigation until you've exhausted all possibilities."

"Those are the president's instructions."

"Thanks," Archer said with clenched jaw.

Day Three

Chapter 25

Peter dialed the Minneapolis restaurant where he and Sam had partied last New Year's Eve. He gave the manager his number, and she promised to call Sam immediately.

Minutes later, his phone rang. "I checked on Huston," said Sam. "No file. Officially, he doesn't exist."

"But he came to space station organizational meetings."

"Maybe Cartwright hired security off the books."

"Why would security shoot at me?"

"He wouldn't have been able to recognize you in your spacesuit with the visor down. Right?"

The impeccable logic forced Peter to say, "True." He came back with a question of his own, "Have you learned any more about Swanson?"

"No, but I have managed to bug his office."

"The Movement just provided me with a phone," said Peter. "That's the number you just dialed. If you find out anything from the Swanson bug, let me know ASAP."

"Count on it."

"Sam, I owe you, big time. Thanks, buddy."

* * * * *

Peter unlocked the door of the LWM storefront. As he expected, it was deserted.

He was concentrating so hard on his assigned task of choosing and packing electronic gear for the Washington rally that he failed to hear the front door open. Consequently, he was startled to hear, "I'm with the Securities and Exchange Commission."

The man flashed an ID.

Not knowing what to say, Peter remained silent.

"What's your involvement with the LWM?"

"I'm responsible for computers and communications."

"What's your name?'

"Uh, Pete. Pete Albertson."

"ID, please."

Not wishing to produce his wallet which was in a knapsack under a table, he lied, "My stuff's already on a bus. We're leaving for a Labor Day rally in D. C."

"How long have you been with the Movement?"

"Quite awhile," Peter lied again, "but I've been helping out in Watertown for only a few days."

"Do you consider yourself a loyal American?"

"Of course!" he blurted out angrily, as if insulted.

"Do you know Sarah Stevenson?"

Deciding it would be foolish to lie, he said, "Yes."

"What are her responsibilities with the LWM?"

"She's our temporary acting treasurer."

"How long has she been with the Movement?"

"Don't know. We both got here a couple of days ago."

"Have you any knowledge of the Movement's finances?"

"None."

"The SEC and your country need your help, Pete."

A flabbergasted Peter just stood there.

"We need your assistance in a government investigation."

Refuse, and they'll be suspicious, he thought. Cooperate, and you'll have a perfect cover. "I guess. What's it all about?"

"The SEC needs to monitor the Movement's financial transactions. To do that, we need to integrate our equipment with yours, especially with that strange-looking machine." He pointed to the round computer.

"I'm in charge of setting things up. That shouldn't be a problem as long as your stuff doesn't interfere with ours."

"It won't. We also need a man on the bus with the equipment. That would be me."

"This place was fire-bombed yesterday. Right now everybody is pretty suspicious of strangers."

"Introduce me as a friend. My name is Frank, Frank Whittier. What I'm about to tell you is classified. You can be prosecuted if you tell anyone. Do you understand?"

"I do," Peter said solemnly.

"We're tracking a shell game. We believe that criminals are deliberately creating a hard-to-follow money trail by making numerous unauthorized transfers among bank and investment accounts. Eventually, they'll steal funds by transferring them out of legitimate institutions and into their own pockets. We suspect that LWM accounts are such a transfer point. Obviously, we need to thwart these illegal activities as quickly as possible. In order to do so, we need to monitor transfers into and out of Movement accounts."

* * * * *

Peter and a man Sarah didn't recognize were loading equipment onto the communications bus parked in front of LWM headquarters. "Hi, Pete. Who's your helper?"

"Sarah, this is Frank. He's a friend. Just got here."

"Hi, Frank."

"Pleased to meet you, Sarah," he said, shaking her hand.

"Frank's a computer whiz. Brought some of his own equipment."

"Oh. Why? What exactly does it do?"

"Well, mostly it adds speed and minimizes system glitches."

"I see." Sarah's smile hid her suspicions. Frank's answer was vague. It could mean almost anything. Did he know something about all that money in Movement accounts?

Chapter 26

The silver-and-blue chartered LWM buses now lined the streets in and around Burns Park. Robyn stood beside the park bandshell reviewing details with the Movement's security force. "Have two people been assigned to each bus?"

"Yes," answered Ted, the staff person in charge.

"One of you must stay with your bus at all times," cautioned Robyn. "We've received threats again. Never forget that, no matter how bored you may feel. And keep your eyes peeled. Thanks so much for volunteering, and good luck!"

As the security force fanned out to the buses, Robyn joined celebrities gathering near the bandshell stage. The Movement had become a Hollywood *cause célèbre*. Star presence guaranteed national media coverage of today's festivities. Robyn could not help noting the high fashion jeans, tops and casual jewelry that would certainly be photographed all day and would appear on the news pages of all the industry magazines next month.

Tom Cartwright arrived as Robyn and her son Nicholas were helping distribute programs. Tom was accompanied by several large men, whom Robyn took to be bodyguards. "Glad you're here," she said cheerfully, shaking hands. Looking at his men, she said, "Public life isn't all it's cracked up to be, is it?"

"You've got that right," agreed Tom. "I heard about the firebombing yesterday. If you need professional protection, I'd be happy to provide it."

"Wasn't that bad, but thanks for the offer. This is my son Nicholas," she said, putting a hand on his shoulder as one eye peeked out from behind her skirt. "Say hello to Mr. Cartwright."

"Hello," said Nicholas, grabbing and partly hiding behind a handful of skirt.

"Hi, Nicholas," Tom said, bending down and shaking his hand. "Your mom is doing something really wonderful and important." Nicholas shyly shook his head in agreement. Straightening up, Tom said, "Thanks again for inviting me, Robyn. When will I be speaking?"

"Toward the end," she said, handing him a program.

"What's a good time for a private word?"

"Got a few minutes now before things start. That enough?"

"Sure."

They moved to a less-populated area behind the bandshell. Tom looked her in the eyes, and said, "I'd be honored if you'd consider becoming a member of my campaign team. Washington needs new faces, new points of view. You don't have to give me an answer now. Just think about it. If you have any questions, please don't hesitate to ask."

Robyn stood with mouth open for several seconds, then replied enthusiastically, "I really don't need to think about it, Tom. You're championing the causes we support. I'd love to campaign for you. I trust your judgment." Looking down at her son, "Wouldn't that be wonderful, Nicholas. You'd get to make all kinds of new friends." Nicholas just smiled, still clinging tightly to his mother's skirt.

"I wasn't expecting an immediate reply. Are you certain?"

"Yes! Quite certain!"

"Swell! Good to have you. Welcome aboard." He drew her close and gave her a long, lingering hug.

She tensed, then relaxed, throwing her arms around his waist and hugging him back.

Tom spoke first, "I'll definitely be at the Washington rally. I considered traveling with the caravan, but, unfortunately, certain pressing matters require my immediate attention."

"Please consider speaking at the Washington rally. It would serve as a strong boost to our cause."

"As would your cause for my candidacy. Count on my speaking. Afterward, we can perhaps get together and discuss the details of my campaign strategy and how you and the Movement might fit in."

"Fantastic."

* * * * *

TV crews busily filmed each performance at the LWM sendoff festivities. Near the conclusion of the program, with Tom by her side, Robyn announced to the energized audience, "It's an honor and a privilege to introduce Mr. Tom Cartwright. Not only is he CEO of GCIS; he's also one of us. We are overjoyed that he has recently announced his candidacy for the presidency of the United States on the American Progressive Party ticket. Please help me welcome the next president of the United States!" The crowd stood, erupting into thunderous applause and chanting, "Cartwright, Cartwright, Cartwright…"

Tom smiled and waved, acknowledging the support of the enthusiastic crowd. As the tumult subsided, he stepped up to the podium, "I'm here supporting the LWM because its values are the values of the American Progressive Party." The crowd grew silent. "Our party believes that the U. S. government has been bought and paid for by special interests. Those special interests have shamelessly slanted our government and our laws in favor of corporations and the wealthy. Both the LWM and the American Progressive Party advocate a living wage— not a starvation wage—and both aim at a larger target, namely economic justice for all."

The crowd roared its approval.

Suddenly, the tone changed. Without warning, several members of the audience jumped up, unfurled signs, and ran toward the stage shouting over and over, "Minimize the minimum wage! Work not welfare! Freedom not fascism! Big business not big government!" A couple of audience members tried to trip them and grab their clothing to hold them back. When the demonstrators had pushed and shoved their way down to the front of the crowd, Cartwright's men forcefully frustrated their attempts to get on the stage.

The demonstrators continued chanting and marching in the aisles, playing to the television cameras now trained on them. Police on the periphery of the crowd raced toward them, and began leading some away while bodily carrying others, who, nonviolently, refused to cooperate.

Several young men at the rear of the crowd threw filled balloons toward the stage, striking and covering the demonstrators and their police escorts with a purplish, foul-smelling liquid. They jumped up and ran as the police gave chase. Vaulting the low fence ringing the band shell seats, they ran to nearby motorcycles and sped off.

Robyn raced over to one of the GCIS television crews, requested airtime, and announced, "Those men who threw balloons are not LWM members. We don"t know who they are. My guess is they were trying to make it look like Movement members are rowdy and violent. We aren't, and we never were."

Hearing Tom quieting the crowd, Robyn abruptly ended her commentary. The cameras swung round toward him. "Freedom and justice are not necessarily identical. Freedom may mean that some are able to gain an unjust amount of wealth and power. Why should CEOs and corporate board members be paid hundreds, even thousands, of times the salary of the average worker? I tell you, there is no good reason. The huge incomes of executives and board members are largely due to the power they have to determine their own pay. I say this as an insider, a prodigal son." The crowd grew silent. "People who take business risks deserve reasonable compensation—I emphasize 'reasonable'. Should obscene wealth be permitted in a democracy, especially when so many Americans are struggling just to provide the basics for their families?" He pounded the podium and shouted, "*I say no! It is simply wrong!* I pledge that, starting here today, I will henceforth devote my energy, my time, and my fortune to the cause of economic and social justice. Workers must receive their fair share of business profits. The wealthy and powerful must pay their fair share of taxes."

The crowd exploded.

When quiet was restored, Tom spoke for several more minutes, interrupted periodically by the boisterous crowd. He then called for Robyn to join him on stage. After she did so, one of his staff carried a giant rectangular poster board onto the stage. Turning the front of the poster board toward the audience, Tom said, "Robyn, as a token of my pledge to promote economic and social justice, I"m presenting the LWM with this check for ten million dollars."

Visibly surprised and moved, Robyn accepted the giant check which he handed to her. Facing him, she said in a voice brimming with emotion, "Thank you, Mr. Cartwright. Thank you, Tom, very, very much. Your generous contribution is an inspiration to us all. Together, we will fight the good fight for economic justice, for a government representative of all the people."

Chapter 27

As Tom walked offstage to tumultuous applause, his men surrounded him. Camera crews crowded round. Reporters blocked his path and bombarded him with questions. He had refused to meet with them prior to the sendoff, not wishing to divert attention from the festivities.

Some distance from the stage, he stopped and shouted, "One at a time," pointing to the nearest reporter.

"Mr. Cartwright, won't your candidacy siphon off Democratic votes and make it easier for the Republican presidential candidate to win?"

"There's a growing dissatisfaction with the status quo in this country. That groundswell is going to carry me into office."

"Barbara Townsend, St. Louis *Guardian*. Our news organization has learned that a satellite relay from Earth to your corporation's space station just prior to the disaster was intercepted by the military. Apparently, someone claiming to be acting on your authority urged the use of force. Mr. Cartwright, did you order or condone the destruction of your company's space station?"

"Ms. Townsend, I have no knowledge of any such communication. But you can be certain I'll look into it."

Other reporters shouted: "Why was the space station sabotaged?"

"Was the flooding a publicity stunt gone wrong?"

"I wouldn't sabotage my own company's space station," Cartwright responded curtly. "That's crazy. I'll make a statement after I've studied the communication, if indeed there was such a communication."

His men pressed closer and helped him push his way through the throng of reporters to waiting limousines.

"Mr. Cartwright, a word please?" called out Maggie Blevins.

"Call me Tom, Maggie," he said, bringing her inside the circle of bodyguards. "This isn't the best place to talk. Get in and drive with me to the airport. Afterward, my driver will drop you off wherever you like."

Once in the limo, he said, "Shoot."

"Are you aware that a well-financed negative issue ad campaign has been launched against you?"

"Nope. Too early to pay attention. Haven't even been nominated."

Maggie pulled out her laptop. "I'm investigating issue ad organizations." She played two ad samples for him. While not mentioning Cartwright by name, they insinuated his responsibility for the space station disaster and for the developing financial institutions crisis. "I suspect that a few extremely wealthy individuals are behind these ads and are covering up their involvement." She handed him several pages of computer printouts, explaining the repeated marker highlighting of five names.

"I know these men," said Tom. "They're charter members of the Club I was telling you about. They also founded the Bilateral Freedom Institute, which lobbies for unrestricted global free trade." Thinking for a moment, he picked up the limo phone. "I need your word that what you're about to hear is off the record."

Unused to being an insider, she said with a bit of trepidation, "You have it."

Tom put on the speakerphone.

"Global Communications and Internet Services, how may we assist you?"

"Tom Cartwright, Jennifer."

"Yes, Mr. Cartwright?"

"I need you to contact the Snoop Squad."

"Who?" Maggie asked.

"Company Secrecy and Security. We call them the Snoop Squad in house." To Jennifer, "Their investigation must be absolutely secret, our eyes only. I'm going to put Maggie Blevins on the phone. Do you remember her?"

"Yes, Mr. Cartwright."

"She will describe an investigation she's conducting. Convey the information to the Snoop Squad." He turned to Maggie, "Anything they turn up that's relevant to your story is yours. Just don't implicate us or get yourself sued."

She nodded.

"Maggie will explain the details of her investigation and what still needs to be done. Record the conversation and play it back to the Snoop Squad. Any questions?"

"No, sir."

He handed Maggie the phone. "The limo has a fax if you need it."

While Maggie and Jennifer were speaking, Cartwright retrieved his personal phone and dialed. "Hello, Conrad. Tom Cartwright."

"Good to hear a friendly civilian voice. What can I do for you, Tom?"

"I hear that the military intercepted a satellite relay to my corporation's space station just prior to the disaster. Can you check on it for me?"

"Hang on."

Tom waited patiently for the general's response as the limo continued on its way to the Watertown airport.

"Tom?"

"Yes, Conrad."

"I have a copy. They've assured me it wasn't leaked by the military. It's brief, plus it's already public, so I have no reservation about downloading it to you."

"Thanks. I really appreciate it. One more question. Was the communication encrypted?"

"No."

After receiving the download, Tom thanked the general again, hung up, and played it.

Voice 1: What should I do?

Voice 2: It must be silenced!

Voice 1: Am I authorized to use force?

Voice 2: Yes, use your own judgment.

Voice 1: Is he prepared to support me against his own people?

Voice 2: Whatever support is required. Do your job!

"Everything is set with Jennifer," Maggie said after Tom had finished listening to the download. "I can see why those reporters were confrontational. You could be the person permitting the use of force."

"Why wasn't the message encrypted?" he asked no one in particular while dialing another number. "Swanson, Cartwright. What do you know about a communication to the space station just prior to the disaster?"

"I have a copy if you'd care to…"

"I already have a copy," he interrupted, his voice betraying a hint of anger, "which I should have gotten from you."

"Yes, sir."

"What about the space station. Anything new?"

"We suspect that Peter Abelard, the radio telescope operator, may have sabotaged the station, though we haven't any idea why. He seems to be the only survivor. The police in Watertown, Iowa have found what they believe to be his escape capsule."

"Either of the voices in the communication his?"

"We don't think so."

"Could you identify the voices?"

"Not so far."

"I'm in Watertown. Send me a photo of Abelard. He might still be here. I'll see that it's distributed. What's Archer up to?"

"He believes he's found at least one place where the criminals are preparing to put some of the illegal fund transfers into their own pockets."

"Well?" demanded an obviously irritated Cartwright.

"The LWM," Swanson replied in a subdued tone.

"What! That man's a damn fool!"

"That's all I know, Mr. Cartwright," Swanson said apologetically. "Archer's not saying much."

"Where's he now?"

"Don't know."

After trying in vain to reach Robyn, Tom said to the limo driver, "Take us back to the buses. I need to speak to Robyn."

Chapter 28

The Living Wage caravan was underway. Peter was in the communications bus, immediately behind Robyn in the lead bus. He was relieved that Sarah was with Robyn, instead of looking over Frank's shoulder.

"We're ready," Frank assured Peter. "Should be able to trace any call."

"How will you know if it's the Movement's stock market guru?"

"We won't, unless he identifies himself."

The new equipment Frank had brought with him blinked red as the round computer, now the Movement's primary communications computer, came to life. He motioned for Peter to sit down at the round computer.

"To whom am I speaking?" announced the round computer speaker with what Peter took to be a slight accent.

Leaning toward the microphone, "This is Pete. I'm the LWM's communications person. Please identify yourself."

"I wish to speak to Robyn," said the computer, ignoring his request.

Never having heard a Piscean speak English, he dismissed his impression that the speaker had an alien accent. "She's on another bus."

"I *must* speak to Robyn."

Frank motioned for Peter to stretch out the conversation.

"We can arrange to have her return your call."

"Please contact her now and put her through."

"We're not set up for that," he lied. "Perhaps she could contact you, or we could arrange for a time when you might call back." Frank nodded his approval.

"We will contact you."

Frank held up a finger. Peter asked, "How about one hour?"

"That is acceptable."

Frank again motioned to keep the person talking.

"I have a message from Robyn, on behalf of the LWM."

"What?"

"She wants to thank you for your financial support."

After a moment's silence, "Robyn and I must speak. I'll call back in an hour."

Not knowing what else to say, Peter replied, "Okay, one hour."

As the connection went dead, Frank told Peter, "I need to talk to the boys." He flipped a switch and spoke into his headset microphone, "Any luck?" After listening, "There'll be another call in one hour. Enough time?...Good." Turning to Peter, "Something's funny about the signal."

* * * * *

Two caravan buses already on the expressway caused a stir among Movement members in nearby buses when they split off from the caravan at the last Watertown exit. Some noted the slightly different design of the two buses and figured that they had been leased from a different company than their own bus. Driving into the mall near the exit, they stopped in front of the main entrance of Watertown's MegaSmartMart store.

Occupants of the buses ran toward the entrance, shouting LWM slogans. Inside, they began tipping over racks and smashing display items. Workers and patrons who attempted to intervene were confronted with weapons of various sorts, including guns, and backed off.

The demonstrators produced and lit Molotov cocktails which were indiscriminately thrown at the merchandise littering the floor and at racks still standing. The merchandise caught fire quickly, especially racks of clothing, which were engulfed in columns of flame shooting almost to the ceiling. Acrid, foul-smelling smoke quickly started to fill the huge space. All the while, the demonstrators shouted, "You torch us, we torch you, you torch us, we torch you..."

As people ran for the exits, the demonstrators retreated en masse to the main entrance. Outside, they quickly boarded the buses, a few pausing long enough to toss Molotov cocktails onto the MegaSmartMart roof. When all were on board, the buses sped away.

Minutes later, fire engines headed to the MegaSmartMart with their sirens blaring and police sirens wailed atop patrol cars as they pursued the buses. Before the patrol cars could catch up, the buses were back on the expressway, gunning through the long line of caravan buses into the center lane. They passed bus after bus after bus, forcing slower traffic off the expressway or into the right-hand lane. When patrol cars tried to pass, the second bus swerved from side to side, successfully foiling every attempt. The lead patrol car called in, "Gonzalez here, haven't been able to stop them." He explained the situation. "We're coming up on exit 224. If they don't get off, consider setting up a roadblock." After a moment's silence, he shouted, "Holy shit! You won't believe this, but they just disappeared." He looked back at the police car behind them. The officers gestured in bewilderment. "Car thirteen doesn't see them either."

"Repeat," said the dispatcher.

"I said the buses just disappeared." He looked quizzically at his partner, Bob, behind the wheel, who just shook his head.

Other officers called in, acknowledging what had happened.

Without a quarry in sight, the police cars slowed, but continued down the expressway.

After they had gone under the overpass at exit 224, officer Gonzalez looked back then shouted into his radio, "I see them. I don't know how they did it, but they took the exit." To his partner, he said excitedly, "Turn around, Bob. Let's get the bastards."

Followed by other patrol cars, they skidded across median strip grass, accelerating in the opposite lanes back to exit 224.

Upon reaching the last seen location of the buses, Gonzalez yelled, "Dammit! Bob, do you see them?"

"No. Nothing."

"They disappeared again," Gonzalez reported over his radio. "But they definitely left the expressway at exit 224. At least the last time I saw them, they had. Damndest thing I…We're looking down the road in both directions. Couldn't have driven that far that fast. What should we do?"

Over the radio, Captain Fitzgerald issued orders sending cars in both directions down the exit road, while others remained on the expressway. He concluded with, "Report anything unusual, and I mean anything."

The search continued, but without further result.

Chapter 29

A coyote spooked by the noise ran for the protection of its den as low-flying helicopters raised clouds of dust on the Wyoming plain.

"Ground station dead ahead," said the lead pilot.

As the copters landed in a cluster a few yards from the perimeter fence, the communications officer reported to the lead pilot, "Sir, the schematics have downloaded. Captain Thompson has a printout."

"Captain," said the lead pilot into his headset, "have you got what you need?"

"Standard equipment. Shouldn't be a problem." Glancing at his watch, Thompson announced to the personnel on the other helicopters, "Fourteen minutes til the transmission. Set up PDQ."

Squads of uniformed men jumped out of the copters and approached the perimeter fence, carrying dish antennas and other electronic equipment. One cut the gate chain, and everyone entered. Some set up dishes near the ground station's antennas. Others placed explosive charges. The door of the windowless building blew open. Captain Thompson entered with a squad. He proceeded to the control panel and began manipulating dials. "Check in," he said into his headset. Each squad did so. "Stay alert. Report anything."

* * * * *

After stopping briefly so Robyn could transfer to the communication bus, the LWM caravan was again underway.

At precisely one hour, the round computer announced, "Robyn, please."

133

Already seated at the computer, she replied instantly, "This is Robyn." Noting an unfamiliar accent, she assumed she was not speaking to the Movement's stock market guru.

"Please activate the computer camera and allow me to see you."

Robyn complied.

"Thank you. Have those in the back of the bus move forward."

"Is that really necessary?"

"Yes. Position the camera so that I may see."

When everyone had complied, she asked with evident annoyance, "Are you satisfied?"

"Yes. Please turn the computer screen so that it's facing the back of the bus and sit in front of it." She did so. The voice continued, "I'm downloading an encryption program which will activate automatically. Please put on the earphones." Robyn did so as the program finished downloading. "We may now communicate in complete privacy. Type the answers to my questions. Share what I'm about to tell you only with people you trust absolutely."

Frowning, Robyn typed, "OK."

"Tell me about the computer we are presently using."

"It was a gift from a friend of the Movement. Why do you ask?"

"It has...curious features."

"Meaning?" typed Robyn.

"It possesses certain unusual capabilities. How is it being used?"

"Our friend has been using it to provide us with information regarding stocks. We have used the information to do market trading, pretty successfully too."

"Do you use the computer to do the trading?"

"Yes."

"Have you considered the possibility that the trading might be illegal?"

"What?" Robyn blurted out, instead of typing.

"I advise against using the money."

"Advice noted," typed Robyn, "but we'd be more inclined to give it credence if you identified yourself."

"Sorry, that would be premature. This contact was made to inform you that we will be attending your Washington Labor Day rally."

"What do you mean, 'we'?"

Ignoring her question, the voice continued, "We support your cause. We have evidence that your stand on economic issues has merit."

"What sort of evidence?"

"When we meet, it will be self-evident. Goodbye for now. The encryption program will delete itself."

Robyn sat speechless.

* * * * *

"Report," ordered Captain Thompson as he eyed the control panel in the satellite ground station.

"The dishes are receiving a faint signal," said the lieutenant by his side. "But it doesn't seem to be coming from a satellite."

"Explain."

"Insufficient data."

"Squad three report," said the captain.

"We don't have a fix, but we're working on it, sir. The beam is surprisingly narrowly focused. I'm having our dishes moved closer to the station antennas. The best we can hope for is a rough fix."

Thompson turned to the lieutenant. "What about the message?"

"It began as an ordinary signal, and then switched to encryption. I'm recording everything. Seems like one of those new encryptions, so our chances of deciphering it aren't good."

"Squad Three reporting, sir."

"Yes?"

"We have a rough fix, sir. Moving our dishes closer to the antenna helped. Seems to be in line with the moon."

"Stationary or moving?"

"Hard to tell."

"The signal has ended, Captain," announced the lieutenant.

As instructed, Captain Thompson immediately conveyed their findings to General McNulty at the Pentagon, who forwarded the report to military satellite command and SEC chair James Archer.

* * * * *

"Jim Archer, Mr. President."

"More bad news, Jim?"

"Puzzling news, Mr. President," he said, briefly describing the Wyoming operation.

"What do you make of it?"

"Only a guess, sir. Could be some connection between the so-called ICD transmission and the encrypted transmission to the LWM. Both seem to have come from near-Earth space. In addition, the direction of the LWM transmission was in line with the moon, which may or may not be significant, and both beams were very narrowly focused."

"What's the status of the transmission to GCIS?"

"It's no longer broadcasting, sir, and we haven't been able to locate the transmitter."

"Keep looking. Keep my chief-of-staff informed. And Jim," the president said with added emphasis, "keep this low profile. We don't want to frighten people unnecessarily, even though this might be the greatest threat to our country since the terrorist attacks at the beginning of the century. However, if we continue to have no idea who we're up against, if we can't stop the illegal activities, I'm going to have to act, and soon."

Chapter 30

Robyn stared thoughtfully at the computer screen after the encryption program had erased itself. She motioned to Sarah, who had moved to the communications bus with her.

"Show me our financial records," she requested. Sarah accessed the accounts. "How can we be making such very high profits in the stock market? Isn't that unusual? And what about these recent contributions of millions of dollars to the Movement? Why didn't you tell me?"

To Sarah, Robyn seemed genuinely surprised, genuinely innocent of wrongdoing. "Sorry, you were so busy organizing the bus caravan," she lied, "and I was trying to make sense of it all. You're right. Such extraordinary profits from stock trading are unusual. And I have no idea who contributed those millions, though I tried to find out."

"Could some of our large profits from stock trading be illegal?"

"That's certainly possible. They do seem suspicious."

"I was just warned about them."

"What?" Sarah's puzzlement was obvious. "Weren't you just talking to the Movement's stock market guru?"

"Don't think so. Voice wasn't familiar. Plus the communication was encrypted. The Movement's friend never encrypts."

"Who was it then?"

"Don't know. Wouldn't say."

A series of loud car horn blasts interrupted the conversation. Robyn and Sarah could not tell what was going on, but the lead bus, followed by their bus and the rest of the caravan, pulled slowly to the side of the expressway. As they watched, they saw two black limousines in front of the lead bus also pull over.

Those seated near the driver informed everyone in the bus that a man had jumped out of a limousine and climbed into the lead bus. Almost immediately, they reported that he had exited and was running toward the communications bus. The door opened, and he bounded up the bus steps. Standing breathlessly before Robyn, Tom Cartwright said, "We need to talk."

"Tom, this is Sarah Stevenson, our acting treasurer."

"Pleased to meet you, Sarah," he said politely. Glancing at the people seated nearby, he turned to Robyn, "Complete privacy would be best. There's a rest area just ahead. The buses can park safely while we talk."

* * * * *

Alone in his limo with Robyn at the rest stop, Tom said, "I've just learned from our news staff that the occupants of two LWM buses fire bombed the MegaSmartMart store in Watertown."

"What? I can't believe it, but it does help explain some strange goings on that our security people called to tell me about!"

He provided details. "My people assure me that the report has been verified and is accurate. The fire gutted most of the store before the firefighters succeeded in extinguishing it. Apparently, no one was injured except for a few cases of smoke inhalation. The buses responsible have somehow eluded the police."

Robyn pulled out her phone and said, "I'm dialing the person in charge of bus security. Dave, I want to double check something. See if all the buses we leased are accounted for…. Yes, check again if any left for any reason while we were pulling out of Watertown?…OK, get right on it."

"Will it take long?" asked Tom.

"No. He'll call me as soon as he finds out."

As Robyn sat waiting with the phone in her lap, Tom said, "I've also been informed that the federal government is investigating the finances of the LWM. Has the Movement received substantial amounts of money recently?"

"Oh my goodness, yes! Sarah, our acting treasurer, and I were just discussing…Want me to get her?"

"Guess so," Tom agreed, unenthusiastically.

When Sarah joined them, he said, "I'll get right to the point. What do you know about the sudden increase in Movement assets?" Sarah explained about the high percentage of profits resulting from recent stock trading based upon the advice of the Movement's friend.

"Sounds suspicious."

Sarah concurred.

"There's more," said Robyn. "The Movement also recently received large anonymous contributions amounting to millions of dollars. Sarah was showing me the accounts when you arrived."

"Those contributions probably triggered alarms with Archer's people," Tom observed.

"Do you mean Jim Archer?" asked Sarah.

"Yes. Do you know him?"

Sarah hedged, wishing to reveal as little as possible, "Yes, we've met."

"Please hold what I'm about to tell you in strictest confidence," said Tom. Both agreed. He described the round instantaneous communication device his company had recently built and explained that it was now considered to be a fraud. He also sketched the possible threat that it posed to the country's financial systems. "So these contributions to the Movement as well as the stock transactions could be part of the financial irregularities Archer's people are investigating."

"The Movement is also using a round computer," volunteered Robyn.

"And it has strange circuitry," added Sarah.

"I'd like to see it," said Tom.

They left the limo and walked to the communications bus, deserted now except for a Movement security guard. The strains of a Brandenburg concerto emanated from the phone in Robyn's purse.

"Yes Dave, what did you find out?…Thanks, Dave."

Putting away the phone, she reported, "All the buses we leased are with us. However, as suspected, two unidentified buses did pull out of the caravan as we were leaving Watertown."

"Good!" said Tom. "If they were Movement members, and I do mean IF, they were wildcatters, acting on their own." After examining the round computer, he concluded, "It's similar to the device my company built."

Sarah decided to be more forthcoming. "There's also a round computer similar to this one, only bigger, at the New York Stock Exchange, where I used to work. When I saw this one, I got curious. No—perhaps a better word is suspicious. I checked and discovered that the round computer at the Exchange didn't resemble the computer with its model number in the catalogue of the company from which it was supposedly ordered."

Tom asked, "What company was that?"

"The Minuteman Company."

"Never heard of it. However, I doubt that all these round computers popping up at the same time is merely coincidental. All of them seem somehow to be tied into the financial irregularities."

"This may be nothing," Sarah said hesitantly, "but a new person named Frank just started working with the Movement's round computer." Turning to Robyn, "Pete claims he's a friend. Arrived with a bunch of equipment. Maybe we need to keep an eye on him."

Robyn and Tom nodded in agreement.

"I'm going to have my people try and trace those large contributions to the Movement," said Tom.

"I hope they have better luck than I did," said Sarah.

"To change the subject, Robyn, I stopped your bus for another reason as well. You probably heard the reporters at Burns Park practically accuse me of sabotaging my company's space station."

Robyn nodded, "Everyone did."

"Apparently, a member of the space station crew, Peter Abelard, survived. The police found what is presumed to be his escape capsule near Watertown. They suspect that he's in hiding, perhaps on one of your buses." Tom opened an attaché case and handed her photos of a long-haired, bearded Peter. "Be on the lookout. Could provide us with important information. If possible, I would like to speak with him before the police do."

"Looks like a hippie," observed Robyn.

"A rather bright hippie, so my people tell me. I have more photos if you need them."

"I'll see to it that they're circulated," said Robyn. "By the way, Tom, who's that?" She pointed to a woman standing beside the limos talking to his men. "I don't recognize her."

"Maggie Blevins, a reporter who's been of considerable help."

Chapter 31

Learning that they would be at the rest stop for approximately half an hour, Peter decided to go for a jog. After doing warm-up exercises, he ran briskly through the maze of caravan buses. Having circumnavigated the rest area several times, he felt that he had gotten a respectable workout. On his way back to the communication bus, he noticed snack machines near the washrooms. Since he hadn't eaten that morning, he joined the shortest line.

While waiting, he was startled to see Huston in a nearby line. When Huston looked in his direction, Peter froze. His eyes lingered for only an instant before he turned and spoke to a man standing beside him, whom Peter did not recognize. The man reached for his wallet, presumably to buy a sandwich. His loose-fitting, short-sleeved shirt worn over his pants rose for a moment, revealing bare skin and what looked like a pistol. Peter watched intently as Huston reached for his wallet. His shirt barely moved. After inserting bills into a machine, the two walked away with their sandwiches.

Mind racing, Peter gave up his place in line and followed. Running through the crowd toward them, he hollered, "Coming through." Pretending to trip, he crashed into them, deliberately grabbing at both as he fell.

Getting up, he apologized perfunctorily over his shoulder and jogged away, quite shaken, certain that the two had gill indentations on the sides of their chests. He could hardly believe it. They were Piscean.

* * * * *

As Huston and his companion walked slowly to the far end of the rest area parking lot, Peter followed at a distance, curious about what they were up to. Suddenly altering their pace, they dashed toward a nearby cluster of trees. Before reaching them, Huston's companion dropped to the ground, clutching his right leg. Peter saw blood.

Huston turned and pointed what appeared to be a large pistol at two men ducking behind a bus. Peter did not hear a shot, but one of the two seemed to falter before reaching the bus.

Huston dodged behind a large tree as the two fired back. Again, no sound, but bark flew in all directions, and the tree itself began to smoke.

Huston pointed his pistol, and the corner of the bus behind which the two had taken cover began to glow a bright orange-red. When the two did not reappear, Peter concluded that the heat given off by the glowing metal had forced a retreat.

Huston took several steps toward his companion, but when the two men reappeared at the other end of the bus, he again retreated behind the tree. A wild firefight forced the pair to again retreat behind the glowing end of the bus, as Movement onlookers ran for cover. Huston suddenly ran from behind the tree, leapt into the air, and vanished. An amazed Peter could not figure out what had happened.

Then Huston's companion also mysteriously disappeared. The two shooters reemerged from behind the bus and began firing into the air. It seemed to Peter that they were shooting at nothing, but suddenly smoke and sparks appeared. Huston's companion again became visible, still lying on the ground. The two shooters continued firing into the air until sparks were no longer visible.

Weapons still drawn and aimed at Huston's companion, the shooters showed badges to the crowd and shouted, "Police business, stand back." One reached under Huston's companion's shirt and removed what Peter remembered seeing at the food machines, a pistol with a rather large handgrip. Hoisting him up by the shoulders, the two hauled Huston's badly limping companion away.

Peter followed and watched as they got into one of two unmarked cars with darkly tinted windows. The two cars were identical except for a peculiar antenna on the roof of the second car. Even through the tinted glass, Peter could see them shouting at Huston's companion. At one point, he was struck in the face with the butt of what looked like a pistol.

When those in the other car began staring in his direction, Peter decided to back off. As he did so, three occupants jumped out, pistols drawn. For an instant, he thought they were coming after him; instead, they pointed the pistols up into the air and, he assumed, began firing. No sparks and smoke this time, just silence. When they returned to their car, Peter decided it was time to leave and faded into the crowd of onlookers.

Back in the communications bus, his brain whirled as he thought about Huston and his captive companion. It now seemed obvious why the government was searching for Huston back at the restaurant. The feds would certainly be concerned if they knew that Pisceans were on Earth and that Huston was one of them, especially if Piscean intentions were suspect.

Should I tell someone? he wondered. Sam? He's not here. Frank? Hardly know him. Sarah? Could be some sort of fed, could even be working with Frank. Robyn was probably the best choice, the most trustworthy person. At least he knew which side she was on.

* * * * *

Although he was seated amidst the communication equipment in the back of the bus, Peter could not help overhearing the excited discussions up front. Movement members were arguing about what they had just seen.

"They must've been shooting."

"No they weren't. I didn't hear gunshots."

"Didn't you see the puffs of smoke, the sparks? They must have been using weapons."

"Who knows what those puffs of smoke were. Could've been anything, fireworks for all we know. Weren't that many."

"With no bang?"

"Okay, smoke bombs then."

"Anyway, the two in the open start running for the trees at the other end of the parking lot. One went down. His buddy started shooting back at the other two, who ducked behind a bus. When they fired back, he ran for a tree."

"We didn't hear anything though, remember?"

"Yeah, yeah, but the way they all took cover seems like they must've been shooting."

"The guy behind the tree tried to rescue his buddy but was hit in the shoulder and retreated."

Peter registered his failure to notice Huston getting hit.

"And then the guy disappeared."

"Yeah, came out from behind the trees and just vanished."

"When the guy on the ground also vanished, the two behind the bus started shooting into the air."

"Right. I couldn't believe my eyes. There wasn't anything there, but sparks began to fly all over the place."

"Then, like magic, a hazy something materialized up in the air where they were shooting."

Peter noted that the "hazy something" had also escaped his attention.

"When the hazy something moved away and vanished, the guy on the ground reappeared."

"The two behind the bus ran over, grabbed the guy on the ground, showed badges, and dragged him off."

"Nobody interfered. We thought they were police."

"And were afraid of the guns."

"Yeah. Did you see where they took him?"

"Naw, back behind the buses somewhere."

When the excited conversation died down, Peter stared out the bus window, trying to make sense of what he had just heard, particularly the "hazy something." Could other Pisceans in an aircraft have been involved? Why didn't the aircraft fire its weapons? And were the guys with the badges police officers? Didn't seem likely. Probably they were federal agents.

As Peter continued staring out the window, two black cars drove past his bus on their way back onto to the interstate. The first had that strange antenna on its roof. Although the tinted windows made it difficult to tell, he thought he saw the space station solarium crew chief in the front seat on the passenger side of the second car. Pressing his face against the window, he strained to be certain. Huston's companion, blood streaming from a swollen nose, was sitting in the backseat with his head against the window. Peter thought about the altered solarium video. If the crew chief was a federal agent, did that explain his disappearance from the video?

Seconds later, the cars were no longer visible. Preoccupied with what he had just seen, Peter did not move.

Chapter 32

"We interrupt this program for a late-breaking story," network news anchor Charles Phelps announced. "President Hedges has ordered the temporary suspension of stock market and banking operations. He will address the nation shortly. White House officials assure us that the president's action is purely precautionary.

"We now bring you President Hedges live from the Oval Office."

* * * * *

Reporters traveling with the caravan quickly learned of Cartwright's presence and invited him to ride on their bus for an informal press conference. When he climbed on board, they were abuzz with news of the president's action suspending stock market and banking transactions. Maggie followed him onto the bus. As the reporter wolf pack began to salivate, she was suddenly struck by the high price paid by citizens seeking public office. Without delay, the snarling, growling questions poured forth from ravenous mouths.

"Mr. Cartwright, Bill Williams, Washington *Gazette*. The *Gazette* has obtained a copy of a second communication to the space station just prior to the disaster. The communication seems to implicate you in a plan to sabotage the space station. Do you have any comment?"

"I haven't seen the communication," he replied.

"Here's a copy," said Williams. After Tom glanced at it, Williams asked a second time, "Any comment, Mr. Cartwright?"

Tom continued reading before looking up, "My name's not mentioned. But you're right, the communication could be interpreted as implicating me. Was it encrypted?"

"Not to my knowledge," said the reporter.

"Why, under any circumstance, would I send an unencrypted message implicating myself? Next."

Several reporters vied for his attention. He pointed to the least vocal. "Bill Polanski, *Consolidated Internet News*. My service is reporting that you recently made large donations to several right-wing political organizations. Any comment?"

"First, I no longer contribute to right-wing groups or causes. Second, anyone could make contributions in my name, knowing that it would cause controversy. Third, you have just learned of the president's suspension of banking and stock market transactions due to certain irregularities. These contributions could be among those irregularities. I certainly have no personal knowledge of any such contributions. We must be patient while the government investigates these attacks on our financial institutions."

Maggie winced. Political neophyte, she thought. Experienced politicians do their best to use bland, apple pie platitudes. He's too honest to be elected.

"'Attacks,' Mr. Cartwright? Are you implying that some enemies, some terrorists are waging war on the United States?"

Immediately, he was buried by an avalanche of questions.

* * * * *

"General Mark McNulty, sir," said the chief of staff, handing the president the phone.

"Mark, Hubert Hedges.

"Yes, sir."

"I assume that your best crew will be on the new rocket ship and that it will be armed.

"Yes, sir."

"However, no lasers or missiles, unless it's attacked. Agreed?"

"Yes, sir."

"How soon will it be ready?"

"Within the hour."

"How long will it take to reach the moon?"

"About five hours."

"Speedy little devil. Good. I want a live feed to the White House upon arrival."

"Yes, sir."

Chapter 33

At the next rest stop, Tom left the press bus and invited Maggie to join him on the lead bus. "After all," he said, "I abducted you. At the very least, I should offer my hospitality. Besides, it's nice to have a friendly face around after what I've just been through on the press bus. Also, I could use your help."

"Nothing illegal or immoral, I hope," she bantered, impressed by his regal charm.

"No—you're safe," Tom smiled. "What I had in mind was help discovering how the messages, presumably ordering the destruction of the space station, were made public. In addition, I would like to know who notified the media of my alleged donations to right-wing organizations."

She laughed, "You don't ask much, do you? I'll see what I can dig up."

"Good. I hate being blindsided."

They moved to opposite sides of the aisle and commenced making a string of calls.

"Roger, Tom Cartwright. Have you heard about the contributions I'm supposed to have made to right-wing political organizations?"

"Yes, Tom," said Roger Payne, chief strategist and campaign manager for his presidential bid, "we just heard. The alleged contributions were made a couple of hours ago. Someone posing as you sold all your shares of Emmons and Bezzel. The seller had proper identification codes."

"Is there any way to prove it wasn't me?"

"Sure. If your account card chip doesn't have any record of the transaction."

"Didn't someone have to use a counterfeit card to initiate the transaction?"

"Must have."

"If someone could fake a card and its codes, couldn't that person also alter the records on a card?"

"Likely."

"Then my card wouldn't prove anything."

Payne hesitated, then said thoughtfully, "No, I guess not."

"That's not the answer I wanted to hear. Do what you can to try and prove it wasn't me. Top priority."

Ending the conversation, Tom dialed GCIS headquarters, "Jennifer, how's the Snoop Squad investigation coming?"

"They have a preliminary report, Mr. Cartwright. It's brief. May I read it?"

"Shoot."

Initial research indicates that Maggie Blevins is correct. The five men named in her research appear to be responsible for organizing the political advocacy groups and for funding them through persons working for companies which they control. The leader of the group of five appears to be Kenneth Lacey.

However, these findings are conjectural. Proving that money donated to these issue advocacy groups is the result of special consideration shown to employees by their employers will be difficult and time-consuming. The groups and companies involved would need to be infiltrated and informers recruited. Tracing the monies directly to the five men would require additional hard work plus considerable luck.

We await Mr. Cartwright's decision concerning the extent to which Global resources should be devoted to this investigation.

"That's it, Mr. Cartwright."

"Tell them to proceed, Jennifer."

"Yes, Mr. Cartwright."

"I'll expect regular reports."

With Jennifer listening, Tom wondered out loud about the possibility of a connection between Lacey's United News Services and the space station disaster. United News was GCIS's biggest competitor in the commercial rebroadcast of Piscean programs. Obtaining intelligible weak signals via the space station would give GCIS a distinct additional competitive advantage over United News. Might Lacey go so far as to sabotage the space station? Finally, he said, "Jennifer, I would also like the Snoop Squad to check for possible connections between Lacey or his company and the destruction of our space station."

"Yes, Mr. Cartwright."

"Tell them no one is to know about the investigations but you and me."

Tom disconnected and leaned across to Maggie. "My investigative team confirms your suspicions about those political advocacy organizations. But it's going to be hard to prove. Ken Lacey appears to be the leader. I've decided to go to New York and confront him."

Maggie, phone to ear, put a finger on her lips, "Carol Muir, please." She impatiently tapped her fingernails on the bus seat. "Carol, it's Maggie. I need a favor. You probably know that I'm covering Cartwright. I read your piece about the messages to the space station. I need to know your sources. It's confidential, of course."

"There's not much to tell. We broke the story, but the source was an anonymous tip to United News Services, which the editors forwarded to Scott Smith, presumably because we're the major news outlet. I'm surprised he didn't tell you, since you're covering Cartwright."

"He didn't."

"Anyway, the tip also said that the authenticity of the messages could be confirmed if the military checked satellite data gathered at certain times and locations. We asked the military. They checked, discovered the messages were authentic, and provided us with their findings because the messages had already been made public. We ran the story."

"Who would have known about the messages even before the military?"

"Good question. I have no idea."

"Thanks. I owe you. Covering Cartwright is more interesting than I anticipated."

"I'll pretend I didn't hear that," whispered Tom.

Grinning, Maggie continued, "Carol, is Michael around?"

"Should be. Hold on."

While waiting, Maggie described for Tom what she had learned.

"Your editor, Scott Smith. Isn't he related to Ken Lacey?"

"Yes, his nephew."

"Lacey again. First, those political advocacy organizations. Now the public release of those messages to the space station. It would be in Lacey's and United New Services's interest to slow down Global's acquisition of intelligible weak signals."

"Are you suggesting that Lacey might be responsible for the destruction of the space station?"

"Why not? Whoever released those messages probably hoped I'd be blamed. "Assuming you're not responsible," Maggie said with a wry smile. "Another possibility is that you're looking for conspiracies where none exist."

"True," Tom admitted.

Turning her back to him, "Hello, Michael. Maggie. I'm covering Cartwright, and I need to know the source of your information about his alleged contributions to right-wing political organizations."

"Anonymous tip sent to our esteemed editor," said Michael. "He asked me to verify it. Fortunately, I started checking before the president suspended market and bank transactions. Government investigators were convinced that the contributions came from one of Cartwright's accounts, and that they involved a stock sale. Their word was good enough for me, so we went public."

"Was the tip note similar to the one Carol received?"

"They were similar in appearance, but that doesn't prove much. Standard letter format."

"Why would the tip come to Smith?"

"He thinks maybe it's because he wrote a series exposing white collar crime."

"Yeah, sure. Office supplies and petty cash. Anything else?"

"Nope."

"Thanks. If I can do you a favor, let me know."

Maggie stowed the phone in her bag and moved over to Tom, telling him about the second tip.

"Mere coincidence, their looking alike, huh," Tom said sarcastically.

"Don't jump to conclusions," cautioned Maggie. "They were garden-variety."

"Excuse me a minute," Tom said. He speed-dialed.

"Mr. Murphy's executive assistant. How may I help you?"

"Tom Cartwright, Jane. I need to speak to him."

Seconds later, "Tom, good to hear from you. What's up?"

"George, several rather troubling matters have recently come to my attention. I'd like to run them by you."

"Go," encouraged Murphy.

Tom told him about the fake ICD which GCIS had built and the possibility that it had hacked into the country's financial systems. He told him about the five members of The Club who appeared to be financing negative issue ads against him, most particularly his business archrival Ken Lacey. He detailed the messages to the space station seemingly implicating him. Finally, he mentioned the money he was supposed to have contributed to right-wing political organizations.

"What do you make of it, George?"

"Tom, from the tone of your voice, I can tell that you suspect the worst."

He did not respond.

"Are you implying that these could all be related?"

"Could be," Tom replied noncommittally.

"If there was a conspiracy, why would they pick on you? Are you that important in the grand scheme of things?"

"You have a point," admitted Tom.

"It's true that some of your old friends don't want you to be president. But this grand conspiracy thing is a bit much."

"Thanks, George. I probably needed to hear that."

"We all need to be told to go to hell from time to time. Isn't that why we get married? Anything else? Sorry to cut you short, but this financial institution closing thing is keeping me busy."

"I understand. Thanks again. Good talking to you, as always."

"Sounds like you just received some good advice," said Maggie.

Without responding to the comment, Tom said, "I'd appreciate it if you'd come along to New York City when I confront Ken Lacey, Maggie. Your contacts could prove useful."

Without hesitation, she replied, "Sure, why not? Following you around is my job." However, she had no intention of telling her editor.

Chapter 34

After the next rest stop, Peter decided that he had to confide in Robyn, to tell her about Huston and his companion being aliens. They were together on the communication bus. She was there hoping for another round-computer message.

He walked down the aisle toward her, "Robyn, I need to talk to you, privately."

"Yes, what is it?" she said when they were alone in the back of the bus surrounded by electronic gear, having asked Frank to leave for a couple of minutes.

Peter spoke slowly, carefully, not wishing to reveal too much, "You may have heard that Pisces II aliens look a lot like humans, except they have gills running down the sides of their chests."

"I have."

"Well, a couple of rest stops ago I saw two males with gills."

"What??!!" she whispered harshly.

Peter described how he had purposely collided with them in order to confirm his suspicion about the gills, acknowledging that he recognized one of them, Arthur Huston. Feeling the need to lie, he said, "I worked for a company which built equipment for the space station. We got to know the crew. Huston was one of them."

"But how did a Piscean get to Earth?"

"Spaceship, I guess. How else? I only know he was on the space station at the time of the disaster. We were present when the crew launched."

"Tom Cartwright told me that a guy named Peter Abelard is also believed to be a survivor. So that makes two. How did they get back to Earth?"

"The station had escape capsules in case of an emergency."

"Yes, now I remember. Tom said police discovered what is believed to be Abelard's capsule." She looked at him strangely. "Pisceans on Earth? And with our caravan? Why? I think we need to talk to Tom. His company built the station. They know more about Pisceans than anybody."

Despite his fears that Tom Cartwright might recognize him, Peter felt he had no choice other than to agree.

* * * * *

The caravan had stopped at a rest area on the outskirts of Indianapolis in preparation for a rally downtown where additional buses would join the caravan and a brief news conference was scheduled. Robyn and Peter walked toward the lead bus to talk to Tom Cartwright. Sarah passed them, walking in the opposite direction.

"Hold on," Robyn said to her. Turning to Peter, "Strange things have also been going on with our finances. Seems to me that our acting treasurer should also be part of this conversation."

"Okay," Peter said reluctantly, "but nobody else."

"Please come with us," Robyn said to Sarah. "Something important has come up." Stopping Tom as he stepped off the lead bus, she said, "This is Pete, a Movement member. We need to speak with you privately." When they were alone on the now empty lead bus, she continued, "Pete has some unbelievable news. We are hoping you can help us figure out what to do."

Peter explained about Huston and his companion. Cartwright listened without interruption.

"You seem to know a good deal about the space station, Pete."

"I worked for a subcontractor."

"You're correct; Huston was on the space station at the time of the disaster. If you saw him, it means there's a second survivor."

157

"Robyn told me about the other survivor."

"Could he also be an alien?" speculated Tom.

"Why would Pisceans be interested in us?" queried Robyn. "Might they be involved somehow in the strange goings on with our finances?"

"And there are also those damned round computers," said Tom. "Global Communications built one following instructions supposedly from Pisces II, and the LWM has a smaller version."

"Remember there's also one at the New York Stock Exchange," Sarah added. "Could Pisceans be responsible for all three?"

"Better slow down," advised Tom. "Seems fairly clear now that my company's so-called Piscean instantaneous communication device is a fraud." He repeated for Peter what he had already told the women. "So on that subject, we're likely dealing with terrestrials, not Pisceans. Pete, you could even be mistaken about Huston being Piscean."

"I don't think so," he retorted, regretting having told Robyn about his surprising discovery. "Couldn't Huston's buddies have sent the message about the communication device from their spaceship, or even from somewhere on Earth?"

An obviously startled Tom Cartwright whipped out his phone, "Swanson, check our antenna array immediately." Peter winced at the mention of that name. "Look for a device capable of faking the ICD transmission. If the source of the signal was right under our noses, it would explain why the signal couldn't be detected a short distance away from our antenna and why the other radio telescopes could detect no trace of it."

"Will do, Mr. Cartwright."

"So, you do think Huston or his buddies might have been responsible for the ICD transmission?" Peter said cautiously after Tom had put away his phone.

"One step at a time. If there's a device attached to our antenna, we'll know where the signal originated." Staring at him, Tom continued, "Abelard's escape capsule landed near Watertown. He's suspected of sabotaging the space station. Apparently, he's in hiding." Moving closer, "If he's innocent but fearful, arrangements can be made to ensure his safety."

Does he know who I am? Peter groaned inwardly. Will he tell anyone? I was going to mention the gunfight at the rest stop and about seeing the solarium crew chief in one of the cars, but it might draw too much attention to me and blow my cover.

Turning to Robyn, Tom said, "I'm leaving for New York. I need to cut this short. You have my private number. Stay in touch. Contact me if you need anything, including additional protection. I promise to be at the rally day after tomorrow." Walking to the bus door, he leaned out and called, "Maggie, I'd like you to meet some folks." She came over and got on the bus. "Maggie is covering my presidential campaign," he said to the others. "You can trust her to do a fair, honest job of reporting. She's our kind of people. She's certainly been helping me."

* * * * *

Together with Robyn and Peter, Sarah watched Cartwright's limos leave the rest stop on their way to the Indianapolis airport. Leaving the other two, she casually walked away from the lead bus. When they were no longer in sight, she pulled out her phone. "I must speak to Mr. Archer at once. He knows me. My name is Sarah Stevenson. I'm with the New York Stock Exchange."

"He's not in. Would you care to leave a message?"

"No. I don't want to leave a message. Put me through to whoever's in charge."

"Paul Perth. What can I do for you?"

"Mr. Perth, I need to speak to Mr. Archer immediately. This is Sarah Stevenson. He knows me. I possess information which may have a bearing on the financial crisis."

"One moment please."

"Jim Archer, Sarah. Good to hear from you. What's up?"

"I'm with the Living Wage bus caravan on its way to Washington. I've uncovered what look like stock market irregularities traceable to Living Wage trades."

"We're also investigating."

"I suspected. Then what I've got may help." Sarah described what she had learned about Living Wage stock trading and about her inability to completely trace the recent multimillion-dollar deposits.

"We already know much of what you just told me."

"Great. However, the main reason I called is to tell you that there are aliens, Pisceans, right here on Earth, with the LWM bus caravan."

Before she could continue, Archer said, "Stop! Don't say another word! Do you know Frank on the communication bus?"

"Yes."

"Find him, now. We'll set up a secure line by the time you get there."

Chapter 35

"What is it, Jim?" the president asked the SEC chair.

"Two Pisceans were allegedly sighted with the Living Wage bus caravan. The source also claims that one of them was on the space station at the time of the disaster."

"How reliable is your source?"

"Sounds convincing. I have my people on it."

"I wouldn't believe a word if it weren't for that transmission from the direction of the moon. Did my chief of staff fill you in on the rocket ship we're sending?"

"Yes, Mr. President."

"An alien spaceship could mean trouble right here in River City. Have you succeeded in establishing any substantial connection between the financial mess and those signals from the moon?"

"Only the circumstantial connections I've already mentioned, Mr. President. We're working on it."

"Anything new, I want to know ASAP. Clear?"

"Yes, sir."

* * * * *

"President Hedges, General McNulty."

"As you instructed, Mr. President, I'm having us patched through to the rocket ship."

"General, you've been briefed on the reported sighting of Pisceans on Earth?"

"Yes, Mr. President."

"Must have a spaceship."

"Yes, Mr. President, they must."

The voice of Captain Townsend, on the rocket ship, intruded, "Approaching possible target area. Can't see anything in orbit or on the surface. Instruments ditto."

"Could the alien ship have some means of avoiding detection, General?"

"A definite possibility, Sir."

"Anomalous reading," said Captain Townsend.

"Meaning?" asked the president.

"Unclear," said the general.

"What the hell?" exclaimed Townsend. "Looks huge."

"Your altered flight path has been noted, Captain," said Mission Control. "Confirm."

"Roger that. I…"

"Captain Townsend, report…. Satellite surveillance, what have you?"

"Lieutenant Harvey, sir. Rocket ship's no longer visible on our screens."

"Captain Townsend, come in."

Silence.

"Now what?" demanded the president.

Before the general could answer, Mission Control asked, "Anybody, what was that disturbance when we lost contact?"

"Radiation burst, sir," a team member answered.

"Origin?"

"Hard to tell for sure, sir, but I'd say the moon's surface."

"Lieutenant Harvey reporting, sir."

"Yes, Harvey?"

"For an instant, at the time we lost contact, our radar revealed an object in the target area."

"General, are you thinking what I'm thinking?" said the president.

"They disabled their means of avoiding detection, their cloaking device."

"Exactly."

"Ionization in the target zone, sir," shouted another member of the team.

"Our rocket?"

"Don't think so."

"What then?"

"Unknown."

Chapter 36

Seated alone by a bus window, Peter dialed. He said softly to the person who answered, "I would like to talk to the manager." When she answered, he identified himself and said, "Please tell Sam to dial that number."

"I'll do so immediately."

"Thanks. I'll be waiting."

Minutes later, his phone beeped.

"Hi, Pete, Sam."

"Safe phone?"

"Yeah, no problem."

"I have new information about Huston."

"I've got news as well."

"Not news like this. Huston is Piscean!"

"My God! That might help explain what I discovered. As I told you, Global Communications doesn't have a standard file on him. They only have a brief summary of his supposed credentials. What's more, Cartwright's personal staff hired him."

"Sam, I told Cartwright that Huston is Piscean. He didn't say much, except that he'd check into it. But he seemed genuinely surprised."

"Could be," Sam said noncommittally.

"Check with Cartwright's secretary. See if she'll tell you anything. What about the space station? Anything new?"

"Nothing. However, some guy's been leaving cryptic messages for Swanson. Don't make much sense. If he returned any of the calls, it wasn't from his office phone.

"He did make one interesting call though, to Kenneth Lacey. A New York City number. I heard him ask Lacey if he should remove 'it' before 'it' was discovered. Lacey told him the possibility had been taken into account. He also told Swanson to go through 'channels' and never call him again. Swanson tried to say more, but Lacey hung up."

"Do you know what that was all about?"

"Not a clue, but, as you know, Lacey's a competitor of ours."

Peter said slowly, "Wonder if Swanson's working for him, spying for him?"

"That's an awful lot to conclude from one phone conversation," cautioned Sam. "Sorry, got to go, got a meeting. Let me do some more checking. I'll call if I find out anything."

"Watch yourself. Things are getting weirder and weirder. These people might not hesitate to kill."

"Spooking is getting to be addictive. I promise to be careful, though."

* * * * *

"News from the moon?" said the president's chief of staff.

"Yes, sir," said General McNulty.

"I'll have to relay the message to the president. He's in a meeting."

"I believe he'll want to hear this himself."

"Hold on."

Shortly, "General, what is it?"

"Mr. President, our seismic sensors detected an impact on the far side of the moon. The energy level is consistent with the crash of our rocket ship. If the ship was still orbiting, it would have reappeared by now."

"Is there sufficient evidence to indicate probable hostile intent?"

"Affirmative, sir. After analyzing all available satellite surveillance data, we believe that our rocket ship was fired upon before it disappeared. What are your orders, Mr. President?"

"Send unmanned armed probes to the moon immediately. Bear in mind that our highest priority is to learn what's out there, what we're up against."

"Yes, sir."

* * * * *

As Tom's limos sped toward the Indianapolis airport, his phone buzzed. "Swanson, Mr. Cartwright. I have news about the antennas."

"Just a moment," Tom said punching the limo's speakerphone button and telling Maggie, "I would like you to hear this—off the record." She nodded. "Proceed."

"When we checked our antennas, we discovered a box. The engineers have a preliminary finding."

"And?"

"The circuitry seems similar to that of the so-called alien communication device. The box is designed to send and receive very high-frequency signals. Such signals normally require line-of-sight broadcasting. So the transmitter sending signals to the box would have had to be nearby."

"Prospects for locating it?"

"Not good. Transmitter's probably gone."

"What about Archer?"

"His people aren't saying much. They've taken quite a beating in the press due to the suspension of bank and market transactions."

"Keep me informed."

"Yes, sir."

"What was that all about?" Maggie asked.

Tom explained about the so-called alien ICD and the discovery that Pisces II was probably not the source of the signal. He also explained how the ICD might have gained access to Global Communication's internet accounts through the software library, and thus might have further contributed to the irregularities which ultimately resulted in the president's suspension decree.

"Do you feel responsible?"

"Of course. We built the device."

"Are you considering going public?"

"Yes. Everything out in the open, no matter what the government wants."

"This is sensational," she said excitedly. "May I call my editor?"

"Why not? Let's get this thing over with. We live in a democracy. The public needs to know."

Still on the speakerphone, she dialed. "Scott, it's Maggie. I have a front-page story."

"Source?"

"Tom Cartwright. He's with me now, and he's ready to talk."

"Put him on."

Maggie handed over the phone, "Tom Cartwright here. To whom am I speaking?"

"Scott Smith, Maggie's editor."

"Hello, good to talk to you. Give my regards to your uncle Ken."

"Happy to do so. What about the story Maggie mentioned?"

"I'll vouch for everything she's about to tell you and add additional details as necessary."

"Please put her back on." Tom did so. "Maggie, I want your assurance that I have just spoken to Tom Cartwright."

"You have it."

"OK. But I can't promise you front page until I hear the story."

"Either you promise me front page, or I'll find someone who will."

After a pause, he said, "You win. We'll record everything."

Maggie spoke for several minutes, with Tom occasionally providing additional detail.

When she had finished, Smith said, "Well, you were right, Maggie. This is definitely front-page. Keep me up to date on further developments. By the way, I apologize for the way I treated you when I sent you off to Minneapolis. Keep that Italian restaurant in mind the next time you're in town."

Surprised, she said, "Will do. Apology accepted and appreciated."

Conversation concluded, Tom said, "Glad I could do my civic duty as well as contribute to your career and…"

Maggie blushed and punched him in the shoulder, as he grinned at her good-naturedly.

Chapter 37

An enthusiastic crowd greeted the caravan in downtown Indianapolis. The brief, upbeat ceremony was well attended, particularly by local politicos. Busloads of boisterous Hoosiers were welcomed "aboard." As the caravan was about to leave, Robyn climbed onto the communication bus in case she received another communication via the round computer. Peter, Sarah, and Frank were already on board.

Peter noticed that Sarah and Frank were friendlier than previously. He remembered that Sarah had said that she knew Jim Archer, Frank's boss. Had she told them about Huston and his companion?

A call on the round computer interrupted Peter's musings. "Robyn, please." Frank's hands were a blur as he configured the equipment.

Robyn seated herself at the computer. "This is Robyn Sherwood. To whom am I speaking?"

"Your friendly stock market guru," replied the computer. "I have news."

"Please provide some proof," Robyn demanded.

"Never necessary in the past."

"Can't be too careful on the road."

The computer voice detailed several recent stock trades. Concluding with, "Is that sufficient?"

"Yes," said Robin, looking at one of the Movement members responsible for making trades using the round computer.

"Back to my news. The president will sign a bill partially privatizing Social Security in the Rose Garden tomorrow morning."

"We already know about that awful bill."

"But you don't know that later today a rider to the bill, abolishing the federal minimum wage, will be brought out of committee and voted on."

"What???!!! Why haven't we heard?"

"Even the press doesn't know. The Congressional majority recently streamlined procedures. With enough votes, a rider can be brought out of committee and passed in no time. There are enough votes."

"My God!" said Robyn, "A clandestine coup, right here in the U. S. of A. Who would have believed it?"

"Exactly why I called. Voters need to know."

"We'll make certain of it."

"How?"

After a brief pause, she said, "By picketing the White House tomorrow morning. I'll get right on it."

"Good luck. Until tomorrow."

Turning to Peter, Robyn said, "Activate the caravan communications network. We were going to rest for a day before the rally, but instead we're going to picket the White House. Tell everyone about that damned rider."

Reaching for her phone, she informed Tom of what she had learned.

"Bastards!" he said. "I remind you, Robyn, that you should be suspicious of advice from your so-called friend. Assuming he's right, what are your plans?"

"We'll picket the White House tomorrow. Can you give us TV coverage with interviews and all that?"

"Absolutely. What time is the bill signing?"

"Ten tomorrow morning."

"Our TV crews will be there at eight."

"Great! See you at the rally."

"Count on it."

As Peter contacted the buses, he watched Frank place a call, with Sarah standing beside him, listening. Her behavior convinced him that she was now, if not earlier, working with the SEC. Should he tell Robyn and Tom? If so, he would have to explain how he knew about Frank. That posed a problem.

* * * * *

As the tail end of the LWM caravan was making its way back to the interstate, two buses with Movement signs drove slowly through downtown Indianapolis. Waving liquor bottles, young passengers leaned out the windows. Others beside them inside the buses lit the cloth wicks dangling from the bottles. The bottles were then hurled at the glass windows of businesses along the street, spewing flame into buildings and onto the street. Volley after volley exploded in flame as the two buses meandered through downtown Indianapolis.

Leaflets were thrown from the buses. Bystanders picked them up and read:

DECLARATION OF WAR
ON
CAPITALIST THIEVES
RESTORE WORKER RIGHTS
LEGISLATE A LIVING WAGE

Police officers ran toward the buses, ordering the drivers to stop. When they failed to do so, the officers shot at the tires. The tires failed to deflate. Taking aim at the drivers, the officers again ordered the buses to stop. Bullets bounced off the windows around the drivers without so much as scratching the glass. The officers radioed for assistance.

Open side windows slammed shut as the two buses picked up speed. Officers shot at the engines as the two buses sped by. Bullets simply bounced off the metal engine covers, causing nearby terrified pedestrians to fall to the ground. The buses raced away, seemingly undamaged by the barrage. As they approached an interstate entrance, police cars were in pursuit.

An officer in the lead police car radioed, "The two buses are approaching the interstate. Can't tell which direction they're headed yet. On a ramp any second. What the hell! Sweet mother of God!"

Silence

"Car thirty two, report!"

"The buses just vanished."

"They exploded?"

"No, they just disappeared. Damndest thing I've ever seen. One second they were there. The next they weren"t."

Chapter 38

Sarah and Frank took turns on the phone. After one such conversation, she observed Peter staring at them and said to Frank, "I've got to talk to Pete. I think he knows about you and me and Archer, that I've been cooperating with you."

Frank nodded.

She stood and walked over. As she approached, he said, "I assume that you told Archer about Huston."

"I did."

"Give me a good reason why I shouldn't tell Robyn and Tom Cartwright."

"Why didn't you tell them that you have been Frank's little helper?" she retorted.

"Touché," Peter responded. "So—what did Frank learn about the call to Robyn?"

Sarah said nothing.

"If you don't tell me, I'll tell them."

Reluctantly, she replied, "They traced the call to a warehouse in New York, Manhattan Storage and Transfer."

"Address and telephone number?" She told him. "Doesn't ring any bells."

"Me neither."

Robyn came over. "Pete, were you able to inform all the buses, including the Indianapolis buses, about the bill signing and our plan to picket?"

"Yes."

"Great! We need to converge on the White House before the bill signing so we can spotlight this chicanery."

Preoccupied with the latest revelations, Peter had difficulty concentrating on what Robyn was saying.

* * * * *

When the caravan stopped for a break near Pittsburgh, Peter decided to tell Robyn about Sarah, Frank, and Archer. He also told her about his own involvement.

Robyn stared at him silently, an alarmed look on her face. Finally, she said, "Wow. How can I fully trust you, Pete? My head says I can't, but my gut says I've got to." She paused. Then said with determination, "In any case, Tom Cartwright needs to know."

"I agree. He has connections, and he knows more about Archer than we do."

Robyn activated her phone's tiny speaker so Peter could listen, then dialed Tom's private number.

"Tom, Robyn. Pete has just shared something with me that you should know."

"Shoot."

Robyn related what Peter had told her.

"Why didn't you tell us sooner, Pete?" Tom queried.

"I guess I was intimidated by Frank and his government connections," Peter said, telling only as much of the truth as he thought was safe. "I also learned that Frank traced a call Robyn received on the round computer after you left the bus caravan. It came from a warehouse in New York City." He gave Tom the address and phone number.

"Doesn't mean anything to me. You?"

"No."

"I'll have my people check it out."

Peter continued, "According to Frank, Archer suspects the LWM may be a place where the 'bad guys' are actually planning to siphon money out of the system, not merely transfer it from one legitimate account to another."

"Thanks for that info, Pete."

"Tom, I can't tell you how I know this, but it could be important. Your vice president, Swanson, called a Kenneth Lacey in New York City."

"Interesting. I'm planning to visit Lacey tomorrow. Why did Swanson call?"

"I couldn't figure that out." Peter described it for Tom.

"Doesn't make a hell of a lot of sense to me either, unless the 'it' they were talking about was the box which we recently discovered attached to our antenna array. We're pretty sure it's the source of the supposed Piscean transmission instructing my company to build the ICD.

"Needless to say, I'd like to know why Swanson is communicating with our biggest competitor. Perhaps there's something to the wild-sounding conspiracy theory I've been tossing around. Perhaps Swanson and Lacey had something to do with the space station disaster. Robyn, Pete, that's confidential."

Peter reluctantly decided that it was time to come clean. "Tom, I'm the Peter Abelard who was aboard the space station at the time of the disaster. I know that I'm a suspect, but I wasn't responsible."

"I was about to have you investigated," said Tom. "However, I tend to believe you. Tell me about the space station. Convince me that I'm right about you."

Peter described what had happened on the space station, including his discovery of the altered solarium video tape. "I think that Huston, the space station security person, was very likely responsible." He also told Tom about his encounter with Huston at the Watertown restaurant, about the people in the car who came to the restaurant searching for him, about the shootout at a rest stop, and about his possible recognition of the solarium crew chief in the car with Huston's captured companion.

"I'd really like to know what Huston is up to and how those other people are involved," said Tom. "I'd especially like to know about that shootout. You're a surprising young man, Peter. Got to go, plane's taking off. Robyn, take good care of him. And Peter, you take care of Robyn. This could turn ugly. Don't take unnecessary chances. Got my work cut out for me in New York."

Chapter 39

After midnight on the last leg of the trip to Washington, Sam Cohn called. "Peter, I have something new on Swanson. A few minutes ago, he called New York City again."

On a hunch, Peter gave Sam the number of the warehouse from which the computer communication with Robyn had originated.

"That's the number. How in the world...??" Sam's amazement was evident.

"It's a long story. I'll tell you when we're both more wide awake. What was the gist of the conversation?"

"He said he needed instructions. The people on the other end said they had none. He asked about what would happen at the Living Wage rally. They told him it was none of his business. Then he got mad. He said he'd put everything on the line and expected to be kept in the loop. After a heated argument, they told him to fly to Washington for a briefing. That satisfied him."

"Thanks, Sam. You need to know that I told Cartwright who I am."

"How did he take it?"

"Fairly well, I'd say. I told him almost everything."

"Do you trust him?"

"I have to. I don't seem to have any choice. When is Swanson coming to D.C.?"

Sam gave him the details.

"I'll meet him at the airport and tail him. Didn't tell Cartwright about you, Sam, and I won't." Peter gave Sam Tom's private number. "Give him a call if you feel comfortable with it. If he wants you to do anything that's relevant to my situation, let me know."

"Feeling like a CIA spook is a real rush."

"Careful, Sam. This is scary stuff. The people we're dealing with could be capable of almost anything. Please don't forget that."

"Don't worry. I certainly won't forget."

Day Four

Chapter 40

Although the LWM caravan had arrived well after midnight, Sarah woke early and decided to go for a run. Each bus had gone to a prearranged location. Occupants of the lead and communications buses had spent what remained of the night in sleeping bags on a Baptist church floor. She was thankful that church members had provided generous amounts of padding. She admired the sights and smells and sounds of her surroundings as she jogged down the hilly, curved, tree-lined street of the well-to-do Virginia suburb. She was aware that even a modest home here sold for a small fortune.

As her feet made their faint jogging slap, slap, slap against the street with every step, she mentally reviewed the day's agenda. Firmly ensconced in Wall Street, she would have enthusiastically supported the rider abolishing the national minimum wage. Now she wasn't so sure and, for that reason, was grateful that Robyn had asked her to take charge of the communication bus during the picketing of the White House. Otherwise, she would have had to decide whether or not to join in.

Sarah thought of the various phone consultations with Jim Archer the previous evening. He had filled her in on the SEC investigations and asked for her advice. She had shared her suspicions regarding what had gone wrong at the Exchange, and she felt that he was growing more appreciative of her analytic skills and more comfortable confiding in her. She felt they were bonding—perhaps more than bonding? He had even sought her assistance in some aspects of the investigation because, although his team had accumulated huge amounts of data, they had been unable to detect any pattern that made sense of the illegal transactions, especially after she had vouched for the innocence of the LWM in this regard. The challenge was invigorating: another puzzle to solve, a giant puzzle with the financial future of the United States at stake.

Returning from her run, Sarah spotted Robyn walking toward the communications bus. "Damn," she whispered, knowing that Frank's automatic trace equipment was down. For a moment, she considered going over to the bus under some pretext and switching it back on, but she didn't want to arouse Robyn's suspicions.

* * * * *

"Thank goodness," Robyn said softly as Sarah looked in her direction, paused, then turned and walked into the Baptist church. Heading straight for the round computer to check for messages, she was not disappointed. After following instructions, she waited.

"Are you alone?" said the computer.

"Yes."

"Show me."

She took the camera off the top of the round computer and panned the bus interior. "Satisfied?"

"Yes. Downloading the encryption program."

When the program had self-activated, the computer continued, "Our plans have changed."

"Meaning?"

"As I told you, we are planning to attend your Washington rally. However, we have learned that your government will attempt to prevent us."

"Why? Because of who you are?"

"Our representative will contact you. He'll explain everything."

"How will I know your representative?"

"He will identify himself by referring to this conversation. Please share the information he provides with Mr. Cartwright. When the two of you are convinced of its veracity, we trust that you'll persuade your government to allow us to attend your rally."

"When may I expect to hear from your representative?"

"We will contact him shortly."

Robyn decided to probe. "I may be hard to find. I'll be picketing the White House because of your tip concerning the bill signing this morning in the Rose Garden."

"The tip?"

"About the rider to the Social Security bill abolishing the national minimum wage." There was a long pause. "Hello? Are you still there?"

"Expect our representative. He'll explain everything. The encryption program will erase itself. Goodbye."

* * * * *

Despite the hour, the operator had instructions to wake the president.

"Captain Thompson, Mr. President. I'm at the Wyoming satellite ground station. We just intercepted another communication to the LWM."

"Yes?"

"We've been able to do a better job of pinpointing the source of the transmission. It's coming from an area on the side of the moon facing Earth."

"And the content of the message?"

"No clue. It was encrypted."

"Thank you, Captain. Inform General McNulty at the Pentagon as well as your commander as to the exact location of the transmission."

"Yes, sir."

Chapter 41

At the Baptist church, Robyn had recruited Peter, Sarah, and Frank to help her contact everyone and make final preparations for a coordinated arrival at the White House. "We don't want to be late," she advised. "The ceremony in the Rose Garden will probably be brief. The president will want to attract as little attention as possible to the minimum-wage rider."

When the opportunity arose, Peter took Robyn aside and brought her up to speed on Swanson's call to New York, emphasizing that it was to the same number in New York City from which the Movement's financial guru had called. Concerning Swanson's planned trip to Washington, he told Robyn, "I won't be picketing because I'm going to meet his plane and follow him. My hope is that he will lead us to the masterminds behind the destruction of the space station."

"Take one of our cars," she offered.

"Thanks. I need to leave soon, and I need a favor. I didn't want to disturb Tom late last night, but he needs to know that Swanson's coming to Washington and that I'm going to follow him."

"Of course, I'll tell him. Do you want company in case of trouble?"

"I think the fewer the better, less chance of being detected. But taking a witness along sounds like a good idea."

"Do you have someone in mind?"

Peter thought for a moment, "Sarah would be perfect. Archer seems to trust her. If we discover any funny business, she could contact him and get the government to investigate."

"OK, but you'll need to convince her."

"I'll tell her who I really am. That should do it."

Leaving Robyn, Peter walked across the church parking lot to the communication bus, where Sarah was working. "I need your help," he said, looking down at her and the pile of picket signs she was constructing along with other Living Wage members.

"What is it?" she said, irritated. "I'm busy."

The two walked outside the bus to a swatch of grass with large rocks framing a sort of border. Peter took a deep breath and then began to disclose his true identity. He briefly told her what he knew about the space station disaster. Sarah's eyes widened in surprise. Finally, he told her about his intention to trail Swanson, concluding with, "I need a witness to verify whatever I find out. Will you come?"

"Very cloak-and-dagger," she said. "Could be dangerous?"

"Could be."

Reaching into her purse, she produced a small-caliber handgun.

Now, Peter's eyes widened in surprise. However, he asked in an even tone, "Got a permit?"

"Of course. Any other stupid questions?"

"Hmm. Black belt?"

She just grinned.

* * * * *

As Tom's limos pulled out of the Manhattan hotel parking lot, he dialed Lacey's office. When Lacey's executive assistant answered, he said, "This is the office of the president. When do you expect Mr. Lacey?"

"The president of the United States?" she asked in an extremely deferential tone.

"When is Mr. Lacey expected?"

"Within the hour."

"Tell him to expect a call. We're on a tight schedule."

"Certainly, sir."

To Maggie, Tom said, "We're heading for the Snoop Squad's New York office to pick up a team and surveillance equipment. Going to bug Lacey's office."

Maggie's eyes sparkled, "Oh, what fun! Like playing trick or treat."

"Except, this Halloween may turn dangerous." His phone buzzed. "Cartwright."

"Robyn, Tom. Am I disturbing you?"

"Not at all."

"We're on our way to see Lacey. What's up?"

She quickly summarized Peter's news regarding Swanson's call to Manhattan Storage and Transfer and his planned flight to Washington.

"I'd love to know what he's up to," Tom replied.

"Peter and Sarah are meeting his plane and intend to tail him."

"Sounds like a good idea. Keep me informed. What about the picketing?"

"Heading for the White House as we speak."

"Our TV crews should already be there."

"Thanks, Tom. Really appreciate your help."

"Let's hope all the publicity gets them to think twice before pulling a stunt like this again. I'll be in Washington this evening. Let's keep in touch. Good luck with the picketing. Give 'em hell!"

* * * * *

Peter wore a borrowed broad-brimmed western hat and sunglasses to further disguise his appearance. The new additions to his outfit plus his leather vest made him look like a wildcatter just off a plane from Texas. Sarah also sported sunglasses and a broad-brim hat. She had purchased one-way tickets so they could pass through terminal security.

Swanson's plane landed on schedule. "That's him," said Peter, indicating the fourth passenger to emerge. "The creep must have flown first class."

"Looks like a grandfather, not a villain," said Sarah.

"Yeah, right. How about you go first, and I'll hang back. Don't want to take any chances on being recognized."

"Fine."

They followed Swanson to car rentals.

Soon he was on the road, with Peter and Sarah following at a safe distance.

Chapter 42

By 9:30 A.M., the buses had dropped off their passengers, and chanting Movement members with placards ringed the White House grounds. Traffic backed up due to the large number of buses, but police managed to keep a lane open for arriving VIPs. Boisterous Movement members heckled arriving dignitaries and waved their placards.

As promised, Cartwright's TV crews were in place at the main White House and West Wing entrances, as well as in the Rose Garden where the bill signing was to take place. Robyn walked over to TV news anchor Charles Phelps at the White House main entrance.

"We meet again," Phelps said, with a trace of a smile and cold, humorless eyes.

"I'm here for an interview."

"Yes, of course," he said, ordering the crew to turn its cameras toward him and away from the crowd.

After introducing Robyn, Phelps recited a brief history of the LWM, concluding with, "Ms. Sherwood, we've learned that there's a rider abolishing the federal minimum wage attached to the Social Security bill to be signed this morning. Is that why you are here?"

"Most certainly. We are appalled and outraged to learn that our president and his congressional cohorts maneuvered to sneak through legislation that will adversely affect so many. The American public needs to know what their elected representatives are doing. We are here to make certain of it.

"Are you implying that Congress doesn't represent the American people?"

"Mr. Phelps, the corrupting influence of big money is silencing the voice of truth, the voice of the real America. How many members of Congress have lived on minimum wage dollars? Abolishing the federal minimum wage is an abomination. It will roll back what little progress has been made in achieving fair compensation for low-wage workers. Congress needs to hear, loud and clear, that their constituents will hold them responsible for their irresponsible action." Walking closer, she looked directly into the camera, "Contact your representatives now. Shame them into reversing this monstrous provision, this discrimination against the poorest among us. Demand the passage of a new federal minimum-wage law, a real living wage law with built in cost-of-living increases!"

"Wouldn't such a law pose real dangers to our economy: increased unemployment, price hikes, even recession?" Phelps asked.

"Look at the record," Robyn replied. "Recent minimum wage increases brought about by Movement efforts have resulted in local economic booms, not recessions. When low-wage workers have more money to spend, they spend much of it, stimulating the economy."

"That *is* interesting," remarked Phelps. "But isn't education important?"

"Education is important. However, it doesn't mean much if good-paying jobs aren't there. Why aren't the jobs there? Because the top 5%, which has 50% of the national income, saves and invests most of its money rather than spending it. If average consumers—that bottom 95%—had more money, they would spend much of it. Such spending would create more income and more jobs, exactly what's been happening everywhere our living wage law has passed. Those economies are not booming by chance. They're booming because the average person has more money to spend."

"How many American workers do you claim are living at or near the poverty level?" asked Phelps.

"About fifty percent. For practical purposes, the middle class has disappeared. Historically, of course, such economic disparity is nothing new. Jesus lived at a time when a few wealthy aristocrats controlled society while the overwhelming majority, the peasants, lived at a bare subsistence level."

"And your point is?" asked Phelps.

"My point is that Jesus and his followers were engaged in a nonviolent struggle against the economic injustices of the Roman Empire. My point is that similar injustice exists in our own society today. My point is that our country is becoming increasingly divided between a few wealthy aristocrats and the low-income majority who are just barely getting by."

"Speaking of money," said Phelps, "Tom Cartwright, CEO of GCIS, our network's parent company, has just contributed ten million dollars to the LWM. However, is it true that the Movement also recently received several large contributions from other, some might say less transparent, sources?"

"We're very grateful to Mr. Cartwright, and we've thanked him publicly. And we want the American people to know the sources of all contributions to the LWM. However, we can't identify the most recent donations due to the president's temporary suspension of banking and investment activities. But we expect and demand transparency in our finances and in the overall operation of the Movement."

"Is it true that the Movement is under investigation by the government?"

"We don't know. But the government can count on our full cooperation."

"After the Washington rally," Phelps said, switching topics, "you'll be in demand as a speaker. Could be quite lucrative, couldn't it?"

"I look forward to and am grateful for any opportunity to spread our message. As for money, I donate anything beyond expenses to the LWM."

Chapter 43

Maggie, Tom, his bodyguards, and two Snoop Squad men gathered on the sidewalk in front of Kenneth Lacey's United News Service corporate headquarters. Tom gave final instructions, and they entered the building. The group barely fit into the only elevator that zoomed up to Lacey's fifty-fourth-floor suite of offices. Everyone squinted as the doors slid open and they emerged into the bright sunlight of a spacious solarium. The décor was impressive.

"Are you expected?" queried the receptionist.

"Yes. I'm Tom Cartwright, CEO of Global Communications and Internet Services. We're here to meet with Mr. Lacey."

"This way, Mr. Cartwright," she said, leading them to a nearby suite of offices. "This is Mrs. Johnson, Mr. Lacey's executive assistant."

Without any introduction, Mrs. Johnson said, "Mr. Cartwright, how may I help you?"

"I'm in New York for a short time, spur-of-the-moment decision. Ken is expecting me."

"You're not on his schedule. Let me check with him."

"No need."

With that, Tom walked briskly to the nearest mahogany door, opened it, and strode into Lacey's office, followed by Maggie and a Snoop Squad man. A flustered Mrs. Johnson followed. The second Snoop Squad man, in her absence, attached a tiny device to the underside of her desk.

Startled, a grey haired, distinguished-looking Lacey looked up from the papers on his desk. Recovering quickly, he said in a booming bass, "Cartwright! What the hell are you doing here?"

The Snoop Squad man tripped, spewing the contents of his briefcase onto the office carpet. Hurriedly picking up the scattered sheets, he said apologetically, "Sorry," over and over. However, he made no attempt to retrieve the tiny spheres which had disappeared into the thick plush fibers of the carpet. Instead, he brushed them still deeper into the weave. He then walked over and stood, head bowed, behind Tom and Maggie, who had sunk into two leather chairs beside Lacey's desk.

"Ken, meet investigative reporter Maggie Blevins," said Tom as he felt for the underside of his chair frame and attached a miniscule device. "We're here because it seems you're secretly funding a political smear campaign against me."

"Nonsense. That's all right, Mrs. Johnson. Please leave us, but alert security."

She left and went back to her office.

"Actually, your denial is nonsense," said Cartwright, opening his laptop computer and turning the screen toward Lacey.

A simulated exploding space station filled the screen, complete with sound effects. Then a voice-over asked, *Why was the GCIS space station destroyed just as it was about to relay intelligible versions of Piscean weak signals to earth? Would the weak signals have confirmed that the economic and political fears of liberal radicals are nonsense, that the strong, vibrant economy of Pisces II is a perfect example of the benefits of a free-market?*

The scene switched to irate customers banging on barred bank doors and on non-functioning ATM machines. *"Recently, GCIS built a device that may have contributed to the financial irregularities which led to the closing of our banks and stock markets. Contact your congressional representatives! Insist on an immediate investigation of Global Communications and its CEO. The safety of your money is at stake. Demand action now!"* Lettering at the bottom of the screen read: The Committee for the Protection of American Rights and Freedoms.

"I'm not affiliated with that organization," said Lacey.

"We believe you are," said Cartwright, glancing at Maggie. "My staff has monitored and recorded a number of similar ads. Many of them are directed at me. They insinuate that I destroyed my company's space station and that I'm responsible for the financial crisis."

"Any comment, Mr. Lacey?" asked Maggie.

"I won't deny my sympathies for the general gist of such ads," he said calmly. "But that doesn't mean I financed them. Where's your proof?"

Ignoring the question, Tom continued, "I think you also had something to do with the destruction of our space station."

"That's absurd, Cartwright," growled Lacey. In a venomous voice, he demanded, "Get out of my office, all of you. Cartwright, you used to have such promise. Now, your stupid liberal ideology has corrupted your judgment." He pressed a button on his desk, and two large men burst into the room. Lacey ordered, "Escort Mr. Cartwright and his party to the elevator."

Tom smiled, turned, and walked out of the office with his party plus the security men. In the outer office, he announced with an amused tone, "Mr. Lacey has invited us to leave."

Near Mrs. Johnson's desk, the second Snoop Squad man shuffled about. "Lost my pen," he said, reaching around the pot of a small tropical tree. "Ah, here it is."

Mrs. Johnson said agitatedly to the security men, "One of them went down the hall toward the restroom."

A guard headed immediately in that direction. Shortly, he returned with Tom's man. The two security personnel ushered everyone to the elevator. As the doors closed, the larger guard warned, "You'll be arrested—or worse—if you attempt to bother Mr. Lacey again."

* * * * *

On the advice of the two Snoop Squad men, the limos drove to the highest level of the parking garage across the street from Lacey's United News Service headquarters. Open to the sky, the snoop squad men believed it would provide good reception of signals from the devices they had planted. They powered up their equipment.

"Anything?" Tom queried when the equipment had been powered up.

"Not yet, but the window sill transmitter is working fine. Signals from inside shouldn't be difficult to pick up."

Momentarily, Mrs. Johnson's voice could be heard, "I called them, Mr. Lacey. They should be here anytime."

"No serious business until they've finished."

"Yes, sir."

"Lacey probably requested an electronic sweep," explained Matt, one of the Snoop Squad men. "We won't learn much until he thinks it's safe. The micro spheres in the carpet will fully activate after the sweep is concluded."

"You don't think they'll find those?" asked Maggie.

"Unlikely. The microspheres are sensitive to electromagnetic radiation and motion and will shut down temporarily. Also, they transmit a spread-spectrum signal that is easily mistaken for random static."

"Mistaken? Why?"

"Because the signal is broken up into a series of very brief transmissions over many different frequencies. Individually they sound like static."

"The device under Mrs. Johnson's desk is no longer transmitting," announced Bob, the other Snoop Squad man. "They must have found it." Shortly, he announced that the device under the chair in Lacey's office had also been disabled.

After some time, Matt announced, "The microspheres in both offices are back on line."

Lacey's voice was heard, "Mrs. Johnson, wait until they sweep the corridor." His voice sounded distant and somewhat muffled, but intelligible.

* * * * *

The voices of both Lacey and Mrs. Johnson could be heard speaking simultaneously in their respective offices.

"Can we listened to just one of them?" Tom asked the Snoop Squad men.

"Sure," said Matt.

"Let's listen to Lacey."

"Done."

"What about Cartwright?"

"He doesn't know much," replied Lacey, obviously on a speakerphone, "but he's annoyingly suspicious."

"So don't worry," said the other person.

"He could cause trouble. Have you located Peter Abelard?"

"Let's encrypt."

After moments of silence, "Satisfied?"

"Yes. We haven't located Abelard. No matter. He doesn't know enough to be a problem."

"What about the other matter? If anything goes wrong…"

"Everything went as planned. Tomorrow we drive home the knife."

"I'm worried about tomorrow, about the rally."

"We're ready."

"Are you sure? We can't afford loose ends."

"Yes. Do you want something done about Cartwright?"

"Not unless it becomes necessary. He used to be a friend. We must guard against excessive use of force."

"Very well. Leave everything to us."

As the call ended, Tom asked, "What number did Lacey dial?"

Matt told him, and Tom checked it.

"Minuteman Company. Michelle speaking. How may I help you?"

Cartwright answered smoothly, "I have an appointment, but I've mislaid your address." She gave it to him. "Midtown Manhattan, right?"

"Correct. Do you also need the address of our satellite location?"

"Yes, please."

"2104 Elm Street, Pleasant Valley, New York."

Tom turned to Maggie, "Lacey was talking to someone at Minuteman's New York office. I think it's time to pay the Manhattan office a visit."

Chapter 44

After a second interview, Robyn joined the picketers taunting VIPs arriving in limousines at the main White House entrance. Most stared straight ahead as they drove through the gates, ignoring the singing, shouting, and placard-waving protesters. When the number of new arrivals dropped off, she decided to walk around the outside of the White House grounds to the portion of the sidewalk nearest the Rose Garden. From the rear of the White House, well hidden by trees and shrubbery, the Garden could not be seen from the street.

Shortly before the scheduled bill signing at 10 o'clock, the protesters saw what they took to be Secret Service agents walking along the inside of the White House grounds perimeter fence. They shouted warnings to picketers flying long-tailed kites to which protest messages had been attached. The picketers shouted back that they had constitutional rights.

Robyn watched with amusement as Movement members armed with a potato cannon, made out of plastic water pipe and powered by hairspray, launched a potato. It arched several hundred feet into the air, landing near its target, the Rose Garden. Several men among the picketers, dressed in dark suits, ran toward the cannon. The shooters dropped it and scattered. Picketers formed a human shield, impeding the pursuers.

Loading the confiscated cannon into a waiting van, the agents patrolled the picket line looking for other contraband and promising to arrest the next person who threw anything over the fence onto White House grounds. The kites were tolerated, but string holders were warned that any flying near the Rose Garden would be confiscated. Movement members responded loudly.

When Movement members with small video receivers saw President Hedges come down the steps out of the White House into the Rose Garden, they passed the word, and the protest went into overdrive. They crowded the fence surrounding the White House grounds, shouting loudly and waving placards.

Then all of a sudden, Robyn saw Movement members pointing and gesturing toward the White House grounds near where the Rose Garden was obscured by trees and dense foliage. Oddly dressed men in bulky clothes and wearing large helmets were appearing as if from nowhere on the grounds. Holding what appeared to be rifles, they sprinted in the direction of the hidden Rose Garden.

Secret Service agents near the perimeter fence began firing at the oddly-dressed men. The shots appeared to miss, but several of their own number dropped to the ground, apparently wounded. Members of the crowd shouted that the strangely-dressed men must be wearing body armor. A protester with a video receiver shouted and pointed at the screen. Panic had broken out in the Rose Garden.

The sudden appearance of soldiers in battle dress on the rear grounds of the White House caused Movement members to throw themselves to the ground. So many soldiers streamed into view that the protesters speculated that they must be coming from hidden underground bunkers. The soldiers raced after the intruders, who had disappeared into the foliage. Robyn and the person with the video receiver, who were now also flat on the ground, watched the screen as dignitaries streamed out of the Rose Garden and scattered, heading for safety. Secret Service agents protecting the president went down as the intruders burst into the Rose Garden. The video feed focused on the president, who was halfway back up the White House steps. He appeared to either trip or be wounded. Agents picked him up and hustled him inside. Three more agents crumpled to the ground before the doors slammed shut.

Soldiers kept appearing and firing. The intruders fired back as they retreated into the trees. Several protesters looked up from where they lay on the sidewalk and saw the intruders emerge from the Rose Garden tree line. Suddenly, they began to vanish. Soldiers with rocket launchers began firing into the air above where the intruders were last seen.

Surprisingly, the rocket explosions formed shapes and were not symmetrical. The protesters watched as the clouds of smoke created by the exploding rockets began outlining what appeared to be a sort of craft hovering over the White House grounds. As more rockets struck, it began to move. It appeared to rise out of the smoky haze, then disappear.

Everyone heard a grinding sound and, turning away from the White House grounds, they saw three parked cars collapse, crushed flat. Above the cars a large object materialized, gaping holes in its side. Figures wearing apparel identical to that worn by White House attackers leaped out and ran toward a nearby grassy area where two buses with LWM signs on their sides were parked.

"Where did those buses come from?" Robyn asked those around her. "They weren't there a few minutes ago." Others agreed.

The figures dove into the buses. Soldiers fired sparingly, apparently attempting to avoid hitting the mass of humanity between them and the buses. When the last strangely-clad figure leaped in, the two buses raced away across the grass toward the street. As soldiers with rocket launchers prepared to fire, the buses vanished. Some around Robyn expressed their disbelief while others recalled that the strange craft had been invisible before suffering rocket damage. A few soldiers continued to fire, but most stood staring, with open, gaping mouths.

Robyn's gaze and those around her returned to the strange craft, from which smoke and flames had begun to belch. Within seconds, a violent explosion seemed to annihilate what remained. The crowd's attention was drawn back to the White House grounds, where soldiers and television crews were milling about on the lawn. Hand-held cameras began clustering around a single location. Robyn asked a Movement member with a video receiver to scan the TV channels and see if any were broadcasting live from that spot on the White House lawn. He located a channel. A figure could be seen lying on the ground wearing the same bulky clothes as the intruders, minus a helmet, and covered in blood from what appeared to be a neck wound.

"He's not moving. Could be dead," commented the individual with the video receiver.

"Get a copy of that," she told him.

"Done," said the other person, handing Robyn a small detachable memory unit. "I've got others if you need them."

"Keep 'em safe. We may want to look at them later."

Soon, soldiers forced the camera crews to leave. Persons looking like medics arrived and began examining the person still sprawled on the ground.

"That's got to be body armor they're removing," said the person with the video receiver.

Abruptly, the examination ended. After a short conference, one of the apparent medics could be seen speaking briefly into a hand-held device. Within minutes, an impeccably dressed man in a dark suit approached and conferred with the group of medics while staring at the figure on the ground. He stepped away and spoke into his lapel mike.

"Must be talking to his boss," Robyn said to the person with the video receiver.

Shortly, a military ambulance drove up. The prone figure was lifted onto a gurney and loaded into it. A black sedan with no identifying markings met and accompanied the ambulance as it left the White House grounds.

"What the hell was that all about?" said the person with the video receiver.

"Aliens, maybe?" said Robyn.

* * * * *

After the two buses disappeared while speeding away from the White House, police radio broadcast: "Attention, all units in the vicinity of the White House. Suspects are escaping in two blue-gray buses with LWM signs on the sides. They may be wearing body armor. Repeat: may be wearing body armor. Exercise extreme caution. Uncertain whether the buses are traveling together or separately."

The dispatcher failed to mention that the buses had vanished as they sped away from the White House.

"Car fifty-four. Buses fitting those descriptions are headed our way, going east on Payne at Salem Parkway. We are turning and will pursue...."

What the? They just disappeared," the officer shouted into his radio. "I mean, they didn't turn a corner; they just vanished as we passed them."

"Car sixty-eight. We are traveling west on Payne. The buses are turning left onto Spruce."

"Where are you, car 68?" the dispatcher asked.

"Almost to the Spruce street intersection."

"Try to stay as close to the buses as you can."

"What's going on?"

"Don't ask questions. Just follow orders."

"Roger that. The first bus just vanished somehow, but I still see the second."

"Stay as close as you can!"

"I'm just behind it. It's turning right into the first alley."

"Car fifty-four here. We're proceeding to the other end of the alley."

"Car sixty-eight. The buses have stopped and are blocking the alley. The suspects ran into a connecting alley. They are entering a building facing west on Spruce just north of Payne. Waiting for backup."

"Car fifty-four. We see them and are proceeding to the Spruce Street entrance of the building."

The officers heard their commander order, "All cars in the vicinity of Spruce and Payne: see the officers and surround the block. Do not proceed into the building. Repeat: do not proceed into the building. Wait for SWAT."

Fourteen police cars responded, and the officers did as instructed. SWAT teams wearing full-body armor arrived shortly. After checking their weapons, the teams coordinated plans to storm the building. Half proceeded to the rear of the building; the rest remained in front.

The windowless building had metal doors front and back. The teams placed explosive charges. They exploded almost simultaneously, blowing both front and rear doors completely off their hinges. Both sets of teams charged into the building.

The police commander moved to the building's front entrance, monitoring the communications of the SWAT teams inside.

"Teams one and two. Nothing in the rear."

"Teams three and four. Nothing in the front. We are proceeding toward the interior."

"We see you. We're at a freight elevator."

"We're at some stairs, up and down. Must be a basement. We'll check it out. Stay put…. Basement is clear."

"Taking the freight elevator up to the next floor. Follow on the stairs."

"Copy. I figure this building has four floors."

"Agreed. Watch yourselves."

"Yeah. You too."

"Starting up…. Charlie, hold it between floors. Tony, have a look…. Okay, Charlie, take it up…. We're out of the elevator…. Nothing."

"Same here. Watch for us. We're moving in your direction."

"We see you. Check your side of the building; we'll check ours."

"Our side is clear."

"So is ours."

"See you topside. Watch your ass."

"Like playing Russian roulette. We're starting up. Hold it between floors again, Charlie…. Take it up…. We're out."

"We're out, too."

"Nothing to report."

"Same here. They must be on the fourth floor."

"On your say so."

"Starting up."

"Roger."

The police commander at the front entrance heard the sharp staccato of gunfire. It continued uninterrupted for several minutes, then gradually became intermittent. He saw an explosion blast through the roof of the building, toppling a large tower antenna and spewing debris. Smoke and flames shot up from the building. He ordered his assistant to place an emergency call to the fire department.

* * * * *

The police commander felt a rush of air as the fire expelled flames and hot air through the hole in the roof. Entering the warehouse, he saw members of a SWAT team scramble out of the freight elevator, some bleeding from multiple cuts and abrasions. They were soon joined by others filing out of the stairway toward the rear of the building.

A team leader said, "That blast gutted the top floor."

"Did we lose anyone?"

"Several are wounded, but I don't know how badly."

"Will the firefighters be safe?"

"Should be. The suspects couldn't have survived the blast and fire."

"Clear out," the commander ordered. As the building filled with smoke, fire trucks screeched to a halt at the front entrance. Outside, the police commander shouted, "Chief, the gunmen were on the top floor. We think they're all dead. Get the fire under control as quickly as possible. We need to preserve as much evidence as we can."

Firefighters, equipped with air tanks and facemasks, pulling hoses, entered the warehouse. Two ladder trucks began pouring water through the hole in the roof. In minutes, the flames subsided.

Shortly, a firefighter radioed, "The worst is over, Chief. The fire is contained."

"Anyone alive up there?"

"No. Haven't even seen any bodies."

"We'll send in forensics when you give us the word," the police commander said to the fire chief.

The firefighter, still on the radio, said, "Tell the cops there's nothing up here but ashes."

"Our forensics people are ash experts," the police commander said into the chief's radio. "Disturb the scene as little as possible."

"Unless the fire flares up, we won't have to disturb much."

About twenty minutes later, the forensics team leader reported by radio from the fourth floor, "Commander, so far no identifiable traces of human remains. No weapons either."

"What's up there?"

"Just ashes and a twisted heap of metal."

"What metal?"

"Don't know. Sort of looks like a bridge girder or large crane arm. Don't see any motor, though. Might be under all the mess."

"Even thoroughly incinerated bodies don't vanish without a trace, right?"

"Right."

"Well then, find me something!"

Chapter 45

Peter and Sarah followed Swanson as he drove through Washington's Virginia suburbs. Nearing the intersection in Falls Church where he had just turned, Sarah exclaimed, "Look! He's headed for the Minuteman Company. That's the same company that installed the round computer at the New York Stock Exchange. Remember, I told you the computer with the same serial number listed in the company's on-line catalogue was not the one actually installed."

After pulling in some distance from where Swanson had parked, Peter remarked, "He knows me. I should stay in the car. Go in and see what you can see. Maybe pretend you're looking for a job?"

"Sounds good," Sarah agreed.

"Be careful."

"Don't worry," she said, patting the gun in her purse as she got out of the car.

"Wasn't what I meant."

She turned, walked across the parking lot into the building, and asked the first person she encountered to direct her to the employment office.

"We don't have one," the man said, looking at her strangely. Pointing to an office near the entrance, he added, "Try over there."

When he disappeared round a corner, she walked briskly toward the rear of the building, spotting Swanson talking animatedly to three men behind a glass partition. Since she could not listen without being seen, she continued on. Trailing three employees through a pair of large double doors, she found herself in a huge open area full of machinery. On the far side, she saw a towering metal structure resembling the superstructure of a bridge. Under it sat what seemed to be a strange-looking aircraft.

From behind, someone firmly grabbed her arm. "Can I help you?" a man's voice asked.

"I'm looking for the employment office," she said meekly as her hand wandered toward the gun in her purse.

Without another word, he escorted her to the office near the front entrance.

"Thank you," she said politely, as he opened the door.

A dark-haired woman pointedly informed her that the company only used employment agencies, mentioned several and encouraged her to register with them. Deciding not to press her luck, Sarah left.

In the car with Peter driving back to Washington, she described what she had seen. "But no round computers."

He listened silently, then announced, "We're being followed."

* * * * *

Sarah glanced over her shoulder at the car that had caught Peter's attention.

"Don't be so obvious," he warned.

"Don't be a worry wart," she scolded, adjusting the side mirror in order to avoid turning around.

"Let's not argue. We need to figure out what to do."

"It's not like they're going to run us off the road. Too many witnesses. We aren't in any immediate danger."

"Don't be so damn certain. I wonder if they know who we are."

"Haven't the license plates already given us away?"

"Not unless they have connections."

"Well, if they've done what we suspect they've done, adding connections to the list doesn't seem like much of a stretch," Sarah said sarcastically.

"Agreed. But they probably don't know that the owner is a Movement member or what the owner is doing in Washington."

"Are you suggesting we need to lose them?"

"Yep."

"Well, why didn't you say so?"

"I just did."

She shot him an irritated look. "Smart ass!"

"Let's just concentrate on losing them. OK?" he replied in a consciously conciliatory tone.

"OK. Let's fake an emergency stop just before the next exit. They'll probably drive past. We take the exit, and they're history."

Swerving to the side of the expressway, Peter came to a sudden stop just before an exit. The other car sped by, pulling up beneath the overpass.

Gunning the engine, he took the exit and said, "This should give us a few minutes head start."

Sarah consulted a map of Washington. "The only direct way back is the expressway."

"Find another route."

"Check." Fumbling with the map, she said, "Take the next left. Then take a right at the first major intersection."

Peter followed her instructions. "Call Robyn. Tell her what you saw at Minuteman."

"Shouldn't we call Archer too?"

"OK, but Robyn first. She needs to tell Tom that Swanson visited Minuteman here. He might turn up something in New York."

She tried calling several times before getting a response. "It's Sarah, Robyn," she yelled. "I can hardly hear you. What's happening?"

"An attack on the White House," she heard Robyn shout. "Everybody's going crazy."

"My God!" Sarah cried. "Are you OK, Robyn?…Thank goodness." Turning to Peter, "Someone attacked the White House. "

Straining to hear, Sarah finally said, "I need Tom's private number." Robyn repeated it several times before Sarah got the number. She tried to tell Robyn what they had learned about Swanson, but gave up. "I'll call back later," she shouted at last.

"Tell Tom he may need to bail us out of jail," she heard Robyn shout. "They're trying to take my phone." The connection went dead.

Sarah hurriedly described Robyn's situation for Peter. She then called Tom. He knew about the attack on the White House. She told him

Robyn's phone had been confiscated and that she was probably under arrest.

"Whenever you can reach her again," Tom said, "let her know my lawyers are on their way. We'll do our best to see that no one spends the night in jail."

Next, Sarah told him about Swanson, the Minuteman Company, and their situation.

"We're checking out the company. Give me your number." After she did, he said, "Keep me posted and take care. Do not underestimate the danger."

"Count on it," she said soberly.

"Till tomorrow."

In a voice indicating she would brook no opposition, Sarah said to Peter, "Now I'm calling Archer. He'll likely turn up more than Cartwright."

"OK," Peter conceded, grinning inwardly. Sarah was playing exactly the liaison role he had been counting on.

Chapter 46

D.C. police, aided by the Secret Service, herded Living Wage picketers into groups. Everyone was searched for weapons and asked for identification. The information was recorded, photos taken. Detention of the picketers continued. They demanded to be charged or released. They were bluntly told that civil rights were not top priority under the circumstances.

* * * * *

Sarah talked to Archer, then said to Peter. "We need to help Robyn."

"Agreed."

Minutes later, they were driving across the Potomac. Parking away from the White House near the Lincoln Memorial due to traffic congestion, they walked briskly to a makeshift roped-off area which was serving as a detention space where the picketers were being held. Circling the groups of detainees looking for Robyn, they eventually spotted her. She gestured at a particular police officer.

"He must be in charge," said Peter.

"Let me handle this," Sarah replied, batting her eyes. Walking up to the officer, she announced in a pleasant, self-assured voice, "I represent Robyn Sherwood. She's leader of the LWM, and one of your detainees. If she's not being charged, I demand her release."

"Sorry Miss, can't do that."

Sarah persisted, leading the officer over to where Robyn was standing at the outer edge of her group of detainees. "Officer," she glanced at his badge, "Johnson, this is Robyn Sherwood, leader of the LWM."

Shaking her hand, Officer Johnson said, "Yes, Ms. Sherwood, with all the publicity I'd recognize you anywhere."

"There must be something you can do for us," insisted Sarah. "Ms. Sherwood is certainly not going to run from the law if released, and, very likely, she will not even be charged since she was merely an innocent bystander, as were the members of the Living Wage Movement."

"I'm certainly innocent of any wrongdoing," stated Robyn emphatically, "and I'm certainly not going to run from the law."

"I cannot release you on my own authority," said Officer Johnson. "However, I will contact my Captain, who is in charge of the operation."

He moved away from them while speaking into the microphone attached to his lapel. After several minutes, he returned.

"My captain agrees that the chances of her being charged are slim and that the likelihood of her attempting to evade the law are minimal given her national prominence and reputation. He is sending over a form which the three of you must fill out and sign, swearing to the truth of your statements. Another officer and I will countersign as witnesses. Is that acceptable?"

All three agreed.

After they had signed the document, Robyn learned the identity of the captain in charge. She immediately stalked over to the command headquarters with Peter and Sarah scurrying to keep up. He was obviously annoyed but agreed to talk.

"Captain Barshefsky," Robyn began, "I demand that all members of the LWM be released immediately. We have a constitutional right to picket peacefully. We've committed no violent acts and broken no laws."

"Look, lady," the captain responded, "someone just attempted to kill the president. We will detain whomever we please. This is an emergency. And who exactly are you?"

Ignoring his question, Robyn pressed on, "How long are you intending to hold these people?"

"Until we're darn sure that they weren't involved in the attack on the president." He turned and began walking away. Robyn scooted around him, back into his line of vision. In his personal space, close to his face, she stared him in the eye and said, "The attackers arrived in an aircraft and left in two buses that weren't ours. I have a list of all Movement caravan buses and can account for them. We had nothing to do with any of that."

The radio in his hand squawked out his name. Putting it to his ear and motioning for her to be silent, "Captain Barshefsky," he listened for a moment. "Why?…What should I tell my officers?…Very well."

Walking to a nearby police van, he spoke to a cluster of uniformed officers.

"Wonder what's up," said Peter.

Barshefsky and another officer approached the waiting trio.

"Don't look very friendly," whispered Sarah.

"This is Officer Connery," said Barshefsky. "We have been ordered to search all detained picketers for weapons. In my book, that includes you."

Peter pointed to himself and Sarah, "We weren't even here at the time of the attack. You have no reason to search us."

"Yes," said Sarah, thankful that she had had enough foresight to leave her gun in the car. "We were driving on the expressway when we heard about the White House."

"Sure. Raise your arms," ordered Officer Connery. He patted down both sides of their legs as well as their upper bodies. "Thank you," he said politely to each as he finished, indicating to the Captain with a shake of his head that he had found nothing.

While they watched the police search nearby Living Wage members, Robyn said to the captain, "I want to impress upon you that we expect our members to be released as soon as possible. If our rights are violated, we will consult our lawyers and take appropriate action."

"We'll do our best, ma'am."

"Thanks, Captain. The LWM had nothing to do with what happened at the White House." Turning to Peter and Sarah, "Let's find a place where we can talk." When they were a distance away and could not be heard, she said excitedly, "Do you know what just happened?"

"No, what?" said Sarah.

"They were looking for Pisceans."

"Crap!!!" Peter blurted out.

"After the attackers' aircraft crashed and they drove away in those two buses, one of them was left lying on the White House lawn, apparently dead. The medics that examined the body acted surprised. Somebody—maybe a Secret Service agent—arrived and consulted with them. Then a military ambulance drove up, the body was hustled in, and it sped away, accompanied by an unmarked black sedan. When we were searched a few minutes ago, did you notice that the officer seemed to be mainly interested in our upper bodies? I think maybe they were looking for gills!…My God! What are those aliens up to?"

Remembering the memory chip she had hidden in her waistband when the police began to search detainees, Robyn pulled it out. "Give me your phone, please," she said to Sarah. After she slipped the memory chip into the phone, a picture of the person left behind by the attackers appeared on the tiny screen. "Take a look at this," she said to Peter. "Is that Huston by any chance?"

His jaw dropped when he saw the face on the screen. For a long moment, he just stared. Looking up, he said, "No. That's not Huston! It's the guy I saw him with back at the rest area in Illinois when I discovered they were aliens. I thought two government men took him into custody after a gunfight. Now, I don't know what to think!"

Chapter 47

On the drive cross-town to the Minuteman Manhattan office, Tom and Maggie discussed strategies. Checking the web for information about the company, they found little. Next, Maggie consulted the archives of her news organization with no better result.

"Guess we go in blind," she said.

They decided that she and one of Tom's men, Ziggy, armed with a video camera, would pretend to be a news team sent to get a story.

"Make up a rumor about a research breakthrough," suggested Tom.

"Good idea! When they deny the rumor, that'll give me an opening to ask questions."

"Let's hope they let something slip."

They parked a distance from the building in order to remain inconspicuous. Maggie and Ziggy walked the rest of the way and took an elevator to the company suite on the third floor. At the reception desk, Maggie announced, "I"m a reporter. I would like to speak to your public relations person."

The receptionist thought for a moment, "Oh, you must mean Mr. Jameson. I'll buzz him." A conservatively dressed, middle-aged man emerged from an office down the corridor. "Mr. Jameson, this is a reporter who is here to see you."

"What may I do for you?" he asked politely.

"I'm Maggie Blevins, a reporter with Gaia News Services. This is my cameraman, Ziggy." They shook hands. "We received a tip that your company made a research breakthrough which will send its stock price through the ceiling. Would you care to comment?"

After a moment's thought, Jameson suggested, "We can talk more comfortably in my office. Please come this way." When all were seated, he continued, "First of all, we're a privately-held company, so we're not terribly concerned about the short-term effect of a news story on the price of our stock. Secondly, it would be nice if the rumors were true. But they're not."

"That's too bad. My source is usually reliable. What sorts of projects does your company work on?"

"Our business is to provide our clients with specialized technical information and computers."

"What sorts of information? What sorts of clients?"

"I'm afraid that's confidential."

"What sorts of computers?"

"Various sorts."

"My source tells me that Mr. Kenneth Lacey is connected with your company." When he didn't respond, Maggie said, "A news story means free publicity. My news service has worldwide coverage. Isn't that worth a little news about your company?"

"We're not interested in publicity." He stood. "Ms. Blevins, I'm a busy man. I'm afraid I must ask you to leave, and I must ask you not to take photographs on the way out."

"Do you have company literature that we might take with us?"

"We are a very private company and intend to remain so. Please follow me." He led them to the front entrance and bid them a definitive goodbye.

Through the glass doors, as they were leaving, they saw a stern faced Jameson speaking to and waving a finger at the receptionist.

In the limo with Tom, Maggie summarized her conversation with Jameson, then added, "Oh, I almost forgot. I saw what looked like round metal computers in a room we passed on the way to Jameson's office."

"So did I," confirmed Ziggy.

"Those damned round computers again," said Tom. "Let's pay a visit to Pleasant Valley, their other location. It's only a couple of hours. Who knows what we might find."

* * * * *

Tom's limos drove slowly past Minuteman's rural New York site, a large, plain, box-like building located at the mouth of a small valley.

"Plant appears to be closed down," said Jake, Tom's security chief, "no lights and only three cars in the lot."

"Seems like you're right," said Tom. "Let's drive the cars into town, come back on foot, and see what we can see."

After they had parked, Tom and Jake returned to the plant. Jake pretended to be a local showing his friend around town. Across the street from the plant, he pointed at it and pretended to be explaining something to his friend. Casually, they crossed the street and, with hands shading eyes, began peering into windows.

"Not much to see," Jake announced loudly.

"Except that huge metal arch," whispered Tom. "Reminds me of that gateway-to-the-West arch in St. Louis."

As they continued along the side of the building facing the parking lot looking into windows, Jake said, "Seems like they're dismantling everything."

"Yup," Tom agreed.

When they reached the corner of the building, a high metal fence prevented them from continuing and from seeing into the valley. Other buildings further back from the road blocked any view.

"I think we should check out that valley," said Jake.

"Sounds good. Let's have a look."

Walking to the limos, they got in and drove back to the Minuteman building. Past it, the road climbed continuously. At the top, a level landscape stretch before them. Beyond fields of corn, they could see a line of trees marking the edge of the valley. The tree line was sparse, indicating steep valley walls. A tall chain link fence ran the length of the tree line.

"That fence is likely protecting something," noted Jake.

"Are you a fence-climber?" Tom asked Maggie.

"I've climbed my share, though none recently."

"Ziggy, get us closer to that fence."

211

The limos turned into the first farm track leading through the corn toward the fence. At the fence, everyone got out. Tom, Maggie, and five of his men started climbing over. The sharp ends of twisted wire at the top, which could easily puncture and tear the skin, proved to be the real obstacle, not the climb up.

Hearing chuckles as she straddled the top of the fence, Maggie called out, "Pretend to be gentlemen." Once she was clear of the sharp twisted ends, Tom grasped her with both hands and gently lifted her down.

"Thanks," she smiled, sensing his hands grasp her waist an instant longer than necessary.

"Least I could do, partner," he grinned back.

Walking along the fence line, they found a place where the valley wall was not as steep. As they climbed down, their view of the valley was obscured by a dense growth of trees. Reaching the valley floor, they were amazed to see an array of what appeared to be telescopes stretching from one end of the valley to the other.

"If they're telescopes," said Tom, "the mirrors aren't particularly large, perhaps two meters."

"Let's have a look," suggested Jake.

Approaching the nearest, they peered up at the metal tube towering above them. Ziggy and another of Tom's men climbed the support girders and slid open a metal cover on the tube's side. Ziggy poked his head through the opening. A muffled bass voice reverberated from within, "It's a mirror all right. Beam me up, Scotty."

As the two climbed down, Tom and Jake studied the masses of wires which ran from one tube to another.

"Jake, could this be an interferometer telescope array?"

"Good guess," Jake replied, as Ziggy took pictures. "Wouldn't require really large telescopes."

"What's an interferometer array?" asked Maggie.

"It uses light gathered by the array," said Tom, "to produce interference patterns that increase the resolution capacity of the telescopes. For example, an interferometer array is capable of producing images of the planets of nearby stars."

"What's it doing here? The valley walls obscure much of the sky."

"The best results are generally obtained directly overhead," said Jake, "where the atmosphere interferes least with the light."

"True. But that wouldn't explain the secrecy," said Tom, "unless...unless someone discovered a better way to receive signals from Pisces II. It's pretty much overhead at this latitude."

"But these telescopes are built to receive light signals," said Jake, "not radio or TV signals."

"Point well taken," said Tom. "We need to get inside that building."

"I don't relish the prospect of climbing back over that fence in this skirt," said Maggie. "Let me borrow Ziggy and the camera. We'll take some pictures of this place, then sneak up to the building from the rear."

Tom frowned, opened his mouth to speak, thought better of it, and with a shrug of his shoulders, smiled and said, "Reporters. At least you'll have Ziggy with you. Meet us in the parking lot. If we don't see you there, we'll look for you back at the fence."

"Sounds like a plan," replied Maggie."

Turning to Ziggy, Tom said, "No unnecessary chances." Ziggy nodded.

As they walked together passed a second telescope, Jake pointed upward, calling out, "Stop! Surveillance camera! Don't think we've been spotted."

Everyone backed away from the camera and the telescope.

Jake reached into his suitcoat and withdrew a pistol, simultaneously producing a metal cylinder which he screwed onto the barrel. Seeing the surprised look on Maggie's face, he said, "A silencer. I'm going to disable the camera." Looking at Tom, "OK?" After a nod, he took aim and put two holes through its side.

"Jake," said Tom, "since you've disabled the camera, let's have a look inside this telescope and make certain they're all the same."

"Good to be certain."

As Ziggy climbed the girders supporting the metal tube, Tom said, "Here, take some pictures," and threw the camera up to him. Removing the cover on the side of the tube, he poked his head in and said, "Yup, exactly the same." After taking several flash pictures, he climbed down.

They were deciding what to do next, when a speaker blared, "Shoo! Shoo! Shoo!" Then they heard a man say in a lower voice, "Can't see anything, but the computer is sensing motion in sector six. Probably those damn deer again. Don't care how they got in, just kill 'em. Don't want 'em chewing on the wires."

"Move very slowly and head for the trees," ordered Jake quietly. "The motion detectors shouldn't register if we're barely moving. Watch me. Take small steps. You'll be able to maintain your balance better."

As if in a slow-motion movie scene, everyone eased toward the trees.

The speakers blared once more, "Shoo! Shoo! Shoo!" Then in a lower voice again, "Lost 'em. Maybe they're already in the trees. Shoot 'em even if they're heading for the fence. Let's get rid of the little bastards once and for all."

Maggie heard the motor of an approaching vehicle.

"Make a break for it if they spot us," Jake said softly, slowly reaching for his weapon. The other bodyguards followed his lead.

The sound of the motor grew still louder before it began to fade, along with tense facial expressions. Everyone's snaillike pace to the trees continued, but the motions grew more fluid and relaxed.

Maggie was fixating on an approaching tree when she heard Jake proclaim, "We"ve been spotted! Run for it!"

Turning her head, she saw a small vehicle looking like a golf cart with three men inside moving toward them along the tree line.

"Stop!" shouted the driver of the vehicle as it continued to approach. "You are trespassing on private property."

Everyone made it to the trees and started scrambling up a small ravine when they heard the first shot.

"Keep down," ordered Jake. "Don't know if it's a warning or if they're shooting at us. Stay in the ravine. It'll give us cover." He had two of his men act as a rear guard while everyone else followed the ravine upward toward the fence. He told them, "Warn those guys before you shoot, but don't hesitate to defend yourselves if they come at you. We'll cover you from the top."

Halfway up the ravine, they heard more shots.

"Get the hell up to the cars," ordered Jake, as he and Ziggy went back to help the men left behind.

When Maggie reached the fence, she was grateful to see that the bodyguard left behind with the limos had cut a hole in it. Holding up a small tool, he said, "I heard the shots. Thought you might need to get out fast."

Stooping, Maggie crept through the hole as he held up the fence flap, followed by Tom and the remaining bodyguard.

Once through the fence, Tom ordered, "Turn the limos around. Keep the motors running."

Momentarily, the rest of Tom's men emerged from the ravine. While the others ran for the hole in the fence, Jake pivoted and fired several rounds down into the ravine. After listening for a moment, he also ran for the hole in the fence.

Once all were in the limos, he yelled, "Get the hell out of here. Those guys aren't very good, but let's not take any chances." To Tom, he said, "Didn't have to shoot any. Just scared them."

"Did they shoot at you?" asked Tom.

"A few times. Mostly though, they were tree huggers. There they are," Jake called to the driver, as two men carrying rifles emerged from the tree line. Before they could take aim, the limos disappeared into the corn. "We'd better not drive back through Pleasant Valley," he told Tom.

"Right."

* * * * *

When they were on the expressway heading for New York's LaGuardia Airport, Maggie kicked off her shoes and said, "Good to feel safe and relax."

"Yes," said Tom, leaning back and stretching his legs.

Maggie watched as the limos passed three buses. "Looks like they"re full of elderly couples on an outing." Moving her face closer to the window, she stared at the sign on the lead bus. "Yup, and it looks like they're having a good time."

"Not as good as us," commented Jake. "At least some of us. Haven't had such a rush in a while." He smiled, "No reflection on you, Tom."

"No offense taken. But this isn't over yet."

"I hear you," said Jake. "We'll play it by the book. Take every precaution. These people may be very dangerous, and they may be very smart."

Suddenly, all in the limo were pitched violently to the left as it swerved to the right.

"Wind gust," called the driver. "Sorry."

A moment later, they were pitched to the right as the limo suddenly swerved left.

"I'm slowing down," said the driver. "Don't see any wind out there. Might be a wheel, maybe the suspension. Just don't know."

The limo started jerking back and forth.

"The motor is acting up," yelled the driver, pulling to the side of the expressway.

As he did so, the motor died and the tires screeched and smoked. The second limo pulled up behind them.

"Did you feel anything?" the first driver called out his window to the second.

"Yeah, the car felt like it was swerving."

"Mine too. There didn't seem to be any wind, though."

"Let's have a look," said Jake, getting out of the limo. "Try starting the engine."

The driver turned the key. Silence.

They all got out, and soon found that the second limo engine had quit as well. The cause was also not obvious.

Tom looked at Jake, "Both cars. Coincidence?"

"Don't believe in coincidences."

"Were the limos ever left unattended?" Tom asked Jake.

Taking him aside, Jake said, "That's what's got me worried. Could it be some of our own?"

The conversation was interrupted as Tom and Jake each took a step forward to brace against a sudden wind gust. Two of the group were caught off balance and tumbled to the ground. Maggie felt the gust end as suddenly as it had begun.

"Look," said Jake, pointing.

Maggie saw trees and road gradually fade and then completely disappear, replaced by a white haze. Although where they stood was not hazy, the haze completely surrounded them.

One of Tom's men walked toward the circle of haze but quickly retreated, reporting, "Gets hot as hell when you get close."

Maggie suddenly felt light on her feet, felt herself being pulled upward. The others seemed to be experiencing the same.

"Get into the cars," yelled Jake. To Tom he said, "Remember the White House. We'll try shooting up into the middle of that circle of haze."

When all were in the limos, Tom's men leaned out the windows and, on Jake's order, a deafening barrage of gunfire began, ending only when the guns were empty.

While the men were reloading, Jake announced, "Something is moving up there."

Almost before the words were out of his mouth, the white haze vanished, and clouds and blue sky appeared once more above. For several apprehensive minutes, everyone remained on guard. Then they succeeded in starting the limo engines. Tom and Jake agreed that they should get underway but drive more slowly and circumspectly.

Back on the highway, they proceeded without incident. To Maggie, what had happened minutes before seemed almost unreal. She heard Tom's men start to joke about it over their cell phones, as if they'd stepped into the middle of a TV drama.

Listening to and even enjoying the banter, Maggie stared between the two front seats and out the front window. Suddenly, a pickup truck seemed to materialize out of nowhere, forcing the limo driver to stomp on the brakes and come to a screeching halt. A car behind them skidded to the side of the expressway, barely missing the second limo, which had succeeded in stopping without crashing into the first.

"It's happening again," called Jake from the passenger's seat. "One second the truck wasn't there. The next second it was."

"Yes," said Tom. There's a tunnel ahead. Let's make for it and try to figure out what to do."

In the tunnel, the limos slowed and then stopped, blocking a lane. Because traffic was light a line of vehicles only gradually backed up behind them. Tom and Jake jumped out and began going down the line of stopped vehicles, speaking to the drivers. After talking to the driver of a bus farther back in the line, which Maggie recognized as one of the tour buses they had passed, they returned to the limos and urged everyone to get out and run for the bus. While the others did so, Tom and Jake went back to a car containing four young men. After a brief conversation, two of them jumped out, jogged to the limos, and scrambled in. As the limos drove out of the tunnel, Tom and Jake boarded the bus, joining the others. The line of stalled traffic, including the bus, followed the limos out of the tunnel.

The people in the bus wanted to know what had just happened. Tom deferred to Jake.

"We've been having car trouble. We asked them to drive the limos for us and warned them of the danger, such as the car skidding or coming to a sudden stop. We offer them a thousand dollars each, and they agreed to drive the cars to a service station in the nearest town. If they got into any trouble, they were to leave the limos by the side of the road. Their buddies would pick them up, and they would phone and tell us where the cars were."

"Try to stay away from the bus windows," Tom advised his men and Maggie.

The elderly persons around them asked why. Tom and Jake tried lamely to blame it on the car trouble. An awkward silence descended on the bus.

Constance, an elderly lady, sitting beside Maggie broke it, "We're heading back to the city from the Adirondacks. A day tour. Good group. Game for anything."

"Great!" said Maggie. "We're headed for the city as well."

"Where can I drop you?" called the driver over his shoulder. "Our headquarters is near Times Square. I can drop you anywhere between here and there."

Tom thanked the driver and said, "Times Square would be fine."

Maggie thoroughly enjoyed the company of Constance and her companions. The trip into the city only seemed to take minutes instead of an hour and a half. At Times Square, she said goodbye to her newfound friends and got into a taxi with Tom and Jake.

During the bus ride, they had not been able to privately discuss what had happened because they had been dispersed among the other passengers. Neither had they really discussed it in the limos. Jake now began, telling Tom and Maggie about his fear that they were being pulled upward into the haze above—maybe into an aircraft—ending with, "and that's why I ordered everyone into the limos and the men to begin shooting."

"I guessed as much," said Tom.

"Good Lord," said Maggie, "does that mean we might possibly have been attacked by an invisible Piscean aircraft?"

"Could be," said Jake. "I was thinking of what happened at the White House, the attack by the invisible aircraft."

"If Peter's right about Huston and his buddy," said Tom, "it's a distinct possibility. We don't know whether Huston is friend or foe. And don't forget that strange telescope array at Minuteman upstate. Think about lasers. Under the proper circumstances, light can be a better, faster means of transmitting information than the longer wavelength electromagnetic frequencies of traditional radio or TV."

The conversation went round and round.

"Questions, questions, questions," said Maggie at length, "but no answers."

As they boarded the company plane, they looked forward to seeing Robyn, Peter, and Sarah. Perhaps their shared information would help make sense of it all.

Chapter 48

President Hedges addressed the members of his Cabinet gathered for the late night emergency session. "Ladies and gentlemen, as you know, the bill signing gathering in the Rose Garden today was attacked. We don't yet know why. Miraculously, none of our guests was seriously injured. The same is true of the Secret Service agents and army personnel who fought off the attackers. The injured reported a burning sensation throughout their bodies which rendered them senseless for several minutes.

"Our alert military destroyed the aircraft which brought the attackers. We believe that the attackers were from Pisces II. A dead individual with telltale alien gills was recovered on White House grounds following the attack."

An audible sense of shock passed round the meeting table.

"This meeting has been called for the purpose of determining our response to these events. In order to do so, you need to be made aware of two additional facts. First: an alien spaceship has landed on the moon."

Another audible sense of shock.

"The spaceship's intentions are unknown, but it seems reasonable to link it with the attack on the Rose Garden. Second: two buses displaying LWM placards rescued the attackers when their aircraft crashed as a result of damage inflicted by our military. As in the case of the aircraft, the buses were able to render themselves invisible and evade pursuers, at least initially. Eventually, the police spotted the buses and cornered the attackers in a warehouse. The attackers all perished in a firefight and subsequent explosion.

"Because of the two buses displaying LWM placards, we believe that the LWM may be involved somehow with the aliens. For now this is just conjecture. The LWM leader, Ms. Sherwood, insists that those two buses were not part of her caravan. The Movement has permission to hold a rally at the Lincoln Memorial tomorrow. Organizers expect a large turnout. We need to decide what, if anything, to do about the rally. The two buses could be genuine LWM buses, though probably they aren't. We simply do not have sufficient information. Discussion of the situation is now open."

Gradually, a consensus developed. It was decided that intervening to prevent the rally was not wise because it would simply call attention to a possible danger which had yet to be fully evaluated. It was also agreed that alarming the public by calling attention to an alien spaceship whose intention was unclear had little to recommend it. In addition, ferreting out the connection between the aliens and the LWM, if any, might be expedited by allowing the rally to go forward. Finally, everyone concurred that the military should be maintained on full alert status and that additional personnel and resources should be made available to Washington area police and military.

As the meeting was about to adjourn, the president's chief of staff entered the room, interrupting the proceedings and followed by General McNulty.

"General. What have you learned?" said President Hedges.

"Our unmanned rockets are orbiting the moon. They conducted a scan of the area where we believe the Piscean spaceship is hiding."

"And?"

"We don't want to tip them off, so we're only doing passive scans. We almost missed the ship on the first pass because it's down in a crater. On the second pass, a spectrometer and magnetometer survey definitely pinpointed it. It's buried in lunar dust, but we were able to detect its outline."

"Size?"

"Several football fields."

"Anything else?"

"Not without an active scan."

"Have you considered one?"

"Don't want to, might spook them."

"I understand. Continue the present surveillance, unless you determine there's good reason to do otherwise. Inform me of any change, any change at all. I want our Air Force on alert, especially in the Washington area. Low-profile on all this."

"Yes, sir." He saluted, turned on his heels and left the room.

Day Five

Chapter 49

Shoes wet with dew, Robyn trudged up the steps of the Lincoln Memorial carrying a box of microphones. A small crowd had already gathered. Television crews were setting up, and Tom's network was prominently represented. The crews of rally performers were also busily at work.

When she saw Tom's limos, Robyn called to Peter and Sarah. Together, they walked over and greeted Tom, Maggie, and his men.

Peter said, "Sarah and I think we should go back to the Virginia Minuteman plant. We need to find out more about it and about Swanson's involvement."

"Good idea," said Tom, "but first Maggie and I need to bring you up to speed on our New York trip. We planted bugs in Lacey's New York office. Turns out he was communicating with the New York branch of the Minuteman Company. So we visited their Manhattan offices. Didn't learn much, except Maggie and Ziggy saw more round computers. Then we drove to a Minuteman plant outside of Pleasant Valley, New York. That trip was more fruitful. We found a telescope array set up in a narrow valley behind the plant. We think it may have been designed to receive signals from Pisces II."

Jake added, "Then we had to run for it because they started shooting at us."

Robyn, Peter, and Sarah stared at him, shocked, while he described in detail what had transpired. He also described what had happened on their way back to New York City, including their apparent encounter with an invisible aircraft.

"Sounds like what happened at the White House," said Robyn.

"It does," said Tom. "Things may be getting really dangerous, so watch yourselves. Oh, one more thing. Looking through the windows of the upstate New York plant, we saw an arch made of large metal girders." Looking at Sarah and Peter, "Did you see anything like that at the Virginia Minuteman plant?"

"I did," said Sarah. "It had what appeared to be a strange-looking aircraft under it. Remember, Pete, I told you about it." He nodded.

Looking at Sarah and Peter, Tom said, "If possible, check out that arch when you go back to the plant. Also, check for a telescope array while you're at it. Take two of my men. Could be dangerous."

Glancing at Peter, Sarah said, "Once followed, twice shy. Thanks."

"Take Jake and Ziggy. They both saw the telescopes, and Jake saw the arch."

When the four had gone, Robyn turned to Tom, "About the rally. As our keynote speaker, you'll be on last. OK?"

"Sure. However, I should warn you that I haven't had time to prepare a formal speech."

"Your heart's in the right place. That's what counts."

"Just give 'em hell," said Maggie. "By the way, Tom, I completely forgot to tell you on the way over that my editor called late last night. He told me he was on a cell phone he had just purchased because he didn't want to risk a call from any of the phones he normally used. Sounded scared. Wouldn't say much, just that he's coming to Washington this morning and needs to speak to the two of us."

"What's it about, any idea?"

"I'm guessing it has something to do with his uncle Ken."

"I can understand why he might want to talk to you. But why me?"

She only shrugged.

* * * * *

Maggie's phone beeped, "Hello.... Drive to the Lincoln Memorial.... No problem, not many people yet.... He's here with me.... Yes, he'll meet with you.... See you shortly." She walked over to Tom, who was talking to Robyn. "My editor called. He'll arrive in a few minutes."

"Anything I should know before he gets here?"

"Scott Smith, Eastern establishment conservative snob."

"Any redeeming qualities?"

"He's literate and kind to non-establishment animals, like me."

"A wonder you're on speaking terms."

"Barely. However, he did apologize for sending me off to cover you."

"Yup. You do the talking until I get a feel for where he's coming from."

"I told him to look for the communication bus, so we'd better get over there."

Soon, a cab approached. Scott Smith waved, looking tired, unkempt, and worried.

He got out and walked briskly over to them. "We need to talk. Now!" he said to Maggie.

She introduced him to Tom. The three walked to a park bench a short distance away under a canopy of trees. Inwardly, Maggie chuckled at the picture of two such powerful men sitting down on a public bench where tourists, birds, and squirrels were the usual visitors.

Seating herself between the two men, she asked, "What's up, Scott?"

"It's my uncle, Ken Lacey. He left a message yesterday asking me to call. I tried several times, but without success. Late yesterday afternoon a reporter informed me that a man had fallen from a downtown building.... It was my uncle. The police are calling it suicide."

"I checked with his secretary to see if he'd left a message for me. He hadn't. However, a handwritten note from him arrived at my office by messenger. He said things had gone too far. If something happened to him, I was to contact you, Mr. Cartwright. He urged me to tell you that the weak signals are the key." He paused.

"Go on," Tom urged.

"He also said our country is in danger."

"Excuse me." Tom motioned and called to Robyn. When she had joined them, he asked her, "Did Peter have any weak signals recordings with him?"

"Yes. I think they're in his backpack."

"We need to find them." Turning to Scott, "What else did your uncle say?"

"Nothing else."

"Pretty cryptic," said Maggie. "I don't get it."

"Off the record?" said Scott.

"Sure."

He glanced at Robyn and Tom, who nodded their agreement.

"If I were involved in questionable activities, I wouldn't want to admit it in a note that might be made public."

"Makes sense," said Tom. "Where's the note?"

"In a safe place."

"Are you certain it's genuine?"

"Yes. I'm familiar with my uncle's handwriting. And I know…knew…him well enough to take this very seriously."

"Let's find Peter's weak signal recordings."

* * * * *

"Anyone know where Peter keeps his gear?" Robyn asked Movement members on the communications bus.

One of them pointed and said, "Somewhere in that pile."

After rummaging through the jumble, Robyn announced, "This is his backpack," holding it up. "It's full of discs."

"My limo has equipment and privacy," said Tom.

Robyn threw the backpack over her shoulder, and they headed for the limo.

After two discs have been sampled to make certain they were intelligible, Tom said, "We need an interpreter." Punching a button, he dialed.

"Sam Cohn," announced the face on the tiny screen.

"Morning, Sam. Tom Cartwright here."

"Good morning, Mr. Cartwright."

"Sam, I appreciate what you told me about Peter and the space station the other day. Please call me Tom. We're in this thing together, and we need your help in translating some weak signal recordings that Peter brought back from the space station."

"Peter mentioned those recordings. I've been looking forward to getting my hands on them them. Whenever you're ready." Tom played a disc for Sam. After a few minutes, Sam said, "It's Piscean, all right, but just a recording of commercial sitcoms, the usual mind-numbing stuff. Let's try a different disc."

Tom played the second disc. Everyone watched as Sam listened intently and took notes.

"Hold it!" he said excitedly after several minutes. "This one's hardcore journalism."

"Yeah!" Maggie cheered animatedly.

Scott grimaced.

Sam continued, "Several pundits are discussing the political and economic situation on Pisces II. The planet is divided, geographically and politically, as a result of hostilities between two major factions. The faction that lives on the side of Pisces II facing Earth is called The World Alliance for Liberty and Intelligent Economics. They're responsible for what we call the strong signals. As we suspected, the weak signals faction, called the Federation for Democratic Economic Reform, is located on the far side of Pisces II and is thus hidden from Earth. Please play the next section."

Sam listened intently for several more minutes and then signaled for Tom to pause the disc.

"The FDER weak-signal faction believes that governments should intervene in market economics in order to promote social justice. For example, people who work hard shouldn't be forced to suffer the injustice of having to live in poverty.

"The strong-signal WALIE faction believes in laissez-faire economics. They regret the suffering of those who can't compete effectively in a market economy but contend that free, unfettered competition is best for society in the long run, and that company profits will eventually trickle down and result in greater income for workers."

"This is dynamite," said Tom. "So all our current Piscean programming comes from WALIE?" Sam nodded yes. "What we thought was news or just entertainment now looks a lot more like propaganda." Sam again nodded yes. "Then that supposed weak signal recording beamed from the space station that Swanson gave me, the only one he said that was intelligible, is pretty much fake."

"He also gave me a copy," said Sam. "I agree. If the present recording is accurate, Swanson's can't be. It must be a fake."

Maggie said to Scott, "That no-holds-barred, free-enterprise capitalism of the WALIE sounds a lot like the views of corporate moguls like your uncle Ken."

Deep in thought, Scott did not respond.

"And of the members of the Club I used to belong to," Tom added.

"Wow!" exclaimed Robyn. "The Progressive Party and the LWM have been warning that economic inequities here on Earth could lead to serious class conflict. Pisces II is déjà vu all over again."

"Sounds like it," agreed Tom. "Perhaps the danger Ken Lacey warns about has something to do with the conflict on Pisces II."

"Oh, come on!" Scott said in a disgusted tone. "Most employers and workers realize they're a team and that they need one another. What they don't need is government interference. That's socialism. That's been tried. It didn't work and never will."

Tom, Robyn, and Maggie groaned in unison.

Chapter 50

Peter and Sarah drove to the Falls Church, Virginia Minuteman plant in a LWM car with Jake and Ziggy following in a company limo.

Glancing in the rear view mirror, Peter mused, "They always drive Cadillacs."

Sarah laughed, "I'll bet that's all they have."

"The last few turns are a little tricky. Remember what's next?"

"Take a left at that store."

"Yup. Now I remember."

"Then a right after the railroad tracks."

"Yup. Then through the woods to grandmother's house."

"Look at that," Sarah pointed excitedly as they rounded the corner.

"Lot of vans even for a plant this size. Wonder if they're headed for Washington."

"The rally? Shouldn't we follow? We can always come back."

"Agreed."

"I'll buzz Jake and Ziggy." After telling them that she and Peter intended to follow the vans, she also informed Robyn and Tom about the vans and their possible destination.

A dark blue pickup pulled to the curb in Falls Church, near the Minuteman Company. Its occupants never took their eyes off the LWM car and the limo.

* * * * *

Jake and Ziggy insisted that Peter and Sarah follow their limo as they tailed the vans.

Sarah's phone beeped as they approached the Potomac. "Yes?"

"Jake here. The column is breaking up. We'll follow the last van."

"Right behind you."

"Any trouble, you stay out of it. We can't do our job properly if we have to worry about you guys. Agreed?"

"Agreed," replied Sarah.

"Baloney!" Peter exclaimed when she explained about Jake and Ziggy. "They answer to Tom. We don't."

Sarah smiled, "No point in getting them upset if we don't have to."

"Fine. Better let Robyn and Tom know what's going on."

"Right." She did so.

Once across the Potomac, the van they were following proceeded down Pennsylvania Avenue. Traffic was light. A few blocks beyond the White House, the van stopped. Two men carrying large black briefcases got out.

Intent upon following Tom's men and the van, Peter and Sarah failed to notice the blue pickup, which had followed them from the Minuteman plant.

Sarah's phone beeped, "Yes?"

"Jake here. I'm sticking with the guys on the sidewalk in front of the Old Post Office building. Follow Ziggy and let me know where that van goes."

"You shouldn't be alone," Sarah said. "I'm leaving our phone with Peter and coming with you."

After a brief argument, she hung up.

"You should listen to him," Peter protested. "He knows more about this kind of stuff than we do."

"If something happens, he'll need backup."

"Backup! Give me a break! If a former FBI agent with a gun can"t handle a situation, what kind of backup are you going to be?"

"I have a gun, and I know how to use it."

Braking sharply as a cab cut in front of him, Peter was unable to prevent Sarah from leaping out of the vehicle.

"Damn it," he yelled as she slammed the door.

Sarah waved and smiled as traffic forced Peter to drive on. Half a block ahead, she saw Jake loitering, pretending to gawk at the large impressive buildings. The two men with briefcases stood in front of the Old Post Office Building.

Nearby, still unnoticed, the blue pickup stopped and an occupant got out.

* * * * *

"Captain!" the lieutenant called out, as the lines on the seismic sensor screen began to gyrate wildly.

He hurried over and took a look, "The spaceship?"

Checking a second screen, the lieutenant said, "Probably."

The captain picked up a phone, "General McNulty, we have a seismic disturbance on the moon in the vicinity of that spaceship."

"Thank you, Captain." The general turned toward the mission control monitors and spoke to the engineer in charge, "Activity at the spaceship site. Where are our unmanned surveillance ships?"

"On the other side of the moon, I'm afraid."

"Damn those tricky bastards!" Grabbing a phone, he ordered, "Train all available satellites on that moon location. The spaceship may be moving. Keep this line open. Keep me current."

* * * * *

"Captain Bell here, General McNulty, sir!"

"Yes, Captain?"

"The spaceship is moving. If we didn't have a whole battery of satellites on it, we wouldn't have detected it."

"Direction?"

"Toward Earth."

"When will it get here?"

"Hard to tell. It's accelerating."

"Propulsion?"

"Don't know. Definitely not rocket."

"Size?"

"Don't know exactly, but it's huge."

"Communications?"

"None detected."

"Thank you, Captain. Keep me informed."

"Yes, sir."

The general picked up his red phone. "Mr. President, the spaceship is moving toward Earth."

"When will it get here?"

"Too early to tell. You should know, Mr. President, that it's big enough to hold one hell of a lot of weapons."

"What do you recommend for this situation, General?" asked the president.

"Scramble the Air Force, fully-armed fighters in the air at all times. Ready our conventional missiles for immediate launch. Put our nuclear missiles on standby. Activate the secret satellite laser weapons, stealth mode, of course."

"So ordered," said the Commander in Chief as his usually fearless heart skipped a beat at the prospect of these strange and unprecedented events.

Chapter 51

Robyn left Tom, Maggie, and Scott in the limo and walked over to the rally stage to check preparations. Thus far, the gathering was progressing smoothly. A folk singing group from Tennessee entertained the early crowd. The mood was upbeat. No hecklers were in evidence, and television news personalities were beginning to interview celebrities.

Robyn scooped up a batch of programs and began to distribute them in a nearby tent where celebrities were prepping in air-conditioned comfort. Leisurely visits with performers prolonged the task. Emerging from the tent, she waved to Tom, Maggie, and Scott, who had gotten out of the limo.

"Wait up, Robyn," called Tom, "we've got to talk." He gestured toward Maggie and Scott, "We listened to more of Peter's weak-signal recordings with Sam translating. The WALIE-FDER conflict is serious. The WALIE and FDER halves of Pisces II have become two independent states, each with nuclear capabilities. There's an uneasy military standoff. But the propaganda war is alive and well. In view of the fake weak-signal recording that Swanson gave Sam and me, it seems likely that the WALIE conspired with people on Earth to sabotage the space station. Destruction of the station would keep GCIS from receiving intelligible weak signals and hearing the other side of the Piscean story. If we're right, disruption of your rally may well be on their agenda. We know there are Pisceans on Earth. What we don't know is if they're WALIE or FDER."

"We've got plenty of police protection," Robyn said, pointing to the uniformed officers and mounted patrols in and around the crowd.

"If our space station was sabotaged and the crew savagely murdered, who knows what these people are capable of?"

"What about your mysterious internet friend, Robyn?" said Maggie.

"My mysterious internet friends," corrected Robyn.

"How can you be sure they're friends? And didn't one of them promise to be at the rally?"

"Yes. Frank is monitoring the equipment, but so far, no more messages."

"Couldn't one or more of these so-called friends be part of some conspiracy to discredit the Movement?" asked Maggie.

"I suppose," sighed Robyn.

"Talk to the police," advised Tom. "Sarah just called again and warned us that a fleet of Minuteman vans are definitely headed for Washington. It wouldn't hurt to let the police know. Just say an Internet message warned you that the people in those vans are bent on disrupting the rally. Mention possible bombs. We can't rule them out, and their mere mention will serve as an incentive for the police to increase security."

* * * * *

Tom finally convinced Robyn to talk to the police. Walking through the gathering crowd until they reached the officer in charge, they identified themselves and informed him of the vans and the possible danger.

After listening to them with evident incredulity, he reached for his radio and said, "I need to consult with my captain."

Following a brief conversation, he handed the radio to Tom, who again identified himself and quizzed the Captain, making certain that he fully appreciated the danger. Although it took some coaxing, Tom finally convinced him to beef up security and send out an APB on the vans. Shortly, they learned that vans had been placed under surveillance and tracked to various locations in the heart of Washington.

Chapter 52

Jake's phone beeped. "Yes?"

"It's Peter. The van's going into the Reagan Office Building underground parking garage, back down the block and around the corner from where you got out. Building guards are inspecting every vehicle. Doesn't look like they found anything in the van. Where are you?"

"I haven't moved. The two we're watching are still standing in front of the Old Post Office."

"Where's Sarah?"

"She's walking toward me."

"Check. Gotta go."

With Sarah standing beside him, Jake instructed, "Gesture as if you're giving me directions, but don't draw a lot of attention to yourself." Pretending to speak, she made slight pointing gestures while Jake told her about Peter's call, concluding with, "The guys with the briefcases are probably waiting for the van driver."

"You're right," Sarah said in subdued tones. "Here he comes. Same uniform."

As the uniformed man passed by, Peter and Ziggy emerged from the Reagan Office Building. When the man joined his companions, the three retrieved their briefcases and walked up the steps into the Old Post Office Building. Sarah and Jake followed. Inside, the three turned right and descended a flight of stairs. Jake followed while Sarah remained behind.

When Peter and Ziggy appeared, she motioned to them, before disappearing down the stairs herself. At the bottom, she saw the three standing near the middle of the tower elevator line. Jake was also in line.

She joined him and was able to read the insignia on their uniforms—Environmental Protection Agency.

Peter and Ziggy soon also joined the line. It was short, so they all were able to get on the elevator. After traveling upward several stories, the doors opened, and the passengers got off and followed arrows to a second, smaller, tower-bound elevator. This time only Jake and Sarah were able to get on with the three.

In the tower vestibule, Sarah and Jake watched and listened as the three spoke to a tower guard. They told him they were from the Environmental Protection Agency. He ushered them to the tower's open-air observation deck, and pointed to the side of the deck facing the Washington Monument. Nodding their approval, they walked over. Standing on the opposite side of the observation deck, Sarah and Jake saw them rapidly snap and screw together machined metal parts taken from the briefcases.

When the device was assembled, the men extended what resembled a microphone boom through the flexible metal safety grating, preventing visitors from leaning dangerously out over the walls of the observation deck. The bulk of the device remained on the deck. Sarah and Jake looked at each other and shrugged.

Several floors below, Ziggy entered the tower elevator. Peter attempted to follow, but his path was blocked by an individual standing facing the doors. As he tried to get on the elevator, the doors closed. About to lecture the person for his lack of consideration, Peter suddenly froze.

* * * * *

"I mean you no harm," Huston said calmly as he turned and faced Peter in front of the elevator.

With the swiftness of a reflex reaction, Peter punched Huston in the jaw, knocking off the cap which had hidden his red crew cut. Huston staggered, but recovered quickly. Pinning Peter's arms behind his back, he hustled him away from the elevator. Visitors waiting for the elevator stared at them but did not intervene. One even began taking pictures.

With his mouth close to Peter's ear, Huston quietly repeated, "I mean you no harm."

Peter struggled, but Huston's arms felt like steel bars. Through clenched teeth, he muttered, "Wouldn't you call trying to shoot me on the space station harm?"

"I didn't. They also shot at me."

"Well then," Peter replied sarcastically, "why aren't you dead?"

"I shot back." Peter remembered the solarium crewmember who appeared to have been wounded or shot in the chest.

"You were armed?"

"Of course. Security people generally are. When I ran out of ammunition, I dove into a flooded passageway and swam to an escape capsule bay."

"Without a spacesuit?"

"Yes."

"How?"

"I think you know."

"You're Piscean."

"Yes. My gills provided enough oxygen."

"Which bay?"

"Number five."

"My friend Julia was on duty nearby. Did she make it to the bay?"

"I didn't see her."

"An escape capsule was missing from that bay."

"I used it to return to Earth."

Peter stopped struggling. Huston released him. Peter just stood there, not moving. "My God," he finally whispered, "is she really gone?"

* * * * *

Huston helped Peter to a nearby bench, where he sat down heavily and asked, "Why were you, a Piscean, on the space station?"

"To ensure your reception of intelligible weak signals. We never imagined that the station might be sabotaged."

"We? Who's we?"

"My nation, the Federation for Democratic Economic Reform. FDER is situated on the side of my planet facing away from Earth. That's why our broadcast signals are weak compared to those of our Piscean adversaries, the World Alliance for Liberty and Intelligent Economics. Their side of Pisces II faces Earth."

"What do you mean, adversaries?"

Huston summarized recent Piscean history. He concluded, "My people believe in economic and social justice and equality, with government intervention where and when needed. WALIE practice what you'd call unregulated free-market economics. Think of that popular strong-signal Piscean TV show GCIS broadcasts, 'Lifestyles of the Rich & Richer.' Getting rich is all that counts, no matter how. That's what WALIE is all about. Wealthy WALIE aristocrats do whatever it takes to make certain that their views prevail and that they stay in power. They even accused us of illegally transferring money and securities, claiming that we were unfairly taking money from the rightful owners in order to redistribute wealth. Turned out they were the ones responsible. They were attempting to discredit the FDER and put some of our leaders in jail."

"Nasty."

"Yes. That was the last straw. We completely broke with WALIE and established a separate government, a separate nation. Piscean against Piscean has been a bitter pill to swallow."

"That's all very interesting," Peter broke in. "But why are you here? Why is your FDER getting involved here on Earth?"

"We want your people to see the other side, the better side, of Piscean society. And we want you to learn from our bitter experience before hostilities break out on Earth. We believe that economically powerful groups in your country may have conspired with WALIE to destroy GCIS's space station. WALIE wouldn't want you to receive intelligible weak signals and learn our side of the story. Economic conservatives in the United States may be doing just what WALIE did on Pisces II…maybe even with WALIE help."

"Do you mean the illegal financial transactions that caused the president to shut everything down?"

"Yes, quite possibly."

Peter shook his head in disbelief. "Whoa! Slow down. First of all, how could people on Earth have communicated with WALIE? It takes electromagnetic signals two years to travel from Pisces II to Earth."

"Both FDER and WALIE have advanced systems that make instantaneous communication possible even over vast distances. First, we establish a link between two locations by the continuous propagation of electromagnetic waves from point A to point B. Then we impose a special carrier signal on the waves. The signal can traverse enormous distances almost instantaneously."

"Wow, impressive. Next question: how did you get here?"

"A spaceship, of course."

"Where is it?"

"Your moon."

"Why are you here, with me, with the LWM?"

"We plan to attend the rally."

"Why?"

"We believe economic conservatives on your planet, perhaps together with WALIE, are manipulating your financial institutions in an effort to discredit their opponents, folks like the LWM. We Pisceans have traveled this path. It polarized our planet into two hostile camps. We don't want you repeating our mistakes. And we need your help to convince your leaders of our sincerity and of the gravity of your situation."

"So: supposing I buy into this fantastical scenario. Where do I fit in?"

"We need you to brief Robyn about us and about why we intend to land our spaceship at the rally."

"Your spaceship? Are you crazy? What about our military? They'll blow you out of the sky!"

"We have special cloaking fields that will prevent detection until the spaceship has landed."

"Couldn't WALIE have also sent a spaceship?"

"No. We possess the only Piscean spaceships capable of interstellar travel."

"As you probably know, there was an attack on the White House yesterday."

"Yes, we know."

"Until it was brought down by our military, the aircraft that brought the attackers was invisible, just like you say your spaceship can make itself."

"What did the aircraft look like?"

"I don't know. I wasn't there, and military rockets destroyed it before I got there. But Robyn was there. She should be able to describe it to you."

"I would very much like to know."

"Another reason I have difficulty trusting you is because of what happened at the White House yesterday. Before I start, let me say I'm sorry to bring you this news." He told Huston about the dead person left behind on the White House lawn and about it being the companion he had seen Huston with at the Illinois expressway rest area. As Peter spoke, he could sense emotion welling up within Huston. A tear trickled down his cheek.

Regaining his composure, Huston said softly, "At the expressway rest area, we tried to rescue him. But our shuttlecraft was unarmed, and the others had laser hand weapons similar to ours. The WALIE knew we had a spaceship on its way to Earth. Perhaps by having their allies on Earth leave my friend behind after the attack on the White House, they were attempting to throw blame on my spaceship."

"Your friend left behind, and similar weapons. Someone on Earth must have been communicating with WALIE. Right?"

"Correct, unless they have access to Piscean technology and information about our spaceship by some other means. Are you suspicious of anyone in particular?"

"GCIS Vice-President Swanson and the Minuteman Company. We know he's been in touch with the company, and we discovered many unusual structures and activities at their New York and Virginia locations."

"I had intended to talk with Robyn Sherwood in person this morning to inform her of the planned landing of our spaceship at the rally. But instead, I decided to follow you, and you led me to the Minuteman plant. Now I understand why."

Unable to think of a good reason to lie or stall, Peter said, "We knew Swanson was flying to Washington yesterday, so we followed him. He went to Minuteman's Virginia plant."

"And now a fleet of Minuteman vans has traveled to Washington on the day of the LWM rally. Doesn't exactly sound coincidental."

"Let's get up to the tower," said Peter, "and see what the guys from that van are up to."

Chapter 53

Peter and Houston got off the tower elevator just as the three uniformed men carrying briefcases got on. The two men walked to the observation deck, where they heard Sarah, Jake, and Ziggy talking to a guard while inspecting a strange looking device.

"It's an air pollution monitor," said the guard. "The EPA guys told me they're checking for possibly dangerous levels of ozone and other chemicals. Said they were ordered to leave it awhile. Should be checking instead for hot air and bullshit around Washington." He chuckled and walked away.

Aware of Sarah using his body to conceal her hand as it slipped into her purse, Peter put his hand on hers to tell her to stop. Even though he did not fully understand why, he was becoming convinced that the gruff, soft-spoken Piscean really was on their side. To all, he said, "This is Mr. Huston. I'll vouch for him. He was with me on the space station. You trust me? Trust him." Turning to Jake, "Shouldn't somebody be following those three?"

"Got it covered," said Jake, holding up his phone.

Huston examined the strange device and the filmy cocoon surrounding it. "Don't touch this," he said, pointing to the cocoon. "It can kill if sufficiently disturbed."

"What is it?" Jake asked.

"Standard anti-theft device."

"Never saw anything like it," Ziggy asserted.

"Standard where?" a suspicious Sarah asked.

Before Huston had a chance to answer, Jake, turning his back to the tower guard, moved closer, deftly pulling his gun and sticking it in

Huston's ribs. "Move over to that corner," he ordered, shoving Huston farther away from the guard.

Peter whispered sharply, "Put that away. I told you that I trust him."

Jake's hand did not move. "Mr. Cartwright told us that Huston is Piscean," he said, looking at Peter.

"That's right," said Peter, quickly telling Jake and the others what Huston had told him about FDER and WALIE. He also told them about Huston's suspicion that persons on Earth were communicating with WALIE via instant communication devices.

The gun still pressing into his side, Huston added, "You also need to know that our FDER spaceship is going to land at the Living Wage rally. We want to publicize the true nature of the current situation on my planet. We want everyone to know that people on Earth may be cooperating with our WALIE opponents. They may be implicated in the stock market and banking irregularities. They may even have caused the space station disaster, so Earth would not have access to intelligible weak signals. This device and its anti-theft protection seem to confirm that WALIE have been communicating with people on Earth."

Jake hesitated, then holstered the gun, his hand remaining on the butt. Gesturing toward the device and its cocoon, he said to Huston, "Tell us more about it."

"This," Huston pointed to the basketball-sized metal sphere attached to one end of the boom, "is an energy generator. Its activation will expose the tower to high levels of radiation. When that happens, we don't want to be here. And this," he pointed to the tip of the boom protruding through the tower's metal safety grating, "is a beam-focusing aperture. The mechanism is very likely a weapon. WALIE must be sending weapon designs to its allies on Earth for manufacture."

"Is the beam directed at the rally?" Peter asked. "We're not far from the Lincoln Memorial."

"Perhaps," Huston replied.

"Remember the other vans," Peter said to Jake. "Could be more weapons scattered around Washington. The authorities need to be informed."

Before leaving the tower, they warned the guard about the device and the protective filmy cocoon surrounding it.

"Do not attempt to disturb the cocoon," Huston warned the guard. "It could kill you, or worse, if sufficiently disturbed, it could explode."

He looked at Huston strangely but promised to contact building security and the District of Washington police and pass on the information.

"The police need to exercise extreme caution," said Houston.

Just to be certain the warning got through, Jake subsequently also contacted the police.

* * * * *

While the group purchased taken-out sandwiches on the ground-floor of the Old Post Office building, Peter called Robyn. Although still not entirely certain about Huston, he was sure that Robyn needed to know about the spaceship and the rally. "Robyn, it's Peter."

"What is it?"

"Huston, the alien who was with me on the space station…"

"The one who shot at you?"

"Yes. He's here with me, and he swears he didn't. He claims to be our friend." Peter looked at Huston, "I can't be absolutely certain, but I'm starting to believe him. I want you to talk to him. He has something to tell you."

"OK."

Peter handed the phone to Huston, who told Robyn about the situation on his planet and about the planned spaceship landing at the rally.

When he finished, she said, "Put Peter back on." Huston did so. "Peter, we listened to your weak signal recordings, and I can confirm what he told you about FDER and WALIE."

"Thanks, Robyn," said Peter, feeling still more certain about his assessment of Huston. "Okay if I put him back on?"

"Fine."

"Questions, Robyn?" said Houston.

246

"Yes. Have your people been communicating with me?"

"On your round computer, using our encryption program."

"OK. Next: how can your spaceship land safely at the rally? There are hundreds of thousands of people here. And what about our military?"

"The ship has special cloaking shields, so it will be invisible to your military. It will land over the Potomac."

"When?"

"After Mr. Cartwright's keynote speech. We're monitoring broadcasts of the rally. Please make arrangements for media interviews with our representatives. They'll explain the situation on our planet and why movements such as yours are critical if Earth is to avoid a similar fate."

"Hold on! Even if your spaceship is invisible to the military, everyone will know it's there after it lands. In case you haven't heard, there was an attack on the White House yesterday. It's quite likely the authorities think Pisceans did it. Did Peter tell you what happened on the White House lawn after the attack?"

"Yes, he did. I suspect that our enemies on Earth who are cooperating with WALIE abducted my friend and left him behind on the White House lawn in an effort to blame my people and our spaceship for the attack."

Although Peter could not hear Robyn's side of the conversation, he said to Huston so that Robyn could hear, "Tell her about your communication device."

Huston repeated for Robyn what he had already told Peter, explaining the ability of Pisceans to communicate instantly over great distances.

"Thanks for that info," Robyn told him. "It helps fill in the blanks. Please put Peter back on the phone." She told him about the handwritten note to Scott Smith from his uncle and about Ken Lacey's suspicious death, asking Peter to share the information with Huston.

Peter did so, then said to Robyn, "Thanks. It all makes perfect sense given our suspicions. Good ol' uncle Ken may have been having doubts about his involvement in the whole thing, and his buddies decided to get rid of him." To Huston, he said, "Tell Robyn about the possible laser weapon in the tower. She needs to know about the danger to the rally."

Taking the phone, Huston elaborated. He also told her about their suspicion that similar weapons were scattered around Washington.

"I guess no matter what happens, Mr. Huston," said Robyn, "no matter what the danger, your people are determined to land at our rally."

"We are."

"We'll do what we can to prepare for their arrival. But chances are our military won't just sit around while your ship lands."

"Our spaceship is perfectly capable of defending itself. It's more than an interstellar craft. It's also our most powerful battleship. Given the current economic and social dangers facing your country, we must do this. We must land. We will land."

Chapter 54

Officers in a squad car observed one of the tan vans park near the base of the Washington Monument. Two occupants got out and sprayed the vehicle's exterior with a filmy substance. Then the two walked away from the van in the general direction of the officers, who pretended to be eating lunch.

As they came closer, Officer Clark said to his partner, Officer Davis, "Those guys look familiar?"

"I don't think so."

"Yeah, they do," replied an insistent Clark.

"I can't help you, man."

"Oh Jeez!" Clark fumbled for his gun. "They were on the news! I swear. They were part of the bunch that attacked the White House yesterday!"

"What?!?!? Are you sure?"

"Yeah. A network cameraman got close-ups of some of their faces, and they were shown on the evening news."

"Weren't they all blown up in some building? Can't be the same guys."

"Right. Except remember we heard when we got back to the station that they didn't find bodies, or even traces of bodies."

"Jesus H. Christ!" Sweat broke out on Davis's forehead. "Now what do we do?"

"We keep 'em in sight and call for backup."

After making the call, the officers waited and watched. As the two suspects walked north through the park, the officers drove slowly on a parallel course. Another similar van pulled up beside the suspects. They got in. It drove off before backup could arrive.

Officer Davis spoke into his radio microphone, "They just got into another van." He described it. "Looks like they're headed for the Fourteenth Street Bridge."

Almost instantly, the radio squawked, "All units in the vicinity of the Fourteenth Street Bridge. Car fifty-seven is tailing a tan van traveling from the Washington Monument area toward the bridge. Render all possible assistance. Occupants of the vehicle should be considered armed and dangerous."

Officer Davis continued. "Van just turned. It's headed back toward the city. Could be monitoring police frequencies." Switching to his own cell phone, he continuously updated the dispatcher concerning the van's route. Several minutes elapsed. "Occupants exiting the van at Dupont Circle. Four suspects fleeing on foot." He gave a hurried description. "They're splitting up. We're following the two we spotted at the monument. Looks like they're headed for the Metro."

Pulling up to the Metro, the officers raced after their suspects, leaping down the stairs of the long entrance escalator into the bowels of the subway, all the while pushing and shouting at surprised patrons. Vaulting the bottom turnstiles, they barely managed to keep the fleeing suspects in sight. Catching up with them on the nearly deserted platform, the officers drew their guns.

"Police, hands in the air."

Both suspects whirled, weapons drawn. The officers fired as they dove behind the platform escalator. One suspect went down. Clark felt a searing pain in his shoulder, and his gun clattered to the platform. The other suspect grabbed a woman on the platform, using her as a shield. An incoming train slowed behind them. Fearful of hitting the hostage, Davis held his fire.

The suspect holding the hostage aimed his weapon at the inert figure of his companion on the platform and fired. The officers felt a powerful blast of heat.

"What the hell?" exclaimed Davis, peeking out from behind the escalator. "Watch out, Joe! That's no ordinary gun. His buddy's a pile of ashes."

The suspect fired at Davis, who managed to duck back behind the escalator, although the near miss scorched one side of his face. The suspect backed toward an open door of the waiting train, still holding the hostage in front of him. With a sudden violent motion, she tore away from her captor and fled. Davis fired, striking the suspect in the chest. As he stumbled backward into the train, his weapon discharged. The exposed side of Davis's head disappeared in a puff of smoke, and the officer's body crumpled to the platform.

Simultaneously, the suspect fell backward onto the floor of the Metro car. Officer Clark came out from behind the escalator, retrieved his partner's gun, awkwardly took aim with his uninjured left hand, and fired. A flash of light and a blast of heat from the Metro car momentarily blinded him. When his sight returned, he was unable to spot the suspect. Crouching, he cautiously crept toward the Metro car. At the door, he was astonished to see a large hole where the suspect had fallen, completely melted through the metal floor. There was no sign of a body or weapon.

* * * * *

"Captain Bell reporting, sir."

"Yes, Captain?" said General McNulty.

"We have a trajectory. Washington, in one hour, if the spaceship doesn't alter course or projected speed."

The general picked up his red phone. "General McNulty for the President."

"Yes, sir."

"President Hedges."

"General McNulty, sir. We are projecting the spaceship will arrive over Washington in one hour."

"Thank you, General. I'll get back to you shortly."

"Yes, Mr. President."

In the oval office, the President looked at the gathered Homeland Security officials and said, "The spaceship is headed our way. One hour. Suggestions?"

"Implement the emergency plan, Mr. President," the Homeland Security head replied. "With luck, we'll have sufficient time."

"Agreed?" queried the President, scrutinizing the others. All nodded. He gave the order.

Within minutes, the President and selected members of the White House staff were on helicopters leaving Washington, bound for the underground complex designed to house the "shadow" government. Elsewhere, governmental leaders were escorted off the floors of the House and Senate or out of their offices to waiting special subway cars that would whisk them nonstop to the end of the line, where they would also be met by helicopters.

* * * * *

Upon leaving the Old Post Office, everyone walked to the courtyard of the nearby Reagan Office Building. It was decided that Sarah should contact Archer and inform him about what was happening. She was unable to do so. Instead, she described the device in the Old Post Office tower to one of his subordinates, stressing the possibility that it might be a weapon capable of producing lethal radiation and that other such devices were very likely scattered around the city.

"You may be in danger," said the subordinate. "Where are you?"

"The courtyard of the Reagan Office Building."

"We'll send men to ensure your safety. How will they recognize you?"

"I have long dark red hair, and I'm wearing a green short-sleeved top and jeans. There are five of us, me and four men."

"Stay where you are!"

* * * * *

When the men with Sarah learned what she had agreed to, they objected, not wishing to be "protected" by, and thus under the control of, government bureaucrats. Huston insisted upon leaving immediately, not wishing to reveal his identity.

"Archer already knows you're Piscean," insisted Sarah. "I told him."

The argument continued for several minutes and resulted in a decision to leave just as eight men in dark suits entered the courtyard. They paused and looked around. One pointed at Sarah, and all walked in her direction.

"Damn, Swanson's one of them!" Peter said in a loud, harsh whisper.

Holding a palm sized device to his ear, Huston said, "They're planning to take us prisoner or shoot if we resist."

"Move casually toward that door," ordered Jake with a slight movement of his head. "When I tell you, get inside and run like hell for the cars. Ziggy and I will hold them off."

On Jake's signal, Peter, Sarah, and Huston dashed into the building. They looked about wildly for directions to the underground garage.

"Come on," Peter shouted, "the garage should be this way." Coming to a central hub, he shouted and pointed, "Over there!" Finding the elevator doors closed, they raced down the stairs until Peter identified the correct parking level.

Once in the garage, he ran a short distance one way, then another, before gasping, "Now I remember."

Sarah and Huston ran after Peter as he made for the car. They looked about nervously while he fumbled for the keys, quickly piling in once the doors were unlocked. The tires squealed as he stomped on the gas and headed for the exit.

Rounding a turn, he braked abruptly. Jake and Ziggy jumped in. He peeled away even before they had closed the door. Without warning, the rear window exploded.

"They're shooting," yelled Jake, as he and Ziggy leaned out the side windows and fired back.

The car careened wildly up the ramp. Peter shouted, "Duck," just before smashing through the wooden arm of the exit booth. An alarm sounded as the car sped out of the garage.

Blocks away, Peter pulled into an alley. Still breathing hard, he turned to Sarah, "Whose side is Archer on, anyway?"

"I didn't talk to Archer, remember? Whoever it was said he'd contact Archer."

"We know Swanson and Lacey communicated," said Peter, "but how does Archer figure in?"

"Maybe I was wrong trusting Archer," she said. "He mentioned Lacey to me and my boss, George Murphy, when he visited the Exchange. Said Lacey had been his mentor and was instrumental in his making the acquaintance of the president."

"Having a friend at the helm of the SEC," observed Peter, "certainly wouldn't hurt Lacey and his grandiose ambitions."

"If Archer and the SEC are involved," Huston said, "the conspiracy could be more widespread than we previously suspected. Your country, not merely the rally, could be in serious danger. I need to warn my ship." Holding a palm sized device to his ear, he attempted to make contact. "No luck," he said after several tries. "The cloaking shields must be up. No signal can get through unless they know when and where to expect it."

"Better tell Robyn and the others," Sarah urged.

* * * * *

While Robyn repeated for Maggie and Scott what Sarah had just told her over the phone about the attack at the Reagan Office Building, she noticed a man intently eyeing them. She told the others, and they took a look.

He walked over, flashed police detective identification, and said, "I have a good mind to place you under arrest."

"For what?" Robyn snapped back angrily.

"I overheard your conversation about the vans."

"And?" said Robyn.

"They're under investigation. So is anyone who might know anything about them." He pointed toward a tan vehicle parked near the Lincoln Memorial. "Does that look like one of them?"

"Could be," Robyn replied noncommittally.

The detective stared at her. "What else do you know? Be advised I"m recording this conversation and anything you say can be used against you."

"My name is Robyn Sherwood. I'm a leader of the LWM. We are the ones who reported the vans to the police in the first place."

"Oh," his face relaxed slightly, "good to meet you, Ms. Sherwood. Anything more you can tell me?"

Robyn knew that Peter and the others had warned the guard about the device in the Old Post Office tower and that Jake, as an added precaution, had also alerted the police, so she did not hesitate to tell the detective about the device.

"Anything else?" he asked with obvious surprise.

"If I tell you, you'll think I'm crazy, one of those UFO nuts."

The detective inched closer and lowered his voice, "Please tell me what you know. It might help make sense of some strange goings on around here." He thought for a moment, then said, "Earlier today, an officer identified two men leaving a van like the one by the Lincoln Memorial as participants in yesterday"'s attack on the White House. During a police chase, the two suspects were killed in the Metro. Or, more accurately, they incinerated themselves."

"Wait a minute," Maggie said. "I thought all the assailants were killed in a warehouse fire."

"Our officers at the scene thought so, too. But they didn't find any bodies, not even traces of bodies. Somehow, some must have survived."

"You've left out something important," said Robyn.

"What is that?" asked the detective.

"The dead assailant abandoned by his comrades on the White House grounds yesterday was Piscean. And I wouldn't be surprised if the alleged White House attackers who incinerated themselves in the Metro were also Piscean."

"How..."

"Educated guess. I was a picketer. I saw the fuss over the dead body on the White House lawn. I was there when the ambulance came to pick it up. We were body-searched. The officers seemed to pay particular attention to our upper torsos. I suspect they were searching for gills. And the events in the Metro make sense if the suspects were Pisceans who didn't want to be identified."

"I'm impressed," said the detective. "Tell me more."

Oh my God, thought Maggie, could Huston actually be WALIE? The incident in the Metro did not seem to fit with what Huston had told Peter and Sarah. If the suspects in the Metro were Pisceans and were involved in the attack on the White House, then Huston was lying. Pisceans were involved. What was WALIE up to? The overthrow of the U. S. government? Looking at Robyn, Maggie could tell that similar thoughts were disturbing her as well.

Aware of a potential journalistic sensation, Maggie identified herself as a reporter and Scott as her editor. She then demanded, "In exchange for what we know, we want exclusive coverage and to be a part of the action."

"Can't do that."

"Then neither can we," said Maggie, stamping her foot.

"I can hold you as material witnesses," the detective replied, a trace of anger in his voice. Faced with Maggie's continued stubborn resistance, the detective eventually relented. In a conciliatory tone, he said, "Let me check," and meandered away talking into his phone.

Finally, walking back to them, he said, "Chief Jefferson and the FBI accept your terms. You'll have exclusive coverage and, if possible, be party to the investigation. Now, please continue."

"Hold on," said Maggie. "I need to speak to the chief myself. I want to get a recording in case he gets cold feet."

After speaking to the chief and recording the conversation on her phone, she and Robyn summarized what they had learned about the conflict between FDER and WALIE on Pisces II, about the rural New York Minuteman plant and its telescope array, about the origin of the vans and the discovery of the device in the Old Post Office tower, and about the encounters with Huston, whom they considered to be Piscean, at the Old Post Office tower. Robyn described Huston's conjecture that persons on Earth were communicating and possibly conspiring with WALIE on Pisces II via instant communication devices. And both revealed that they were now puzzled about Huston's identity if the suspects in the Metro were Pisceans who had participated in the attacks on the White House. Finally, Robyn dropped the bombshell about the planned landing of the spaceship at the LWM rally.

The detective and Scott looked at Robyn and Maggie with open-mouthed amazement.

Loud shouts and commotion near the Lincoln Memorial platform stage attracted their attention. People with placards were being harassed by members of the crowd.

"What do those signs say?" asked the detective.

"I've seen them before, at an earlier rally," said Robyn. "They damn the minimum wage as a government giveaway to a bunch of freeloaders who don't really want to work. Big business is OK, but not big government."

As they watched, the harassment became a brawl. Punches were thrown; men went down. Women pulled hair and threw one another about. Soon, everyone in the crowd was either a part of the melee or attempting to flee from it.

"No, no, no!" wailed Robyn. "Our members were instructed in nonviolence. I can't believe this is happening."

As they watched, the brawl continued because the police had difficulty making their way through the crowd and converging on the worst violence. The sheer size of the crowd, estimated at 400,000, was a major factor. As police arrived on the scene, the fighting and its perpetrators appeared to vanish. Surprisingly few persons were actually arrested and led away by uniformed officers.

Robyn glanced at the speaker on the Lincoln Memorial platform stage, who had continued talking during the fighting and who had just concluded. "You must excuse me," she said to the detective. "We can talk more later. I have to apologize for what just happened, and I need to introduce our keynote speaker, Tom Cartwright."

Chapter 55

In the emergency underground complex, President Hedges exclaimed angrily, "You've lost it! How is that possible?"

At the other end of the secure line, General McNulty answered calmly and evenly, "Sir, radiation belts are interfering with our satellite reception."

"So the ship could be anywhere?"

"Anywhere within the vicinity of the radiation belts. Should be able to pick it up again when it's clear of the belts in near-Earth space."

"That's cutting it close. My order stands. If it fires at us, you are to fire back."

"Understood, sir."

* * * * *

As she ascended the Memorial steps, Robyn was pleased to see a police presence remaining near the stage platform where the brawl had started. Grabbing a microphone, she faced the crowd. Thanking the police and condemning the violence in no uncertain terms, she took control, reaffirming the peaceful nature of the movement and reminding members of their pledge to respond nonviolently to provocations.

"Now, let's get on with the rally," she concluded. "Please welcome with me our keynote speaker and the next president of the United States, Mr. Tom Cartwright!"

Launching into his speech with gusto, Tom refocused the gathering. The few remaining hecklers were easily drowned out by the applause and cheers which greeted Tom's words.

"Our opponents have accused us of inciting class warfare," Tom said, nearing the end of his speech. "But they are really the ones engaging in class warfare. That's why we need the LWM. We need to call attention to their deeds. That's why people everywhere are rallying to our cause. Look around you. You are the voice of the people, calling attention to this shameful warfare, this oppression. Give yourselves a big hand!" Cartwright paused, applauding the audience as they also applauded and cheered.

When the crowd had quieted, he went on, "The working poor in this country make up over 40% of the workforce. They are the people who would benefit most from an increase in the national minimum wage. They work hard. They come home tired and stressed. They deserve a living wage. But instead, they have to work two or three jobs just to get by. We need to end this injustice! We need to raise the minimum wage! Workers need a living wage!"

Amid the applause and cheers greeting the conclusion of Tom's speech, shouts and commotion in the audience caused him to gaze upward. An oval-shaped object was descending through slow-moving wispy clouds. It appeared to float, like a hot-air balloon, gliding slowly down toward the Potomac River. As it descended, its considerable size became apparent, as did the fact that it was a silvery metallic craft.

"The FDER spaceship," Tom murmured. "Robyn was right."

Tom saw, then heard an explosion at the base of the Washington Monument. The crowd turned and stared. The monument tilted to one side. Although it didn't come crashing down, it continued to lean, like a giant Tower of Pisa.

Hearing another explosion, he looked and saw a huge ball of flame on the Washington skyline.

"The Old Post Office," cried some in the crowd.

Another explosion, beside the Lincoln Memorial, knocked Tom and scores of others to their hands and knees.

As scores of missiles streaked toward it, the silvery craft, still above the Potomac, rose rapidly. Most missiles exploded before reaching their target. A few passed under it on their way to Virginia.

The crowd screamed and scattered as large chunks of debris fell from the sky. Some started running toward the Lincoln Memorial for protection. Others just stood and watched in horror. Faint beams emanating from the craft transformed the falling chunks of debris into dust particles which floated harmlessly down on the crowd, creating a sooty mess. Within seconds, the craft vanished.

* * * * *

When the van near the Lincoln Memorial exploded, the police detective herded Maggie and Scott into his car for protection. They drove to a part of the park away from the crowd and buildings. The detective had played his interview with Robyn and Maggie for his superiors. At the mention of his two passengers, he was ordered to bring them in. Maggie and Scott protested, but relented when, this time with the knowledge and consent of his superiors, the detective threatened to arrest them.

* * * * *

Covered with dust, Robyn joined Tom on the stage in front of the Lincoln Memorial. Her phone beeped. It was Peter. "What happened? We heard explosions."

"We saw them," shouted Robyn over the din of the crowd. "The Washington Monument, the Old Post Office tower, the Lincoln Memorial. All damaged."

"Damn!" swore Peter. "That confirms what Huston"s been telling us."

Covering the phone's mike, Robyn hurriedly told Tom about the Metro incinerations and their ominous implication that Huston might be WALIE. Then, over the phone, she said to Peter, "Put him on."

"Huston, Robyn."

"We're listening. Tell us what you think just happened."

"Who's with you?"

"Tom Cartwright."

"He needs to hear this too."

260

She switched on the phone speaker. "Okay, go ahead."

"The weapons systems on our spaceship are designed to respond automatically to beam weapons systems. The device we saw on the observation deck of the Old Post Office was most likely a beam generator. The vans you and I followed from Minuteman's Virginia plant probably placed beam generators at numerous Washington locations. My ship's weapons systems automatically fired and neutralized the devices, but they couldn't avoid inflicting collateral damage on nearby structures. Your government misinterpreted my ship's response as hostile and fired retaliatory missiles."

"How do we know you're not WALIE?" asked Robyn.

"What just happened only makes sense if WALIE and their allies on Earth are trying to discredit my people by making it seem as if we were attacking Washington. Blaming my spaceship and FDER for what's been happening here would accord perfectly with what they attempted to do on my planet."

Tom was silent.

Huston persisted, "Mr. Cartwright, what do you say? If the allies of WALIE on Earth are responsible for what's been happening, it is imperative that you find some way to contact President Hedges and tell him the truth about our ship. I realize that you may still have doubts about what I'm telling you. When we meet, we'll contact a friend of yours, George Murphy, who can confirm that I'm telling the truth."

Before he could answer, Peter broke in, "Tom, you and Robyn are quite probably in danger. The conspirators may even be monitoring this conversation. They certainly tried to shoot us at the Reagan Office Building, and they may try to shoot you as well because of what you know."

"Makes sense," said Tom. "Robyn and I will leave the rally immediately."

"They may follow you. Let's meet on the east side of Dupont Circle. We'll watch for you and for them."

"Twenty minutes."

As they turned to leave, Robyn said, "Can we really trust Huston, Tom? I have my doubts. What happened at the Metro station doesn't make a lot of sense unless they were aliens."

"At this point, I don't see any alternative, but I have to admit that what happened at the Metro station is puzzling."

As Tom's limos drove off, American mechanized military units converge on the Lincoln Memorial and the crowd. Every automatic weapon on the vehicles was manned. The soldiers were in full battle dress.

Tom asked rhetorically, "Do they think we're allied with the spaceship? Otherwise, why this show of military force?"

* * * * *

"Mr. President, the alien spaceship has fired on the city. The Washington Monument, the Old Post Office, and several other buildings have been damaged."

"Are you certain the spaceship was responsible?"

"Affirmative. We were forced to fire missiles in defense."

"Result?"

"Not successful. We can't be certain, but we suspect the ship used beam weapons to pulverize most of our missiles. Our own beam weapons systems have been readied and are awaiting your orders."

"Any additional hostile actions?"

"No. At the moment, the ship is heading away from Earth."

"Have you tried communicating with it?"

"Yes. But it's raised its cloaking shields. So the ship is now invisible, and communication with it impossible. But we'll keep trying."

"If the opportunity presents itself, fire our satellite beam weapons. We wanted to keep them a secret, but let's make certain that spaceship can't come back and attack our city again."

Chapter 56

The D.C. Police Chief, as well as the FBI and the military, met Maggie and Scott at the police station. The two were bombarded with questions. However, between answers, Maggie reminded the officials that she and her editor had been granted exclusive rights to the story and that they expected to be kept in the loop. Sound from the whirling blades of a landing helicopter ended the session. They were hustled aboard and flown to a nearby military base.

When they arrived, elite army units were boarding a fleet of helicopters. Per instructions, the two donned metal helmets and flak jackets before joining the officer in charge, Captain James, on his helicopter. He explained that, although the role of the mysterious exploding vans at the time of the spaceship attack on Washington had yet to be determined, the mission of his troops was a raid on a Minuteman plant in Virginia from which, according to satellite photos, the fleet had originated. The purposes of the raid were to determine the function of the plant and to capture vans for inspection.

Minutes after the 'copters crossed the Potomac, Captain James pointed out the plant through the haze. "For your protection, we'll stand off at a safe distance. But you'll have a good view of the action."

Several copters swooped down on the plant and landed. Troops poured out and sprinted toward a set of large, open doors, while other copters circled, their weapons trained on the building. Soldiers about to enter were suddenly knocked backward as if by a giant invisible hand. Charging a second time, they were again knocked backward. As they scrambled to the sides of the doors, Maggie saw a portion of the plant roof implode. The troopers nearest the doors were propelled into the air. She felt the helicopter abruptly move sideways and heard a loud booming sound.

Two helicopters dove steeply, then pulled up, weapons trained on the open doors. Soldiers nearby ducked to avoid the powerful downdrafts of the rotor blades. To Maggie's horror, simultaneous massive explosions tore apart the two helicopters. She couldn't believe her eyes or make sense of what she had just seen. Chunks of flaming metal rained down on the soldiers. As Maggie watched in amazement, a strange vessel appeared to materialize near the disemboweled copters. The slender, silvery, triangular shape skimmed erratically along the ground before skidding to a halt.

Another helicopter flew over and aimed its weapons at the still intact vessel. Soldiers on the ground moved toward it. The vessel began to glow a bright whitish orange just before exploding in a flash of light that hurt Maggie's eyes. The force of the blast threw nearby soldiers to the ground. When the air cleared, no trace of the vessel could be seen.

"Good God!" Captain James exclaimed. "It's disappeared! Did we get video?"

"Yes, sir," said the pilot.

The captain issued rapid orders into his headset microphone. Soldiers began entering the plant. "What do you mean, no one?...Check again. What about the plant itself?...Put out the fire around the heap of metal. We need to salvage as much as we can."

He turned to Maggie, Scott, and the soldiers nearest the helicopter windows. "Okay. Describe what happened to the plant roof."

The descriptions were similar: it imploded.

"Any suggestions as to the cause?"

Most just shook their heads, but one soldier volunteered, "It's like a ray hit the roof. At least, that's how it would have been in the movies."

* * * * *

After making certain they weren't being followed, Tom's two limos drove to Dupont Circle. There they rendezvoused with Peter and his group. Leaving the Circle, the three cars proceeded to a nearby alley, where everyone got out.

Tom said to Huston, "I've exhausted my government contacts. The president has declared a national emergency. Both civilian and military leaders have been evacuated and are incommunicado. And I suspect the government thinks we're in cahoots with the spaceship." He explained.

"The military was surrounding the rally crowd as we left," Robyn added.

"Did you contact George Murphy?" asked Huston. "He's former CIA. He's not in Washington, and he's not a government leader."

"Great suggestion. Should have thought of that myself. And besides, I need to ask him about you." He speed dialed. "Hello Jane, Tom Cartwright. I'd like to speak to Mr. Murphy."

"He's not in, Mr. Cartwright, but I can give you his number." She did so.

Tom dialed it.

"Murphy here. What can I do for you?"

"George, Tom Cartwright. Do you know what's been happening in Washington?"

"I saw it on CNN. What do you make of it?"

He informed Murphy of their suspicions and of the declared national emergency. "I need your help to contact the president and convince him to listen to us."

"Is the person who calls himself Arthur Huston with you?"

"Yes," a surprised Tom Cartwright answered. "He says you'll vouch for him."

"I do vouch for him. Tell him I said so. He'll fill you in about our relationship. I'll try my best to contact the president. How may I reach you?" Tom told him.

After the call, Tom recounted for Huston his conversation with Murphy, ending with, "Murphy said you would fill me in. Please do."

A black car driving slowly past one entrance of the alley interrupted the conversation. Tom's men drew their weapons.

"We can't stay here," Jake said to Tom. "They're probably calling for reinforcements."

Jumping into the cars, they sped to the opposite end of the alley. The black car reappeared and followed. The limo carrying the majority of Tom's men lagged behind when the other two vehicles turned onto the street. Leaning from the windows as the black car approached, they shot out two of its tires. Rejoining the other two vehicles, all three blended into the afternoon traffic and hastily left the scene.

* * * * *

"How many of our satellite beam weapons has the Piscean spaceship disabled, General McNulty?" asked the president.

"All weapons within range of the ship, sir."

"What are our options?"

"Limited. If we power up our other satellite weapons systems, they'll probably be destroyed. Ordinary missiles are useless. We could saturate the area with nukes. A few might explode near enough to do damage. But the areas on Earth beneath the explosions would be irradiated, causing catastrophic loss of human life, as well as a collapse of the ecosystem."

"Any communication with the spaceship?"

"Their shields are still up, Mr. President."

"Prepare our nuclear weapons."

Chapter 57

Murphy requested a phone from the bartender at his club and entered a number he had not used in years. "George Murphy here."

The voice on the other end asked, "Your code?" Murphy entered a string of numbers and letters.

"Thank you, Mr. Murphy. To whom do you wish to speak?"

"The person in charge of Project Fish."

"Project Fish?"

"Perhaps the name has changed."

"Please hold."

Another voice. "How may I help you, Mr. Murphy?"

"To whom am I speaking?"

"That's classified, I'm afraid."

"Of course. I need to speak to the president. This concerns the national emergency. It's urgent."

"I need a landline where I can contact you."

Murphy gave his club's number, ordered a drink, and settled back in his favorite leather chair.

* * * * *

As they navigated side streets through D.C. in order to minimize the chance of being spotted, Tom said to Huston, "OK, what is it that Murphy wanted you to tell me about the two of you?"

"The CIA beamed a message to Pisces II back when Murphy was director. The Agency wanted to communicate with us, even though they knew it would take four years to receive an answer. We followed

Murphy's career via electronic media signals from your planet and decided that he would be the appropriate contact person upon our spaceship's arrival.

"When we landed on your moon, we contacted Murphy. We told him about the division of our planet into two hostile camps. He advised us that capitalistic economic conservatism was a powerful force on Earth and that we needed to choose carefully when and where we revealed our presence. The GCIS space station seemed to offer us a splendid opportunity. I flew from your moon to Earth in one of our shuttlecraft, and Mr. Murphy helped me get a job on the space station. My mission was to ensure your reception of intelligible weak signals." He looked at Tom and Peter a bit sheepishly, "I must confess I modified your equipment in order to improve reception.

"The illegal transactions that forced the closing of your financial institutions, coupled with the space station disaster and possible sabotage, caused us to change our plans. We figured that WALIE might be collaborating with some financially powerful group on Earth. We also suspect that they are responsible for the destruction of the GCIS space station. By landing at the Living Wage rally, we hoped to remedy the situation by informing your people about our history. Through it all, Mr. Murphy has been our ally and our good friend."

* * * * *

"It's Jane, Mr. Cartwright. Mr. Murphy gave me your number in case I needed to contact you for him."

"Yes, Jane. What is it?"

"Something terrible has happened, Mr. Cartwright." Her voice broke, but the words tumbled forth, "Mr. Murphy is dead. He told me you were waiting for a message and to tell you that he was at his club if you called. He died there."

"My God, Jane. What happened?"

"He was found slumped over in his chair. At first, they thought it was a heart attack. But the police found a small wound in his back. Now, they're convinced it's murder. People at the club are being questioned."

"I apologize if this sounds callous, Jane, but I need to know who he called from the club."

"I'm sorry, Mr. Cartwright. The club manager said he was waiting for a call. That's all I know."

* * * * *

When they were certain they weren't being followed, Tom instructed Jake to park at the Washington Zoo. Everyone got out, and he told them, "George Murphy has been murdered. I suspect it was because of us. I'm now more inclined to agree with Mr. Huston that we are dealing with a conspiracy in high places—not just a few dangerous individuals. If that is the case, our best defense is to go public. What do you think?"

Peter was the first to speak, "I think Tom's right. It's hard to know what government officials might be involved. We can't tell our friends from our enemies."

After a brief discussion, they agreed to go public.

"GCIS television stations," said Tom, "are the fastest way to go public. The Washington studio may be under surveillance. Fortunately, I have a mobile studio of sorts in my limo. We can link to my company's TV network from right here."

"Hold on," cautioned Jake. "Can't the signal be traced?"

"With sufficient access and proper equipment."

"If they found Murphy," said Jake, "they can find us. A moving target is harder to track than a sitting duck."

They agreed to drive about at random. Peter, Robyn, Sarah, and Huston got into Tom's limo in preparation for the broadcast.

When they were under way, Tom plugged a miniature video camera and microphone into the stack of electronic equipment stashed neatly between the seats. He arranged for an emergency disruption of his company's regular TV broadcasts, intending to broadcast live on all company owned stations. The live broadcast would be taped and continuously rebroadcast for as long as necessary.

Within minutes, they were on the air. Tom introduced himself and his companions. However, before they could air their message, the connection went dead. Tom fruitlessly punched buttons on his console. Attempting to recontact the company studio, he heard only a recorded message instructing him to dial the operator for assistance.

Turning around in the front seat and grabbing Tom's arm, Jake said, "They've traced the signal. Switch everything off."

Chapter 58

Tom insisted that they drive to a company-owned relay center and auxiliary studio outside Falls Church, Virginia. He hoped the center's old coaxial cable connection to stations would be more difficult to disrupt. They took secondary roads, but would still arrive in less than an hour.

Back at the wheel of his car, Peter followed the two limos. Though they had stopped using their phones, he remained alert. A car, which had been following them for several minutes, was of concern. However, it remained well back.

Hearing a whining noise, Peter suspected a car problem. Sitting beside him, Huston pulled a device out of his pocket, put it to his ear, and spoke such rapid Piscean that Peter was unable to follow.

After the exchange, Huston said, "The shuttlecraft which brought me to Earth is above us. The pilot says we're in danger. Two cars are following us, and there's a blockade ahead. We must take the next right turn in order to avoid driving into the trap."

Knowing those in the other cars would not respond to their phones, Peter, with desperate resolve, jerked the steering wheel to the left and slammed his foot on the gas in an effort to pass the two limos. Because the road curved, he was unable to see sufficiently far ahead. As he passed the limo immediately ahead, Tom's men peered out of its side windows in alarm. The lead limo slowed to let him pass, but before he could do so, a vehicle came round the curve, straight at him. He swerved onto the shoulder, barely missing the oncoming car. The ditch was shallow, and he was able to maintain control. Steering back onto the road, he passed the lead limo, and put on his right turn signal. Behind him, the two limos slowed, pulling to the side of the road. Peter sped up, indicating that he was not intending to stop.

"Hold up my phone so they can see it," Peter told Huston. "Contact Tom and tell him what you told me."

Huston held up the phone while maintaining contact with the shuttlecraft. "The shuttlecraft is unarmed," he told Peter. "But the pilot is going to try to disable the two cars following us using the fields generated by the craft's engines. The pilot must fly quite close to the cars. It will be dangerous, but she's experienced and resourceful."

Before Huston was able to contact Tom, they reached the side road where they were supposed to turn. Peter put on his turn signal and motioned violently with his arm, hoping the driver behind would see and understand. Slowing as little as possible, he skidded into the turn. Glancing into the rearview mirror, he was relieved to see the two limos.

"Haven't seen your shuttlecraft," Peter said.

"You won't. It's cloaking fields render it invisible. The pilot opened a gap in the fields to contact me."

"How did the bad guys find us?"

"Don't know. They couldn't have detected my homing signal to the shuttlecraft. It's virtually untraceable." He held the communication device closer to his ear. "Our pilot has been successful. The two cars have been disabled."

"Great!" said Peter. Glancing at Huston, "These guys seem to have a frightening ability to manipulate even secure communication systems, such as Tom's. Do you think they might be accessing our military systems?"

"Quite likely," Huston said animatedly. He spoke in Piscean to the shuttlecraft pilot.

Peter thought he understood, "You're going to use your shuttle to make our cars invisible to satellites?"

"Correct, but only from above." He smiled grimly, "We wouldn't want to cause a traffic accident, would we?"

* * * * *

"Mr. President, there are energy disturbances in the vicinity of the spaceship."

"What sort of disturbances, General McNulty?"

"The spaceship could be launching something, but we don't really know."

"Why? What could they be doing?"

"Even using all available means of detection, we can barely sense the disturbances. One moment, sir, I'm receiving additional information.... The disturbances are moving toward Earth."

"What about our nuclear missiles?"

"On highest alert status, ready for immediate launch, Mr. President. We need to be certain of their intentions."

"By the time we know, General, it could be too late."

"You may be right Mr. President, but we can't afford to be wrong. The resulting holocaust could kill millions of us."

* * * * *

Under the shuttlecraft's protective shield, the three cars sped toward Falls Church. Huston's communication device whined. He answered in crisp tones. Turning to Peter, he said, "The shuttle has detected WALIE-design fighter aircraft searching for us. They were probably built here using WALIE designs transmitted to Earth by means of an ICD. The shuttle pilot has notified our spaceship of our location, and it is dispatching fighters to protect us."

Huston's communication device whined. He listened, then said to Peter, "The shuttle pilot instructs us to pull off the road, park under large trees, and seek shelter. The shuttle will be more difficult for the enemy fighters to detect if it is stationary."

* * * * *

Shortly after gathering in the dank basement of an old farmhouse, they heard a low rumble.

"Fighters," Huston whispered. "Too soon to be ours."

Tom and Jake started up the basement stairs.

Houston cautioned, "Better stay down here, remain silent, and hope we're not detected. You won't see anything. Cloaking fields."

The two retreated back down the stairs.

"I can't believe Jim Archer is one of them," Sarah said with conviction. "I never spoke to him. Maybe my call was intercepted, and my message never got through. The president needs to know that some Piscean fighters are good guys. I'm going to call Archer on the upstairs wall phone."

She walked quickly to the basement stairs. Jake and Huston moved to restrain her. A loud explosion came from the direction of their parked cars.

"Please," she pleaded, "we've got nothing to lose. They've found us."

Looking at the others, Jake and Huston hesitated. Sensing their grip loosen, Sarah shook free and bolted up the stairs.

Reaching the phone, she dialed quickly, experiencing a wave of relief when she heard, "Archer."

"It's Sarah. Don't ask questions! What did Murphy say to me when we first met in his office?" Archer recounted the conversation. Sarah then described what she had said to Murphy and what Archer was wearing at the time.

"You have a good memory."

"More important, now I know it's you and you know it's me. What did you do when you received my message a couple of hours ago?"

"What message?"

"Is this your wireless number?"

"Yes. Why?"

She gave him the farmhouse number. "Call me back at that number, but do not use your wireless phone or any of your office phones. If you do, your call might be intercepted." She hung up.

Shortly, the phone rang. She described her situation, concluding with, "The president needs to know that we're dealing with bad guys and good guys. Bad guy fighter aircraft are here near Falls Church and are about to attack us. The good guy spaceship that tried to land at the LWM rally has launched fighters to defend us. Our military must not shoot at them."

Archer began asking questions. Sarah cut him off, "No time. Trust me. Tell the president, now!"

"I'll do my best," said Archer, "but he's declared a national emergency and is probably in a bunker somewhere."

"Heaven help us if you fail!"

Chapter 59

Huston whispered, "They can detect body heat. Help me move that freezer." Several helped him hauled the boxy chest freezer over to an old dusty pool table. "Pile frozen food on top of the table and on the floor all around it. Then crawl under the table and pray."

The rumble of fighters was again audible. The sound seemed to hover over the house. The ground trembled. No one moved, hardly daring to breathe. The rumbling slowly died.

"Don't move, and don't talk," whispered Huston.

The rumbling returned. The ground trembled violently. They heard and felt several thuds.

"Landing," whispered Huston. He looked at Tom's men, "Ready your weapons." Producing his communication device, he whispered harshly into it.

A hinge squeaked. A floorboard creaked. Guns in hand, Tom's men silently moved to defensive positions. The basement door opened. Light flooded the stairwell.

* * * * *

Jim Archer dialed the White House. "Office of the President. How may I help you?"

"This is Jim Archer, chair of the SEC. I need to speak to the president, immediately."

"The president is unavailable."

"The president's chief of staff then."

"He is also unavailable."

"I have critical information about the national emergency. I must speak to the president immediately."

"Just a moment."

"Mr. Cain. How may I help you?"

"Jim Archer, chair of the SEC. I have an emergency message for the president."

"He is unavailable."

"Tell his chief of staff that I'm calling and that it's about the national emergency and the spaceship."

"One moment, please."

"Homeland Security."

* * * * *

After what seemed a tension-filled eternity, the sound of retreating footsteps surprised everyone. The rumble of fighter aircraft shaking the building and ground brought a measure of relief, only to be followed by a deafening explosion which splintered the basement ceiling, causing it to partially collapsed on the freezer and pool table. The eerie quiet which followed was punctuated intermittently by bits of falling debris. Next they heard a crackling sound, similar to thunder but not as loud.

"Our fighters," said Huston. "I've given them this location." Listening briefly to his communication device, "We are advised to leave while the enemy is preoccupied."

Crawling under and around the debris, they made their way up the stairs.

Tom said to Huston, "I assume our cars have been destroyed. Can your people transport us?"

"No. The fighters only have room for a crew of two, and the shuttlecraft is too small and needs to keep up its cloaking fields. If it landed and took people aboard, it would make a perfect target."

Inside a small barn-like structure near the house, they discovered a large black pickup. One of Tom's men crawled under the dash, crossed several wires, and started the engine. The two women got into the cab beside him. The men crowded together on the truck bed.

Huston announced that the shuttlecraft was overhead and would again fly cover.

"Get us the hell out of here," Tom called to the driver.

* * * * *

"Mr. President, we're tracking the spaceship. If it continues on its present course, it will return to Washington."

"What are our options, General McNulty?"

"Either we nuke it over the Atlantic or let it get closer and deal with it near the coast. The closer it gets, the better our chances of destroying it, assuming it isn't able to take out all our missiles on launch. In either case, blast and radiation damage to the United States could be massive."

"Sure would blow the hell out of my chances for reelection," the president said mirthlessly.

"One moment, Mr. President, I'm receiving additional information.... A series of powerful energy disturbances has been detected near Falls Church."

"Source?"

"Unknown."

"Damage?"

"Midair explosions, but no reported damage."

"Best guess?"

"Some of the disturbances may be similar to those detected in the vicinity of the spaceship."

"Is Washington in danger?"

"Anybody's guess if they come our way, but I'm inclined to say yes."

"Keep the line open."

Chapter 60

"More WALIE fighters have joined the battle," announced Huston after listening to his communication device. "Our forces are holding their own with difficulty. The fighter squadron commander is requesting that our spaceship join the battle."

"Falls Church," Robyn announced through the open rear truck window.

Tom stuck his head through and said, "Turn left downtown at Depot Street. Take Depot a couple of miles and look for a gray windowless stone building on your right."

"Depot Street," announced Robyn.

The driver turned. Part way down Depot, they heard the same crackling sounds as at the old farmhouse.

"They've found us!" Huston exclaimed. A fighter appeared for a flickering instant. "Ours. He's losing control." Another, more slender fighter became visible flying low over the treetops. It vanished in a blinding burst of light and deafening roar.

* * * * *

"Mr. President, those energy disturbances we've been monitoring near Falls Church have intensified," General McNulty reported.

"However?"

"However, there's another matter you need to take into account."

"Yes, what is it?"

"We're investigating a U. S. company which seems to be connected somehow with the Washington spaceship incident. It's a long story. The bottom line is that we conducted a raid today on one of the company's plants in Falls Church. Two of our helicopters were destroyed, possibly by a slender, triangular shaped aircraft quite unlike any of ours. The vessel became visible after the helicopters exploded, flew erratically a short distance, and crashed intact. Before we could capture the vessel, it vanished in an explosion. Fortunately, we have a video."

"You said the plant is in Falls Church. Are you suggesting that the energy disturbances might indicate the presence of Piscean fighter aircraft?"

"I am, sir."

"However, these hypothetical fighters have not attacked us."

"Two of our helicopters were destroyed, Mr. President, and the spaceship is headed toward Washington again."

"Are you advising the use of nuclear weapons?"

"I am, sir. The spaceship will be over the East Coast shortly. How long can we afford to wait?"

* * * * *

Once the troops confirmed that the empty Falls Church Minuteman plant posed no further danger, the command helicopter landed. Maggie and Scott were permitted to disembark and enter the plant. Captain James warned them to be particularly careful in the area where the roof had collapsed over a large heap of fused metal.

After wandering around the plant, Maggie and Scott walked over to the smoldering heap of metal. Initially, Maggie noticed nothing of interest. Then several pieces of crumpled metal drew her attention. After examining them more closely, she gestured excitedly for Scott to have a look. She pointed out what looked like round computers similar to those she had seen at the Minuteman company in New York City.

Examining a particularly large twisted mass of metal and correcting mentally for portions which had obviously melted or were otherwise distorted, she concluded that the large girder-like chunks of metal could have formed an arch fitting Tom's description of the arch at the Pleasant

Valley Minuteman plant. With her editor in tow, she walked over to Captain James.

"Captain, I have important information that you and your superiors need to know." She described the similarities between what had been observed at Minuteman's New York plants and the Falls Church wreckage.

"I've been told to look for round computers," replied the captain. "But what about the girder-like pieces of metal? What's their purpose?"

"I don't know. Maybe they were part of some kind of communication device." She described the telescope array at the rural New York plant. "I need to call Tom Cartwright."

She did so but received no answer and left a message. She dialed Robyn, with similar result.

A moment later, her phone came to life, "Yes?"

"Tom Cartwright. What's up, Maggie?" She described the chunks of bridge-like girders she had just discovered. "Sounds like the arch we saw at the Minuteman plant in Pleasant Valley." Upon hearing the conversation, Sarah reminded him of the arch she'd seen at the Virginia Minuteman plant with the strange craft under it.

Overhearing the conversation, Maggie said excitedly, "That's similar to an aircraft I just saw." On a hunch and despite her misgivings about the alien, she asked, "Tom, is Mr. Huston with you?"

"Yes."

"Do you trust him?"

"Yes. We have proof that I regard as reliable."

"Put him on." She described for Huston her mental picture of what the arch must have looked like and she also described the strange looking aircraft.

"Can you describe the arch in greater detail?"

She did so. Even over the phone, she could hear the excitement in Huston's voice as he questioned Sarah and Tom regarding what they'd seen.

Back on the phone with Maggie, he asked, "Is there a telescope array there similar to the one you saw in New York?"

"We arrived by helicopter. I didn't see one."

"Please ask the officer in charge whether there's a large fiber-optic cable connection in the plant."

Maggie questioned Captain James. "There is," she told Huston.

"At the other end, you should find a telescope array," he said to her. The captain agreed to check it out.

Huston continued, "Tell me more about the odd-looking aircraft."

"Something destroyed two military helicopters near the Minuteman plant. Afterward, an odd-looking aircraft became visible for a few seconds. Then it vanished in an explosion."

"Maggie, listen carefully. I want you to vouch for me to Captain James. I believe that WALIE may have teleported men and materiel, including fighter aircraft, from Pisces II to Earth. This goes far beyond their sending designs to Earth for manufacture here, as I had previously assumed. On Pisces II, we heard rumors that WALIE was researching teleportation and that it involved huge metal structures. If they have succeeded, Earth is in grave danger."

Chapter 61

The studio in the auxiliary control center was little more than a single room equipped with a TV camera and several props. Tom had difficulty convincing Dave, the engineer on duty, that he was indeed the CEO of GCIS. However, eventually, after sufficient proof, Dave accepted Tom's identity, if not his incredible story.

"Is the studio equipment operable?" Tom asked.

"Yes. It's old but well-maintained."

"I want to use the old coaxial cable system."

"No problem."

With Dave, they hurriedly surveyed the studio with its single camera, boom mike, and assortment of tables and chairs. Sitting down at the control panel and switching on the equipment, he announced, "Ready to go."

"Establish a connection with Minneapolis," Tom ordered.

Seconds later, Dave turned in his swivel chair and said to Tom, "They won't put us through without proper identification. Your camera is on line."

"This is Tom Cartwright. I am CEO of this company, and I want you to put me on the air live."

"Mr. Cartwright, you appear to be who you claim to be," came the reply, "but I need to ask for your identification code. Sorry. Security is tight."

"I understand," Tom said, looking at Jake, who activated his boss's security device and handed it to him. Tom rapidly entered his password and transmitted the code.

"Thank you, Mr. Cartwright. Sorry for the delay."

"Interrupt all normal programming immediately," ordered Tom. "Broadcast this signal live over all company-owned stations. I accept full responsibility. This is an emergency."

"Your signal will be live momentarily, Mr. Cartwright.... OK, you're on."

"This is Tom Cartwright, CEO of Global Communications and Internet Services. Anyone with access to President Hedges must contact him immediately. Tell him to halt military action against the Piscean spaceship traveling toward U. S. airspace. The ship is friendly. It is not hostile. We have proof.

"I repeat: contact the president at once. Tell him to abort military action against the spaceship.

"Friendly Piscean fighter aircraft dispatched from the spaceship are protecting the United States from those Piscean and their American allies who would harm us. Our real enemy is responsible for the recent explosions in Washington. Our real enemy is attempting to kill me and others who know the truth. We owe our lives and this broadcast to the spaceship and its brave pilots. Contact the president *now*. Tell him that all military action against the spaceship must stop immediately."

Without interruption, he kept repeating the message, over and over and over.

* * * * *

"Approaching the fire zone," announced the fighter pilot to Washington ground control. "Are we on your radar?"

"Yes," replied ground control. "All friendly fire in your sector has ceased. Do you see anything?"

"No radar sightings. No visual sightings. Nothing."

"If you don't sight anything in sixty seconds, clear out and we'll resume fire."

"Understood.... Still nothing. We're clearing out."

As the fighter flew along the Potomac River, the pilot shouted, "Ground control, ground control, the West Wing has been hit."

"Come again?"

"The West Wing of the White House just blew up."

"General," announced ground control excitedly, "the White House is under attack. Repeat. The White House is under attack."

* * * * *

As soon as the first warning had been received, Secret Service personnel raced through the West Wing, ordering everyone to the underground bunker.

"What about your area, Ed?" Secret Service agent Ackley radioed to one of his men.

"Almost clear."

"Good. Keep 'em moving."

Secret Service personnel were the last into the bunker. A blast shook the building before they could secure the initial set of steel doors. Even with all doors secured, muffled explosions could be heard and felt.

* * * * *

"Washington is under attack, Mr. President."

"Details, General."

"The West Wing is in ruins. The Capitol building has sustained damage, as well as several other government buildings."

"What is the source of the attack?"

"Everything points to Piscean fighters. They are virtually invisible and appear to be using high-energy beam weapons."

"What about the spaceship?"

"It is approaching Washington. We consider it to be directing the attack."

"Ready our nuclear missiles. Fire at your discretion when it's within range."

"Understood, sir."

* * * * *

Archer finally convinced Homeland Security that he needed to speak to the president immediately. However, he discovered that even Homeland Security had difficulty reaching the president. Precious minutes ticked away while Homeland Security went through prescribed channels.

Finally, "You have reached the National Emergency Control Center. State your business."

"My name is James Archer. I'm chair of the SEC. I must speak to the president regarding the national emergency. I have critically vital information which will affect the president's decision regarding the emergency."

"I'm putting you through."

"Operations. To whom do you wish to speak."

"The president. It's urgent."

"The president is not available."

"His chief of staff then."

"He is also unavailable."

"Listen, damn it. This is Jim Archer, SEC chair. I have information that *must* be relayed to the president immediately. I don't have time to wade through eight thousand bureaucratic levels. I have proof that the Piscean spaceship is friendly. It is not—repeat not—responsible for the damage to Washington. Any plans to attack it must be halted immediately."

Archer heard only silence. His head dropped into his hands.

* * * * *

"General McNulty, nuclear missile status?"

"Launched or preparing to launch."

"Time till impact?"

"Less than ten minutes if all goes well."

"Status of the spaceship?"

"Over Virginia near Washington. It has fired its beam weapons. There have been explosions, but the nature of its targets is unclear."

"Keep me informed. Keep this line open."

286

"Yes, Mr. President."

* * * * *

While Tom continued repeating his television plea, Peter and Huston left the building. Outside, they looked apprehensively in all directions and saw multiple vapor trails rising into the sky.

Huston pulled out his communication device and spoke briefly. "Inside!" he shouted. "Your government is firing missiles at our spaceship, and WALIE fighters are converging on this building!"

Scrambling back into the windowless building, they slammed shut the outer steel doors.

In the studio, Huston shouted, "Take cover! Fighters are coming!" Turning to Dave, "Is there a basement?

"Only the cable compartment." Dave pointed to a trap door in the middle of the studio floor. Everyone climbed down, except Tom, who continued to broadcast.

A series of explosions shook the building. When they stopped after several minutes, those in the cable compartment climbed out, thinking the worst was over. Tom had never stopped broadcasting.

Suddenly, the building shook violently. Walls cracked and chunks of masonry fell. Plaster plummeted from the ceiling. The equipment went dead.

All were groping about in the dark when the outer steel doors opened. A woman dressed in a silvery one-piece tight fitting suit staggered through.

"Julia!" cried Peter.

"I'm sorry," she moaned, collapsing into his arms.

"She's in shock," said Huston. "Help her lie down."

As Peter lowered her onto a couch, he became aware that she was no longer wearing a body brace. Feeling ridges, he looked up at Huston.

"Julia's my second in command. She flew the shuttlecraft protecting us. WALIE fighters must have shot it down."

* * * * *

"Mr. President," his aide said, "Tom Cartwright is on Internet television. He claims to have proof that the Piscean spaceship is friendly."

Another member of the staff said, "Mr. President, Jim Archer is on the line. He says he has good reason to believe that the spaceship is friendly."

The red telephone rang, "General McNulty, Mr. President. The officer in charge of the raid on the Minuteman plant has been in contact with one of the spaceship Pisceans. He is convinced that the spaceship is friendly and that the missile attack should be called off."

"Do you concur, General?"

"Yes, Mr. President."

Hesitating for only an instant, the president ordered, "Deactivate the missiles, General."

Seconds later, the general told him, "The missiles have been deactivated and destroyed, Mr. President. Fortunately, none reached the spaceship, and they pose no danger to Earth."

"Well, good. Now, will somebody please tell me what the hell is going on?"

The Walie Conspiracy: Afterword

By Maggie Blevins
Gaia New York Bureau

Whew! What a week! Our country barely avoided interplanetary nuclear war. We foiled conspiracies which threatened our financial systems and our beloved capital city. Technologically advanced aliens—FDER Pisceans—now live and work among us. Safe, instantaneous interplanetary communication and transport is on the horizon.

Who do we have to thank? The recent list of Congressional Medal of Honor recipients—including FDER Pisceans Walter Huston and Julia Withers—is a good place to start.

And the follow-up? WALIE beam devices in and around the capital have been neutralized. Piscean WALIE who teleported to earth are either dead or in custody. Three of their U.S. billionaire co-conspirators are free on huge cash bonds; a fourth is cooperating in ongoing prosecutions.

U.S. banks and financial markets, with new safeguards to assure transparency, are operating normally. SEC investigators continue their search for the rightful owners of illegally-transferred funds; the government will seize unclaimed assets. President Hedges proposes using seized assets to reduce taxes. His political opponents, citing tax reduction and spending programs, advocate their use to reduce the huge national debt.

Two of the Congressional Medal of Honor recipients, American Peter Abelard and Piscean Julia Withers, have announced their engagement and forthcoming marriage. Mr. Abelard and Ms. Withers met in

Minneapolis as employees of Global Communication's space station project. Their marriage will unite two cultures, two planets, and two species, as well as two individuals, and symbolizes the growing cooperation between the United States and FDER.

The upcoming U.S. presidential election offers voters a choice similar to that evidenced by the factions on Pisces II. The FDER view that some free-market regulation is necessary in order to maintain social justice resonates with Tom Cartwright and the American Progressive Party. President Hedges condemns recent WALIE interference with the U.S. economy but continues to advocate WALIE-style free-market capitalism as the best path to economic prosperity.

Recent proposals by the two presidential candidates highlight this contrast. President Hedges, who supported elimination of the federal minimum wage, argues for elimination of the federal income tax on income over $850,000, contending that tax payments on this amount reflect such persons' fair share of the tax burden. Tom Cartwright counters with a proposal, first entertained by President Franklin D. Roosevelt but never enacted into law, that an upper limit be placed on the amount of allowable income; any income over that amount would be expropriated by the federal government. Allowable income would be defined as some multiple of the minimum wage. Those dissatisfied with the established allowable income limit could increase it by raising the minimum wage.

A battle has been won. But battles driven by competing economic interests will continue, both on Earth and on Pisces II. Stay tuned.